ALSO BY DALE E. BASYE

Heck: Where the Bad Kids Go
Rapacia: The Second Circle of Heck
Blimpo: The Third Circle of Heck

DALE E. BASYE

ILLUSTRATIONS BY **BOB DOB**

RANDOM HOUSE  NEW YORK

FiBBLE

THE FOURTH CiRCLE OF
~ HECK ~

Text copyright © 2011 by Dale E. Basye
Jacket art and interior illustrations copyright © 2011 by Bob Dob

All rights reserved. Published in the United States by
Random House Children's Books, a division of Random House, Inc., New York.

Random House and the colophon are registered trademarks of Random House, Inc.

Visit us on the Web! www.randomhouse.com/kids
Educators and librarians, for a variety of teaching tools, visit us at
www.randomhouse.com/teachers

wherethebadkidsgo.com

Library of Congress Cataloging-in-Publication Data
Basye, Dale E.
Fibble : the fourth circle of Heck / by Dale E. Basye ; illustrations by Bob Dob. — 1st ed.
p. cm.
Summary: When goth teen Marlo wakes up in Fibble, the part of Heck that is reserved
for liars, she is disgusted to find out she is in her younger brother Milton's body.
ISBN 978-0-375-85678-5 (trade) — ISBN 978-0-375-89305-6 (ebook)
[1. Honesty—Fiction. 2. Future life—Fiction. 3. Brothers and sisters—Fiction.
4. Reformatories—Fiction. 5. Schools—Fiction. 6. Humorous stories.]
I. Dob, Bob, ill. II. Title.
PZ7.B2938Fi 2011 [Fic]—dc22 2010009460

Printed in the United States of America

10 9 8 7 6 5 4 3 2 1

First Edition

Random House Children's Books supports the
First Amendment and celebrates the right to read.

THIS BOOK IS DEDICATED TO MY EDITOR—NOT THAT ONE CAN
TRULY *POSSESS* AN EDITOR ANY MORE THAN ONE CAN
COPYRIGHT A BABY'S FIRST SMILE . . . THOUGH, HMM . . .
I SHOULD HAVE MY LAWYER LOOK INTO THAT—
DIANE LANDOLF, WHO, UPON READING MY SURREAL,
STREAM-OF-CONSCIOUSNESS FIRST DRAFTS,
ALWAYS GIVES IT TO ME STRAIGHT AND SEES THE POSSIBILITY
STRUGGLING TO EMERGE FROM ALL THOSE PAGES OF
PROFLIGATE PROSE. THIS BOOK IS DUE TO HER AS MUCH
AS IT IS TO ME (THOUGH IT IS MOSTLY DUE TO ME).
ALSO, MY AGENT MICHAEL BOURRET, WHO MAKES
THE TRUTH GO DOWN AS SMOOTH AS A HOT BUTTERED LIE.

★ CONTENTS ★

FOREWORD 1

1. WHAT LIES AHEAD? 3

2. HOORAY FOR HELLYWOOD 17

3. TOUR DE FARCE 26

4. ONE HOT PROPERTY, PRICED TO MOVE 34

5. FROM AD TO WORSE 42

6. A PET PEEVED 51

7. DÉJÀ VOODOO 57

8. GETTING DOWN TO SHOW BUSINESS 68

9. SEEING IS DECEIVING 82

10. SEARCH PARTY POOPER 96

11. IF THE SHOW HITS, BEWARE IT 105

12. REIGNING CATS AND DOGS 117

13. DUCK UNCOVER 125

14. EVERYBODY WANTS TO FOOL THE WORLD 137

15. ALL THE NEWS THAT'S FIT TO BE TIED 146

16. WRITING WRONGS 157

MIDDLEWORD 163

17. RIDING OUT THE BRAINSTORM 165

18.	CAWS FOR ALARM	176
19.	JOINED AT THE HYPE	186
20.	WOOD I LIE TO YOU?	200
21.	BAD BREAKS AND BREAKOUTS	216
22.	TOGETHER FUREVER	232
23.	THAT'S THE WAY THE KOOKS CRUMBLE	245
24.	THE CATASTROPHE'S MEOW	257
25.	THE STY OF THE STORM	272
26.	A LIE FOR A LIE	289
27.	FOLLOW THE MISLEADERS	300
28.	THE PLOT SICKENS	319
29.	ASUNDER THE BIG TOP	334
30.	THE MOMENT OF TRUTH	354
	BACKWORD	365

FiBBLE

THE FOURTH CiRCLE OF ~ HECK ~

FOREWORD

As many believe, there is a place above and a place below. But there are also places in between. Some not quite awfully perfect and others not quite perfectly awful.

One of these places is a gaudy nest of deception, hurricane-force bluster, and artful manipulation so surgical in its precision that you could use it to remove the modesty from a naked mole rat.

This place is a lot like a rainbow.

A rainbow is a breathtakingly gorgeous arc of vivid colors, an unexpected feast for the retinas. It's like watching a giant box of crayons and a beam of radiant sunlight exchanging wedding vows in Heaven, their divine love melting across the sky for all to see. A rainbow is something that is almost too beautiful to be true.

That's because it isn't. A rainbow is a polychromatic lie scrawled across your gullible peepers. It's simply a host of mysterious atmospheric conditions conspiring to form a false perception, albeit a lovely one. The closer you get to a rainbow, the closer you get to realizing that you can never truly get close to one.

This place of illusions, delusions, and oftentimes contusions (it's located on a slippery slope, so watch your step) is infested with truthless scoundrels spouting bright and shining lies of every hue, though the biggest, nastiest lie of all is growing like a mushroom in the shadows.

The mysterious Powers That Be (and any of its associated or subsidiary enterprises, including—but not limited to—the Powers That Be Evil) have stitched this and countless other subjective realities together into a sprawling quilt of space and time.

Some of these quantum patches may not even seem like places. But they are all around you, and go by many names. Some feel like eternity. And some of them actually are *eternity, at least for a little while.*

Honest.

1 · WHAT LiES AHEAD?

BEING A BOY *feels really weird,* Marlo thought as she dangled her brother's gross feet off the backseat of the stagecoach taking her to Fibble, the circle of Heck for kids who lie. Her borrowed body felt alternately simpler and more complicated—frustrating in its sheer, dull straightforwardness. *Just like boys,* she reflected. Marlo tried her best not to overanalyze the skin she *ached* to jump out of: just thinking about being her younger brother, Milton—at least on the outside—made her skin crawl. Or his. *Whatever.*

Marlo was still fuzzy on the particulars of her current situation, but flashes of what had happened, and who she *truly* was, floated to the top of her brain like the cryptic messages of a Magic 8 Ball. She remembered graduating from Madame Pompadour's Infernship program and becoming Satan's Girl Friday the Thirteenth.

Then she remembered Milton—though for some reason, at the time, she'd had no idea that the little twerp hopping around in his *Stargate Atlantis* underwear *was* her brother—storming the Surly Gates of h-e-double-hockey-sticks with Annubis, the dog god, and dragging her from her Deceptionist post to the Break Down Room with Principal Bubb and her demon guards in hot pursuit, before drugging her with a moldy cheese sandwich.

It was here that things got a little strange.

When Marlo had come to, she hadn't felt quite . . . *herself.* Annubis had once presided over Heck's Assessment Chamber, where souls were weighed on the Scales of Justice, so he had the power to pluck people's spiritual essence from their bodies with his bare paws. *He must have switched Milton's soul with mine,* Marlo presumed. To what end, Marlo could not be sure. But as she dredged the sludgy slough of her mind—still yawning and stretching from its peculiar nap—Marlo knew that her little brother was essentially a good kid, so whatever Milton's specific intent, his heart was sure to be in the right place (even if his soul *wasn't*). Marlo also knew that Milton had an ulcer, not because of any prior knowledge as his sister, but because of the waves of pain radiating from the pit of Milton's stomach.

The man sitting across from her in the musty stagecoach coughed. He leered at her with a freaky smirk: a knowing grin that was totally one-sided.

"How long are we going to play this little game?" the old, dough-faced man said as he ran his fingers through his slicked-back hair. Marlo swallowed down the bile that kept creeping up her throat.

"I'm afraid I don't know what you mean," she replied in her brother's squeaky voice. "And I'm not afraid of anything."

The man laughed mirthlessly.

"You could have fooled me," he said, training his beady black eyes on Marlo. "You seemed plenty afraid back in Limbo."

Her stomach suddenly felt as if it housed an unchaperoned, all-ages dance club. *He must have been some teacher in Limbo,* Marlo speculated. *One of* Milton's *teachers . . . and that's who he thinks I am, naturally, because that's who I am. But I can't blow my cover, or else I'll screw up whatever Milton has planned.*

"Yeah, of course I remember you . . . *sir,*" Marlo replied. "You were my, um, teacher. Back in Limbo."

The stagecoach shuddered. The hoofbeats of the Night Mares pulling the carriage clattered uncertainly before regaining their confident rhythm.

The man squinted so hard at Marlo that it looked as if the bags beneath his eyes would burst.

"What's my name, then?" he asked, suspiciously, as he leaned in close to Marlo and stared into her borrowed hazel eyes.

"What, did you forget?" Marlo replied, using her

patent-pending "tact-evasion" technique. "Didn't your momma sew it in the lining of your jacket?"

"I can tell you're covering up something," the man spat back. "I can see it in your—"

Suddenly, the stagecoach bumped and shook so violently that the old man slammed his head into the top of the carriage.

"Oww!" he yelped as the demon driver—a swollen, bespectacled creature with goat horns and a white goatee growing around his orange duck bill—leaned into the carriage.

"Are you injured, Mr. Nixon?" the demon quacked. "I mean, Mr. President, sir."

Mr. Nixon rubbed the swirling slick of hair atop his head.

"Pardon me, *Mr. Nixon?*" Marlo said, making Milton's voice smugger than it had ever sounded before. "You were saying that you saw something in my *oww?*"

Mr. Nixon's ashen face flushed red.

"I pardon no one! *I'm* the one that gets pardoned!"

The stagecoach fishtailed wildly, sending Marlo and Mr. Nixon crashing to the floor. The carriage skidded to a stop. Marlo crawled up off the floor and gazed out the window.

They were on the edge of a vast, frozen mound of water that shimmered weakly beneath the filmy crust. The swollen sea of frost resembled a massive Hostess Sno Ball dipped in crystal. Studding the distended icy knoll were clumps of scraggly bushes that—when rustled by the breeze—almost seemed to . . . *talk*. What they said, Marlo couldn't make out. It just sounded like yammering nonsense.

Marlo pushed open the door and hopped onto the ice, steadying herself with the carriage. The horizon was clogged with a thick, gently seething bank of sparkling pea-soup smoke. The glimmering, billowing murk spewed from a towering structure in the distance perched atop the summit of the swollen, frozen sea.

Through a fleeting crack in the clouds Marlo could see that the structure was a cluster of grand, gaudy tents propped up on massive, swaying stilts. The wound in the cloud bank quickly healed, leaving Marlo dazzled, disoriented, and wanting to disgorge whatever her brother had last eaten all over his freaky skinny-long feet.

Mr. Nixon moaned as he rose from the floor. He crouched through the open stagecoach door, waving "V" for victory signs at the nonexistent crowd that roared in his mind, and joined Marlo. The demon driver waddled over to them, handing the ex-president a thermos.

"Thank you, doctor," Mr. Nixon replied as he twisted the top.

Marlo gently patted her stomach, as if it were a nervous stallion she was trying to calm.

"Doctor?" she repeated.

"Yes, Dr. Brinkley," Mr. Nixon continued as the

demon shuffled to his team of Night Mares. "License revoked many, many times. Which explains his current condition."

Marlo studied the ducklike doctor.

"The big bill?" she enquired. "You know, because doctors charge too much?"

Mr. Nixon tilted the thermos but nothing came out.

"No, because he was a quack," the old man replied as he spanked the bottom of the empty thermos.

The duck demon patted the ice and grit from his white-feathered hands as he tightened his horses' bridles.

"The team is ready," Dr. Brinkley said in an odd, duckish drawl. "I trust they'll find the least perilous path."

Marlo scowled as she noted the team shifting uneasily on the ice.

"Find the path?" she said. "Haven't you been to Fibble before?"

The duck demon's feathers ruffled in the wind.

"No, young man, I haven't. Snivel is my customary route. The usual driver, Baron Munchausen, called in ill today . . . something about contracting swine flu from a pork chop, which—even as a fraudulent practitioner of medicine—I don't believe is—"

"Maybe we should just walk the rest of the way," Marlo said as the wind tickled the fronds of the ragged brown shrubs, their leaves rubbing against one another in a murmuring chorus that sounded a lot like *"walk the rest of the way."*

"I wouldn't recommend that, from what I've been told," the duck demon clucked. "This is the Falla Sea. It is, by definition, misleading and unsound. My Night Mares, though, can beat a safe path around the bushwas."

"Those creepy talking bushes?" Marlo asked as she stared out, mesmerized, at the churning clouds of vapor spilling out across the horizon.

"Bushwas," Dr. Brinkley repeated as he rubbed clean his round spectacles. "To our ears, they spew mocking, befuddling gibberish, meant to lead one astray—which can be especially harmful in an inhospitable place such as this. My Night Mares have a peculiar horse sense that'll pull us through. They won't be flustered by any sidetracking shrubs."

Marlo shrugged, and she and Mr. Nixon climbed back into the black stagecoach. As the carriage lurched across the Falla Sea—the bushwas blathering outside and the Night Mares whickering amongst themselves— Marlo wondered why the dead president sitting across from her had been transferred from Limbo.

"So what gives?" Marlo asked, as blunt as a pair of scissors in a preschool. "Why are you being sent to Fibble?"

Mr. Nixon stared down his ski slope of a nose at

Marlo. "I remember you as being more polite . . . nice and nervous, just like I like 'em," he grumbled.

He glared at Marlo's primly crossed legs. "Though Heck has also, strangely, made you more *demure,* by the looks of it."

Marlo looked down at her legs and quickly uncrossed them. She kept them apart as if she were cradling a watermelon between her knees.

"You're dodging the question, Mr. Nixon," she replied. "Bubb sent you to spy on me, right?"

Mr. Nixon sighed with resignation.

"Yes and no," he said, his beady black eyes darting nervously about the carriage's interior. "Yes, she did, and no, she didn't ask me to *not* spy on you. But I'm also here to act as a demotivational speaker—giving workshops to the faculty on *The Ins and Outs of Getting In and Out of Things, How to Lie Through False Teeth,* and my *Gettin' Shifty wid It: Go from Educator to Equivocator in Three Easy Steps* program."

The stagecoach stopped.

"We're here," Dr. Brinkley quacked dismally as he hopped off the driver's box and made his way to the door.

Marlo and Mr. Nixon clambered out of the carriage, stepping tentatively down onto the edge of the Falla Sea. They were instantly engulfed by a gargantuan shadow. Marlo looked up.

Hovering above her was, for all appearances, a

ginormous, glittering clown head, smiling in that gruesomely gleeful way that clowns do. *Why is it,* Marlo thought, *that the happier a clown is, the sadder everyone else is around it?*

Marlo shivered as she wrapped her brother's skinny arms around her. Marlo was—in general—fearless to a fault. Many faults, actually. But somehow an unease surrounding circus performers had slunk into the big, bad big top of her subconscious.

Fibble just had *to be a circus,* she thought. *With* clowns. *The face paint . . . the wigs . . . and those wicked long shoes . . .*

The frightening, monstrous head, thankfully, was just a floating mass of sparkling gas streaming from the tip of one of three circus tents towering over Marlo, Mr. Nixon, and Dr. Brinkley. The clown head was smeared briefly into twinkling vapor by a strong gust of hot wind, releasing Marlo's eyes from their horrific hostage situation.

The trio of tents—merrily banded as if sheathed in enormous sheets of Fruit Stripe gum—sat upon a great wooden platform forty feet above Marlo's head. The circus shantytown was supported by a wide circle of gently swaying stilts that creaked in the wind . . . almost screaming, Marlo thought, as her gaze traveled down the spindly stilts to the garish Gates of Fibble.

Why the gates to Fibble were actually forty feet directly *below* Fibble, planted on the frozen Falla Sea, baffled Marlo. The three new arrivals walked past the rim of stilts bracing the circus above and toward the gates, located in the middle of Fibble's shadow. The stilts were made of a light brownish wood that looked like dozens of little anguished faces. Marlo shuddered.

It's just my mind—or Milton's—playing tricks on me, that's all, Marlo thought as she approached the gates, a flickering rainbow of long neon bars. *Just like when you look at clouds and think you see faces and shapes.* Marlo looked up at the clown cloud as it grinned malevolently down on her at the edge of Fibble's wooden platform. *Okay, maybe it's not like that, but how bad can a place be with a rainbow for a gate? I mean, what's more genuinely cheerful than a rainbow?*

The gates were part of a circular fence, made of criss-crossed iron slats, that girded a small, enclosed area. Welded to the top of the arch—beneath a marquis reading FIBBLE! as if the circle was the latest blockbuster film—were a metal rooster and a cow. Marlo scrunched up her brother's face.

"I don't get the rooster and the cow," she said to no one in particular, never completely taking her eyes off the malevolent clown head overhead.

"It's a cock and bull, actually," the duck demon said, waddling to her side with Mr. Nixon's bags.

Marlo stared at Dr. Brinkley, still not getting it.

"Like a cock-and-bull story," Mr. Nixon clarified. "You know . . . malarkey. A pile of cock-a-doodle-doo. Don't you know that old phrase?"

"No, I cock-a-doodle-*don't*," she replied. "Old phrases are for old people."

Inside the fenced area were a pair of masked demon guards in flowing black robes, sitting on folding metal chairs reading *GYP*, Heck's fittingly terrible newspaper. As soon as they noticed Marlo, Mr. Nixon, and Dr. Brinkley, they rose suddenly like Jack-the-Ripper-in-the-boxes. The backs of Marlo's arms turned to gooseflesh at the sight of the demons.

Molded to their bald, decomposing heads were burnished brass metal masks with eyes like the shutters of old-time cameras, clenching and relaxing as they adjusted to the fluctuations in light. The demons strode toward the visitors, their floor-length robes fluttering behind them, and opened the gates with a scrape of metal against ice. Dr. Brinkley trembled and waddled to meet them.

"I, um, QUACK!" Dr. Brinkley said nervously, his bill chattering like a pair of wind-up teeth. He cleared his throat and tried again. "We . . . *I* . . . am here with Mr. Nixon, a teacher visiting from Limbo on Principal Bubb's orders, and a new pupil . . . Milton Fauster."

It was all Marlo could do to not turn around, looking for her brother.

"Shall I tie my team of Night Mares anywhere special?" the doctor asked as he glanced over his shoulder at his stagecoach, caught just inside the shadow of Fibble suspended above it. The intimidating demon guards stared mutely at the doctor.

"Um . . . I suppose they're fine right there, then," Dr. Brinkley muttered.

The demons beckoned the threesome inside the gates, pointing to a large target painted on the ground—a series of concentric red, blue, and yellow rings with a bull's-eye in the middle. Marlo stepped through the gates and looked above her. In the middle of the platform supporting Fibble was a circle about the same size as the target area they were standing in.

Must be some kind of elevator, Marlo thought as Mr. Nixon, fidgeting beside her, squinted up at Fibble looming overhead.

"How do we get up there?" he asked, looking around for some kind of entrance.

The demon guards herded Marlo, Mr. Nixon, and Dr. Brinkley to the bull's-eye of the target, before kneeling down to pick up two large megaphones. Standing back-to-back, the tall, slender guards held their megaphones up to their scabby mouths, training them out toward the rim of stilts beyond.

"*Life isn't fair,*" the demon guards bellowed in a deep, deafening unison, "*and neither is death.*"

Instantly, as if reacting to the guards' thunderous roars, the wooden stilts supporting Fibble quivered. Then, with a fresh peal of creaking screams, the wooden supports violently contracted, and Fibble came plummeting down.

"*Aaaaaeeeiieeeyyyy!!*" Marlo, Mr. Nixon, and Dr.

Brinkley screamed in unison, clutching one another as the massive wooden platform of tents struck the ground with a gigantic thud. It felt—and sounded—as if their heads had been torn off, though, Marlo realized, her ability to think at all clearly meant that she still had a head on her shoulders.

Trembling, Marlo forced open her eyes and saw that Fibble had fallen down around them, and that here—inside the target zone—they were safe.

"*Ta-da!*" barked an unseen man through a megaphone. Suddenly, a spotlight shone on Marlo, Mr. Nixon, and Dr. Brinkley. Marlo winced and vainly tried to shield her eyes from the glare.

Well, I was sort of right about the elevator, Marlo thought as she noticed huge shreds of paper tangled in the tips of the circular fence. *Luckily we just passed through a paper hole or something.*

The three visitors disentangled themselves as one of the masked demon guards opened the gates and urged them forward. This time, instead of passing through the strobing, rainbow neon portal back to the frozen Falla Sea, they entered a circus Big Top, surrounded by grandstands filled with children clapping tepidly.

The man with the megaphone—a stout silhouette standing in front of a spotlight—chortled.

"Hurry, hurry, step right up!" he shouted as the demon guard, after leading Marlo, Mr. Nixon, and Dr. Brinkley to the grandstands, hurried back through the gates to join his colleague at the painted bull's-eye. As Marlo's eyes grew accustomed to the light, she noticed that most of the children in the stands were nothing more than painted cutouts.

"B-but my stagecoach," whined Dr. Brinkley, tears forming in his eyes. "My Night Mares . . ."

The full-bodied shadow-man turned toward the duck demon.

"You didn't bring your mangy mares inside the gates?" he scolded.

Dr. Brinkley shook his downy head.

The man laughed as phlegm rattled in his chest like a seething snot-pit of rattlesnakes.

"*A fool and his ponies are soon parted.* Well, it looks like you are our guest. *Forever.* Poor, poor flattened fillies . . ."

The figure emerged from the beam of harsh, dazzling light. It was a stocky, swollen man with a froggish face, dressed in a top hat and swishing tails.

"I am your vice principal, P. T. Barnum," he bellowed heartily, "and welcome to Fibble: *The Greatest Show Under Earth!*"

And with that, he punched his big, brass belt buckle, and the vice principal's pants were engulfed in flames.

2 · HOORAY FOR HELLYWOOD

BEING A GIRL *feels really weird,* Milton thought as he dangled his sister's aching feet off the high-end office chair. Dressed like a model pretending to be a secretary, Milton had expanded his definition of "uncomfortable" exponentially. As one of the devil's Inferns, Milton—in Marlo's body—was forced to wear the latest designer clothing: that is, clothing designed to exact as much bodily pain as possible.

First there were the shoes: "pumps," one of the other girls (the *real* girls) had called them. They would have been somewhat tolerable if Milton had, say, three fewer toes on each foot. Next was the dress: a scratchy, wool thigh-length thingie that clung to him like corn dog bits to a retainer. Plus, it had an unfortunate tendency to creep up, which creeped Milton *out*. Where was the dress going? And to what end?

Then there were the, um, aptly named unmentionables: the less said about them the better. Even though Milton had once, after solving a Rubik's Cube in twenty-one moves, made his own Rubik's Icosahedron out of Styrofoam and toothpicks, he was infinitely perplexed by girls' underwear. It had taken him most of the morning to figure out why Marlo's lace hat had two caps.

His borrowed body felt alternately simpler and more complicated—frustrating in its sheer, confounding unfathomability. *Just like girls,* Milton thought.

Milton tried his best not to overanalyze the skin he *ached* to jump out of: just thinking about being his older sister, Marlo—at least on the outside—made his skin crawl. Or hers. *Whatever.*

Milton hoped that by working undercover he could save not only both of their skins, but their eternal souls. Maybe he'd even stumble onto a way to save the souls of every kid toiling in Heck—at least the ones who didn't seem to deserve to be there. Judging from Milton's experience down here, that was darn near most of them. Some of them, like his friend Virgil, were even—

"Nice necklace," a fellow Infern named Terri Belle said, pointing to the string of paper clips Milton had hung around his neck after noticing that he was the only girl in the office without jewelry.

"Thanks," Milton replied, not quite realizing that some girls tie their sarcasm with a pretty bow.

"*Anyway,*" Terri continued with a yawn, "these boxes aren't going to unpack themselves." She pointed to a stack of bulging cartons.

"But wouldn't that be cool if they *could*?" Milton replied. "Like if the boxes were actually robots composed of electromechanical cardboard that—"

Terri walked away. Milton had yet to master the art of girl-to-girl conversation. He looked over at the pile of boxes and sighed.

Milton, as Marlo, had been claw-picked by Satan himself to help get the epitome of all evil's new entertainment network off the ground, or as off-the-ground as you can get something way down here. The only problem was that Milton hadn't even *met* the Big Guy Downstairs, and his "role" was as vague as a question mark made of fog. All he knew for certain was that he had been transferred from Marlo's job as a Deceptionist for h-e-double-hockey-sticks to this dismal gray labyrinth of cramped workspace cubes in the southwest region of the Netherworld. Judging from the crumbling sign on the fire-scorched hill just outside the office window, this smoggy place was called HELLYWOOD, INFERNIA: HOME TO A GALAXY OF FALLEN STARS.

Milton heard a snarl of laughter, quickly stifled. Looking up, he noticed Terri and several other girls snickering at him. Milton realized that he was sitting, legs splayed, on the edge of his seat, which is nothing for a twelve-year-old boy, but to a teenage girl in a dress with a mind of its own, it was a case of instant humiliation: *just add Milton.*

He crossed his tingly, panty-hosed girl-legs and scooted his chair under his desk. Milton could feel Marlo's cheeks blushing, which, he knew, would have earned him one of his sister's lethal noogies, as Marlo worked hard on her deathly, Goth-girl pallor. Lucky for Milton's cranium, Marlo wasn't here, not really.

Lucky, Milton reflected with a sharp pang of loss as he thought of his pet ferret. Milton had once shared an etheric bond with Lucky, but—just outside of Blimpo— it had been abruptly severed. Now, Milton assumed, his fuzzy white pet was somewhere in the Furafter. Milton bit his sister's nails, hoping that Annubis, the dog god responsible for switching his soul with Marlo's, could locate him.

Just then, an immense man with a salt-and-pepper beard and sad, troubled eyes lumbered into the office, eating two hot dogs at once. The other girls were suddenly and mysteriously absent, leaving Milton to deal with the imposing visitor.

"Hello, um, and welcome to . . . wherever this is," Milton said. "My name is—"

"Moawrlo," the man sputtered between a mouthful

of semimasticated frankfurter and bun. He swallowed. "Marlo. I'm here to see Marlo Fauster," he punctuated with a sly wink.

"I . . . *I'm* Marlo Fauster," Milton managed with difficulty, struggling with a half-truth that was indeed half true.

"The name is Welles," the man said with a deep, velvety rumble as he lit a cigar. "Orson Welles. Actor, director, spokesperson, magician, fortune-teller . . . genius. Perhaps you've heard of me?"

Milton squinted at Mr. Welles, though Marlo's eyes were far sharper—like a thieving magpie—than the orbs Milton was accustomed to.

"Oh yeah," he replied. "Weren't you in one of the Muppet movies?"

Mr. Welles bit down on his cigar so hard that it smacked him on the forehead. "Even geniuses need to eat," he said as he patted out his smoldering eyebrow. "Some more than others."

He rummaged through his coat pocket and pulled out two Beastern Union Penta-grams.

"These are to inform you of your new role here," Mr. Welles announced as he handed Milton the envelopes. "About the beginning of *T.H.E.E.N.D.*"

"The end?" Milton said as two custodial demons in overalls took off their work boots, stood on their hands, and pounded a sign into the door with their hammertoes. "But . . . but I just got here."

Mr. Welles laughed.

"No," he said with a smirk as he presented the new door sign with fanfare. T.H.E.E.N.D.: TELEVISED HEREAFTER EVANGELISTIC ENTERTAINMENT NETWORK DIVISION.

Milton studied the two Penta-grams in his hands, not knowing which to open first. He shrugged and ripped one open with his thumbnail. (One of the few fringe benefits of being his sister were her sharp, should-be-registered-as-deadly-weapons thumbnails.)

BEASTERN UNION PENTA-GRAM

```
To: Marlo Fauster, Infern, Hellywood
From: The Big Guy Downstairs


This is the second telegram. Stop. You
were supposed to open the other
telegram first. Stop.


The Big Guy Downstairs
```

Milton sighed as he wadded up the Penta-gram and tore open the next.

BEASTERN UNION PENTA-GRAM

```
To: Marlo Fauster, Infern, Hellywood
From: The Big Guy Downstairs
```

Defective immediately, you are to be
reassigned as production assistant to
my ultimate mass media endeavor,
T.H.E.E.N.D., the full, unabbreviated
moniker of which should currently be
hanging on your door. Stop. You may
well ask why I am heaping such
responsibility upon someone as untried
and untrue as yourself. Stop. Firstly,
you have exhibited a temerity where
others have shown timidity. Stop.
Lastly, you are an outsider, and I
always value bringing outsiders in,
until they become insiders. Stop. Mr.
Welles (you may remember him from one
of the Muppet movies) will give you
your first assignment. Stop.

Yours, etc., The Big Guy Downstairs

Milton furrowed his brows, which—he had recently
realized—his sister plucked on a regular basis.
"But I thought Satan already had URN: the Underworld Retribution Network?" Milton said to Mr. Welles,
who was leaning against the desk and unwittingly pressing it into Milton's chest. "Why does he need another
television network?"
Mr. Welles smiled around his fat, smoldering cigar.

"Ah, yes, but T.H.E.E.N.D. goes straight to the top!" he said with a sly purr. "Or the Surface, I should say . . ."

"The Surface?!" Milton yelped. "Satan is broadcasting to the *Surface*?"

Mr. Welles grinned.

"Yes . . . Satan is ready for prime time," he snorted, belching clouds of sickening smoke. "A genius idea if I do say so myself! Those philistines upstairs are going to find out that Orson Welles, while dead, is very much alive . . . with creative fire and burning ambition!"

Mr. Welles continued. "Mysteriously, the Big Guy Downstairs found out about a way to pierce the Transdimensional Power Grid from beneath, sending transmissions from below *up above*. The key just seemed to fall into his lap from some unknown source. And while it's all too easy to pierce the grid to arrive on this side, it's quite something else to send information the other way . . . it's like a catfish dog-paddling upstream—"

"I think you mean like a salmon swimming—"

"Regardless of the particular fish or stroke, it's unprecedented. T.H.E.E.N.D. is not *just* a television network. It is a piece of sprawling theater—impervious to DVR, I might add. A collection of volatile, religious-themed shows that play off and directly against each other, creating a complex web of divisive controversy, pushing the buttons of their specific audiences as if they were on speed dial. The network is like an ensemble cast of antagonistic programming, where each show has its own, unique role to play. . . ."

Mr. Welles flicked cigar ash to the ground.

"And the play's the thing, after all," he added, before pointing to a cast-iron hatch at the far end of the room with the tip of his cigar.

". . . and *that*, young lady, will be your playpen for the next month or so. . . ."

Milton swallowed as he eyed the windowless metal door edged with steel bolts.

Just when we thought TV couldn't get any worse, Milton reflected, *along comes the devil to lower the bar . . . all the way down to h-e-double-hockey-sticks.*

3 · TOUR DE FARCE

MARLO AND THE half-dozen boys that had been waiting in the grandstands squeezed into a red-and-yellow clown car. A pasty-faced, shifty-eyed kid with brown stringy hair that hung in his face like a shredded curtain accidentally put his hand on Marlo's knee.

"Watch it, Grabby," she spat. "Keep those hands where I can see them."

The boy's pupils darted toward Marlo.

"What?" he said, puzzled.

Marlo realized that she was Milton—a lanky, grubby boy—and not a girl surrounded by lanky, grubby boys.

"Um . . . just joking," she replied carefully. "The name is Milton Fauster."

The boy held his hand out at his side like a little flipper, being that personal space was nonexistent in this stuffy, smelly clown car.

"Colby Hayden," the boy said. "Youngest American astronaut. Ever. Died upon reentry after delivering puppies from a Soviet canine cosmonaut trapped aboard a Russian spy satellite as its orbit decayed. Luckily I'm also a veterinarian paramedic."

"*Right.*" Marlo nodded. "I think I read about that in *Deluded Dork* magazine."

P. T. Barnum, pants still ablaze, hopped up on the hood of the clown car. Seconds later, a stooped, shrimp-like demon—a foot and a half tall in its rainbow-colored fright wig—dove into the car, scrambling atop a pile of broken toys, dismembered Barbie parts, and already-colored coloring books to reach the tiny steering wheel.

The vice principal swelled to dangerous life, a hot-air balloon buoyed by flammable gas in a lightning storm. "Okay, Scampi, now that all of our new guests have *finally* arrived," he said, arching his bushy eyebrow Marlo's way, "let us begin our spectacular tour!"

He signaled for Scampi to turn the key in the ignition.

"Welcome to Fibble, Heck's very own Three-Ring Media Circus!" he barked through his tiny blue megaphone. "No bottles, cameras, or pictures of bottles or cameras, or tiny cameras in bottles, *please.*"

The car rumbled to life. Marlo could feel Milton's body getting tight with claustrophobia, while the ache in her brother's gut throbbed and thrummed like a big zit full of bees.

Thanks a lot, bro, Marlo thought as the car lurched

forward. *At least I left my body in decent working order before you switched us.*

The car sped around the bright orange floor of the Big Top in tight circles, spinning faster and faster until it was balancing up on its two right-hand tires. With a sudden swerve and a puff of upturned sawdust, the car careened away, racing toward a solid brick wall.

An African American boy with a burgundy ski beanie sputtered in fear. "Mr. B-Barnum! What are we . . . ? Where are we—?"

The portly vice principal dismissed the child with a wave.

"Please save your questions for after the tour, when they will have more than likely been forgotten," he said, his chins jiggling with every bump.

"But we're going to hit a wall!"

P. T. Barnum sneered. "*Hit a wall?* Don't be ridiculous. We've only just started!"

The boy pulled his beanie down over his eyes as the clown car slammed into the brick barricade. Luckily for all concerned, the wall was simply another piece of expertly painted paper, just like the one at the center of the Big Top floor.

"Here in Fibble, you will be tutored in the fine art of advertising—the massaging of perception for fun and profit," the vice principal shouted through his minimegaphone. "That brick wall was your first lesson. Advertising is about creating problems that aren't real so that they can be solved by otherwise pointless products."

The clown car shot into another spacious circus tent. This one was lavishly decorated, like some kind of comic-book palace painted in bright yellows, reds, and blues, with ornate Middle Eastern archways, high ceilings, and flickering candelabras. The round tent was lined with rooms—classrooms, Marlo assumed—with an open, second level above crammed with bunks. As the gaudy decor whizzed past, Marlo realized that the walls were really just moldy old drywall, their garish paint job and fussy details mere projections cast upon them from above. The archways were plaster—Marlo could see chicken wire poking out from behind—the candles were sputtering electric bulbs, and the high ceilings simply mirrors (unless there was another crazy shrimp-driven clown car snaking up above Marlo's head, she thought).

It was like speeding through a cheap set for a bad TV movie that people on a bad TV show would watch: a tacky, secondhand imitation.

Marlo's quickening pulse slowly cleared her cloudy soul, as if her racing heart were carefully shaving the fuzz from a peach. Crisp images flashed in Marlo's mind before quickly fading away: doing ridiculous errands for Satan as part of her Girl Friday the Thirteenth training, Madame Pompadour's weird Me-Wow spa . . .

"Advertising is another way of saying *marketing*," P. T. Barnum said as his twin trouser torches left trails of sooty smoke behind the speeding car. "Which is another way of saying *manipulation*. Which is another way of saying *the expert sculpting of lies until they resemble a sucker's*—I mean, *customer's*—*unexpressed desires,* those irrational wants and foolish aspirations that gnaw upon our souls like a dog on a bone."

The shrimp demon banked hard to the left, nearly falling off his seat of amputated dolls, while P. T. Barnum struggled to right himself.

"Careful, Scampi, or do I need to put another shrimp on the Barbies?"

The demon shook his rainbow-hued head and honked his squeaky red nose twice. Marlo took that to mean no.

Marlo stared at her brother's hand, knuckles white as it clutched the side of the hightailing clown car. As her sense of herself sluggishly returned, Marlo's immediate circumstances and surroundings seemed all the more hard to believe. It was as if fate had written her a Reality Check that threatened to bounce due to insufficient funds.

Shabby plaster fixtures and flickering projections of opulence streaked past as the clown car scooted toward a massive portrait of a young, slender, ludicrously idealized P. T. Barnum at the far end of the tent.

"In Fibble, we are all craftsmen, fashioning plush pillows of lies for a world sore from sitting upon the hard truth," the real Barnum squawked through his megaphone.

Marlo grew dizzy. Fact and fiction blurred and commingled like a library floor after an earthquake. The glazed faces of Marlo's fellow Fibble freshmen crammed in the backseat like sardines—sardines driven by a jumbo shrimp with horn-nubs poking through its clown wig—confirmed that Marlo wasn't the only one losing her grip on reality.

The lurid light dazzled. Barnum's voice held her in its charismatic sway. The car's steady cradle-like rocking lulled her into a pleasant stupor. Marlo felt drunk on hollow spectacle, disorienting motion, and a steady stream of blustering lies.

Marlo looked up above her and noticed a dome on the ceiling that oozed plumes of heavy, glittering smoke. The projected light danced and twinkled in the shifting haze.

That smoke must be clouding our minds, she thought as she scrunched closed her eyes. In the darkness behind her eyelids, Marlo felt as if her soul was *driving* her brother . . . his body and mind were laid out before her like a dashboard, but her soul was in the driver's seat. Somehow, Milton's innate goodness seemed to help Marlo steer clear of whatever Barnum was trying to sell.

Marlo shook the sticky gossamer cobwebs from her head and opened her eyes. Unfortunately, this was the exact moment that the clown car was about to make impact with the vice principal's larger-than-life-sized portrait. The boys squeezed their eyes shut, yet Marlo's clarity revealed that the painting was merely another portal of flimsy paper.

The clown car tore through the vice principal's pompous visage and careened into the third tent of Fibble's Three-Ring Media Circus.

Marlo's throat tightened. She tried to make sense of what she was seeing. Blue lasers inset in the ceiling sliced through the glittering smog, creating a maze of illusionary paths. Scampi the shrimp demon spun the steering wheel hard to the left, then the right, as he navigated the labyrinth of swirling smoke and light.

The vice principal chortled, like a fleshy frog having just snatched a juicy fly with its tongue. The paths of laser light converged as the car sped toward pitch-black nothingness.

"Advertising is like learning . . . a little is a dangerous thing. That's why all you gifted young liars are here: to learn the power of puffery and to help propel the Greatest Show Under Earth to new heights of dizzying hype! And that, my prevaricating pupils, will be the most dangerous thing of all!"

The clown car hurtled through a wall of black velvet into a concrete hall strewn with castaway props and sets.

Just then, Marlo's stomach flopped harder than *Tourette's Syndrome: The Musical*. It was an awful, swirling, sickening movement in her gut that had plagued her ever since switching bodies with her brother. Something seemed to have awakened the writhing nest of molten yuck in her belly.

The clown car lurched past an area cordoned off

with caution tape marked R & D, patrolled by a sentry of hulking chameleon guards with protruding eyes and camouflage skin (their red kerchiefs gave them away). Marlo could make out beyond the barricade, through dingy chain-link-enforced windows, a maze of brass tubes and tanks, stoppered decanters, and glass vials full of bubbling, silver liquid.

"R and D?" Marlo muttered, patting her stomach gently with her palm.

"Research and Development," Colby clarified. "From what I heard in the stands, no one is allowed in there. But I'm sure Mr. Barnum will let me take a peek once he learns I used to be a scientist. I invented that new electric liquid paper that lets you cover up mistakes you make on your computer."

As Scampi the shrimp demon jabbed the accelerator with a severed Bratz leg, the tiny car zipped away and the dull, slurping ache in Marlo's stomach quieted—that is, until she and the other now-screaming passengers of the clown car realized that they were speeding toward a small flaming hoop. The lapping, crackling flames, to Marlo's eyes, were all too real.

"Well, thus concludes our tour," P. T. Barnum said as he took off his top hat and flung it toward one of the lizard demons, who watched it whiz past with its stereoscopic eyes. "Please exit responsibly. *While you still can.*"

4 · ONE HOT PROPERTY, PRICED TO MOVE

"DO YOU KNOW what that room is?" Mr. Welles posed as he gestured grandly toward the imposing metal door at the far corner of the office. Milton shrugged.

"Off-limits?" he replied hopefully.

Mr. Welles guffawed like an idling old minivan in need of an oil change.

"No and yes," he continued as he galumphed toward the dull, hexagonal door. "For production assistants, no. For everyone else, *yes*."

Milton followed behind as Terri and the other girls shot him hostile glares at this sudden, upward shift in status. Mr. Welles gave the small red wheel at the center of the door a twist and nudged the hatch open. Inside was a cove with darkened TV screens and old video players mounted in each of the chamber's twelve panels, with a thirteenth screen set in the ceiling.

"Behold the Boob Tube," Mr. Welles said as he led Milton—who couldn't help but let out a short-lived snicker at the word "boob"—into the cramped, cylindrical nook. "*Sit*, Miss Fauster. . . ."

Milton wriggled into the swiveling chair at the center of the Boob Tube. Mr. Welles handed Milton a stack of scripts and schedules.

"This will be your T.H.E.E.N.D. Command Center—the bosom of our operation," Mr. Welles relayed in a voice as thick and slow as vintage cough syrup. "Where you can review the latest script revisions, juggle our criminally insane production schedule, review dailies on a weekly basis, and even evaluate submissions, as I simply haven't the time."

Mr. Welles fidgeted with a leather attaché case tucked under his arm.

"Speaking of which . . ."

He pulled out a stack of scripts and a thick old Beta videocassette and dropped them onto Milton's lap.

"Oddest thing," Mr. Welles said as he put on his wide-brimmed fedora and made his way to the door. "No one beyond the devil's inner circle even knows about T.H.E.E.N.D., yet I received an amateur submission just this morning. Normally I wouldn't consider such things—crass art *by* the people *for* the people and all—but my timeline is tighter than the elastic band on my boxers, and I have a lot of airwaves to pollute, so I'll consider just about anything."

Mr. Welles lingered in the doorway, smirking.

"I'll leave you to your entertainment laboratory, miss," he said in his crumpled velvet voice.

Milton cringed. Not only did he hate being referred to as "miss," but—judging from the soft hair rising on his sister's forearms—Marlo wasn't too keen on it either.

Mr. Welles's eyes gleamed with dangerous fire, twinkling like the fuse of a just-lit explosive.

"In fact, you could say that the whole wide world is our laboratory . . . with T.H.E.E.N.D. as the ultimate experiment in mass programming."

Mr. Welles lumbered out of the Boob Tube and shut the hatch behind him, giving the handle a twist and sealing Milton inside.

Milton sighed as he considered the hefty stack of scripts upon his lap. His usual joy in reading seemed dampened by the body in which his soul was currently residing, as Marlo wasn't exactly a bookworm.

Milton felt as if his soul was house-sitting: his sister's weirder-than-weird sociopathic halfway house at that. So, until he got more accustomed to being Marlo, Milton decided to watch a little TV instead.

A moment after slipping in the videocassette, a glowing white title flashed on the black screen, accompanied by the sound of a fuzzed-out guitar lick.

THE MAN WHO SOLDETH THE WORLD

PART ONE: THE DEAL

The title dissolved to show the Eiffel Tower piercing the lazy, pink-frosted clouds of dusk. The sluggish sun gave one last Gallic shrug of light before disappearing behind roofs supporting hundreds of clay chimney pots.

" 'Tis in a wondrous location, with lots of curb appeal," explained a haughty voice offscreen. "Convenient to most everything while maintaining an aloof charm. And the price is in *Seine* . . . get it? The river that floweth through central Paris?"

The camera—obviously operated by the speaker—panned to a creature by its side: a large, woolly pot of gurgling pudding with slimy white tentacles for feet.

"In any case, the right buyer could do much unto it," the voice continued, sounding as if the speaker's throat was made of alabaster and his vocal cords the plucked strings of a harp.

The creature's cube of a head was like a large die, only instead of spots on each side, the creature had various set facial expressions. Floating in its creamy, churning, butterscotch-colored guts, the creature's bobbing head rotated from a Smiley Face to a Face Creased with Skepticism.

"Let thine eyes set upon another room," the voice

sighed as the unseen man tossed a stick of gum into the creature's pot.

"This will help keep your ears from popping during the quantum folding process . . . if thou even *hast* ears, that is."

The image began to wobble, the Paris skyline shimmering in sweeping waves until, finally, the picturesque scene crumpled as if scrunched by a pair of gargantuan, invisible hands.

Cool, Milton thought as he shifted in his chair, enthralled by the show's combination of candid, reality-TV amateurism and expertly rendered locations and special effects.

A new vista began to uncrease and flatten until smooth, one of sweeping sands and majestic stone pyramids.

"Now *this* wing not only boasteth designer features—handcrafted I may add," the unseen narrator said as he traipsed across a dune before turning the camera back at his bubbling client. "Hands are like little meat tools that Earth mammals use to . . . it is of no import. What *is,* especially if your race happens to be prone to allergies, is an arid environment devoid of molds and airborne spores. And please take note of the high ceilings."

The creature's block head flopped between a Skeptical and a Seriously Considering It face.

"Thy Surreal Estate Agent said that thou wert highly motivated, what with your home world being renovated and all," the voice relayed with a trace of irritation. "But I have one more wing to show you: a cozy nook that, with meager finishing touches, could be a righteous showpiece."

The scorching desert air began to hum and quiver around them, until the sand, pyramids, and great stone sphinx crinkled and folded away.

In Egypt's place unfolded a creased panorama of oil-slicked mudflats and offshore refineries belching out acrid soot.

"I . . . I humbly prostrate myself," the voice apologized. "I must have accidentally taken us to-eth the very ends of the Earth, or at least the same zip code."

The creature vibrated like a teakettle.

"You . . . *like it*?" the voice inferred. "Let me restate, I *knew* that thou would liketh it. It just required someone with sweeping vision who could see to the bones . . . *the possibilities.*"

The creature tottered toward the foamy surf that sluggishly caressed the shore.

"And do not concern thyself with the humans," the unseen man continued as he joined the extraterrestrial pudding pop on the gloomy shorefront. "*The bald monkeys.* They hath been squatting here for ages. A true nuisance. I will see that they are cleared away."

The creature's square, dielike head rotated in its pool

of gurgling guts, its Face of Delight rolling to one of Suspicious Inquiry.

"How?" the man replied in his smooth yet ancient voice. "I assureth thee that the humans would only be relocated and in the most humane way possible; that is to say 'kind' and 'without hurting' as opposed to 'what a human would do.' The transfer would be seamless—going off with nary a hitch—and no creature would be-eth the wiser. . . ."

The man turned away from the creature, his camera briefly trained upon the dismal cloud cover overhead.

". . . Not even the Big Guy Upstairs," he mumbled beneath his breath as he turned his small surveillance camera back to the creature. "I taketh it we have a deal, then," the man continued as he pulled out a contract from the inner pocket of his white robe. "There art only six billion or so of them to evict, so I'm sure that I could have the place ready for ye by, say, when Polaris entereth the third phase of Ophiuchus?"

The man rolled up the contract and tossed it into the creature's churning sea of tapioca entrails.

"Or, as the locals sayeth," he added with an audible smile, *"by the first of the month."*

The image abruptly ended, and the VCR spat out the bulky cassette like a fussy kid rejecting a slice of meatless meat loaf.

Wow, it was all so real, but—at the same time—absolutely

ridiculous, Milton reflected, his sister's dark eyes wide with awe. *But of course it* can't *be. I mean, the exotic locations, aliens on the Surface, teleportation, someone actually selling* the Earth. *It's got to be an elaborate hoax.*

Milton stared at the monitor that glowed faintly in the dimness of the Boob Tube. He tried to shake off the creepy feeling that gripped him about the waist—though it very well could have been the itching, cinching tights that he had tugged on so poorly this morning.

I switched places with Marlo so I could go as deep and as far into the dark heart of this place as I could, he reflected as he stared at his sister's reflected face in the monitor. *So I've got to just keep my cool, keep my eyes open, and let everything play as far as it can, then—when the moment is right—somehow turn it all around. . . .*

5 · FROM AD TO WORSE

MARLO SUNK DOWN as best she could into the unyielding vinyl upholstery of the clown car as the circle of sizzling flame sped ever closer.

She wasn't sure if she could believe her brother's nearsighted eyes. The blazing hoop just *had* to be another one of Barnum's lies, but it seemed so real. In any case, Marlo didn't relish the thought of getting the third degree from Milton about his third-degree burns, in the off chance that they ever reunited.

P. T. Barnum reached through the nonexistent windshield and grabbed an orange crash helmet.

"I will see you gentlemen on the other side," he said as he secured the helmet's strap in between two of his chins.

With that, P. T. Barnum gave a thumbs-up to Scampi, who jabbed a button on the dashboard with a decommissioned G.I. Joe. The hood flung open, sending Fibble's vice principal soaring through the air. Fortunately for the passengers, the hood also acted as a parachute, bringing the hurtling car to a halt before its hot date with the hissing hoop of flame.

Marlo and the other boys were dragged out of the car by a sudden rush of shrimp demons in clown wigs. *It's like being attacked by bait,* Marlo thought as she and the boys were herded into the darkened Big Top and shoved into the stands.

A spotlight stabbed the dark. Teetering thirty feet above the Big Top floor on a high wire was a tiny man smoking a cigar, holding a balancing pole with two shrimp demons in face paint on either side.

Just then, P. T. Barnum popped out of a paper painting of himself popping out of a paper painting of himself. He strutted out beneath the high wire, tugging at his flame-retardant suspenders with one thumb and holding a bullhorn to his toadlike face.

"Fibble's three rings work in perfect concert with one another," Barnum bellowed. "It's how we turn mere marketing into the ultimate show!"

The little man inched along the wire above, trembling as he steadied himself and his squirming shrimp cargo. His smoldering cigar sizzled toward his lips.

"The first ring, as our diminutive dynamo Tom Thumb is illustrating up above, is a precarious walk between truth and lie. Too much candor will turn customers away, while heaping on too many fallacious claims . . . well, customers will sniff those out like a dog-hair toupee, and then your whole enterprise crashes to the ground."

Just as Tom Thumb crept toward the end of the high wire, his cigar sputtered like a fuse to his pursed lips. Sweating, he swallowed his cigar butt. After a violent belch of smoke, Tom Thumb listed sideways. Several shrimp demons rushed beneath him holding an over-flowing tub of cocktail sauce, just in time to catch the plummeting pint-sized acrobat and his shellfish compan-ions.

"The second ring," Barnum continued, "is where you take your carefully crafted messages—blended like the perfect martini—and create breathless spectacle: a dizzy-ing display that cuts through apathetic haze, a stupefying cure for shrugs and malaise! In short, a media circus that short-circuits common sense!"

There was something about the vice principal that Marlo despised—and that something was *everything*. He acted like he knew all the answers, which is easy when you make up all the questions.

"Moving right along," P. T. Barnum bellowed as he waved the spotlight toward the far end of the Big Top. The circle of glare settled on a pair of tiny orange-and-green cannons.

Marlo noticed the dried, desiccated remains of some fishlike creature hung on the wall above the cannons. Beneath the black, mummified body was a sign reading THE FEEJEE MERMAID. Marlo had thought it a patch of particularly industrious mold until the creepy eyesore began furiously pumping a hurdy-gurdy.

The Feejee Mermaid squeezed its accordion in languid, drawn-out gasps. Two shrimp demons with crash helmets were prodded toward the cannons by what looked like floating pitchsporks, but—Marlo could tell if she squinted Milton's eyes just right—they were wielded by tall, lanky chameleons that nearly blended perfectly with the background.

This has got to be the weirdest thing I've ever seen, Marlo thought as the creepy mermaid music wheezed faster and faster. *Unless I saw something incredibly, jaw-droppingly freaky-deeky in the last week or so that I still can't really remember.* While flashes of Marlo's memory were indeed returning, her recollection of the last few days in particular was patchier than a hobo's pantaloons.

"The third ring is how all this razzle-dazzle is dispatched, so that every message is dished out just right— oh so shiny, oh so bright—so they oompah like a big brass band!" Barnum bellowed, liltingly, through his bullhorn.

The two struggling shrimp demons—sporting tutus and false eyelashes glued to their black olive-like eyeballs— were shoved in the cannons. Tom Thumb struck a match on the heel of his boot and lit the twin fuses.

P. T. Barnum, already froglike with his sagging jowls

and protruding eyes, hopped spryly upon an overturned basin.

"When the three rings are linked together," he said, flamboyantly waving his disproportionately small hand toward the cannons, "it's bigger than a movie, than a TV show . . . it's pure, breathtaking marketing theater! And, with a potent advertising cocktail such as this, what could possibly go wrong?"

With that, the cannons exploded. Yet instead of discharging the two shrimps in drag, the cannons merely disgorged a foul-smelling spray of fish bits and face paint.

It's like a beluga's backwash, Marlo thought in the stands as she waved away the salty stink.

The Feejee Mermaid's demented music slowed to a creepy crawl before stopping altogether. The Big Top went suddenly dark.

The brief moment of silence was shattered by the skull-cleaving din of horns and noisemakers as the Big Top was engulfed by floodlights.

The Scampi-driven clown car zipped along the rim of the ring, stuffed with squealing shrimp demons holding buckets.

"Who wants their new Fibble uniforms?!" Barnum squawked through his bullhorn.

The boys shared blank looks of disinterest while Marlo tried to control the sharp, gender-specific curiosity she had toward what she would be forced to wear.

Marlo tentatively raised Milton's scrawny arm.

Scampi hopped out of the speeding car, coiled up into a ball around the spinning bucket, and skidded to a halt in front of Marlo. Unfortunately for his fellow demons, the now-unchauffeured car careened into a bale of hay.

Scampi pitched the contents of the bucket all over Marlo. The boys on either side of her dove away as she was coated by sodden, slimy white clumps. She watched her arm, in shock, as it shimmered with tiny, writhing worms. Marlo screamed, though the piercing timbre was dampened by her brother's preadolescent vocal cords.

"What are these?!" she howled as the pale, wet worms slithered all over her body.

"Little white lice," Barnum croaked. "Now you're dressed for deceit—Fibble-style!"

The lice knitted themselves into a shimmering, constricting unitard all over Marlo.

"It *itches!*" she whined as the unitard tightened.

"They are hungry," Barnum added, his sneer somehow amplified by the bullhorn. "And want to be fed . . . *with fibs.*"

Marlo's stomach lurched. The swirling queasiness in her belly, the suit of slimy white lice . . . it was all too much. She bolted down the stands and out of the Big Top, running through the next tent past the R & D lab. Marlo's stomach folded in two like a gastrointestinal deck chair. The little white lice girdling her belly bit angrily. She spun around, almost delirious with nausea, and saw the Boys' Unrestroom.

Marlo charged through the door toward the sink with the intent of splashing water on her face and getting a grip on her gut. Instead, hit by the filth and depravity of the facilities—which, truth be told, weren't a far cry from your average Little Boys' Room up on the Surface—Marlo lost the lunch she hadn't had yet in the sink.

As Marlo opened her eyes, she saw, amidst the confounding kernels of corn (*Is there some undiscovered organ that collects corn strictly for regurgitation purposes?* Marlo pondered fleetingly), a tarnished glass-and-metal pendant. She delicately scooped it up from the basin and washed it clean. Marlo held up the puzzling, puked-up jewelry to her face and rubbed the crystal droplet with her thumb. Inside was a gently swirling liquid, like melted silver, that burbled to her touch. The sheet of little white lice crawling on her sleeve unraveled themselves to move away from the pendant, giving Marlo's arm the occasional stinging bite in protest. She looked over the pendant into her brother's face staring back at her in the mirror.

Of all Milton's freaky quirks, I never pegged him to be a compulsive jewelry swallower, Marlo thought as she leaned against the disgusting roll of soiled cloth towels bolted to the wall. *He must have gulped it down just before he got to h-e-double-hockey-sticks, before we switched souls, when I was still a zombie from Madame Pompadour's spa, and that weird milk bath—*

It was all coming back to her. Fuzzy, like your tongue the morning after Halloween, but—nevertheless—the fog shrouding her short-term memory was slowly beginning to lift.

Milk of Amnesia . . . that's what it said on the bottle in Madame Pompadour's spa. No wonder I couldn't remember anything.

Marlo was mesmerized by the soothing liquid inside the pendant. It was the only thing that seemed real here, a glimmer of truth in this circus of lies. Somehow, just holding it in her palm pushed out the noise crowding her mind, all the chatter left there by the bitter bureaucrats and antagonizing authority figures populating her so-called afterlife. The pendant made her feel like a once-living bar of Ivory Soap: 99.44 percent pure, give or take a few dozen percentage points.

The silver liquid inside seemed familiar in some hazy way, Marlo thought. It looked kind of like the stuff the PODs—the Phantoms of the Dispossessed—collected back . . . back . . . *in Rapacia. Yes, that's where I've seen it,* she thought as the murk in her mind thinned. *Like the stuff dribbling from the tubes in . . .*

"*The R & D lab!*" Marlo whispered.

Marlo wiped away a layer of disgusting, wriggling lice and stuffed the pendant in her pocket. The second the pendant touched any of the little white lice, they immediately curled up, shriveled, and burned away, scattering to the ground like bits of Cajun fried rice.

Barnum said the lice were fed with fibs, she thought curiously, *which means that—if they're dying—this stuff must be full of* . . . the truth!

Marlo looked back at her brother's face in the mirror.

"I have the truth in my pocket," Marlo murmured to Milton's image. "I just wish you were here—*really* here—to help me figure out what the truth even *means* in a place like Fibble!"

6 · A PET PEEVED

CERBERUS GROWLED IN a three-part harmony, heavy on the *harm*. It was rare that his three heads agreed on anything. If you were to serve him a bowl of porridge, for instance, one head would find it too cold, the other head too hot, and the third head would bite your face off for having the audacity to serve it porridge in the first place. In this peculiar case, though, all three heads agreed to be disagreeable.

"There, there, my whiddle stack of whuffles all covered in syrup!" Bea "Elsa" Bubb cooed in a sickening gush of treacle that threatened all diabetic demons within a mile radius. "Why so tense? Do you need me to wub your whiddle footie pads?"

Cerberus bounded off the Principal of Darkness's lap. His distress would not be allayed by a footie massage, even the kind with the imported baby dolphin oil.

Something familiar and tormenting tickled his six nostrils before taunting the back of his throat. The nagging musk of lost prey. Cerberus coiled himself in front of the door to the principal's not-so-secret lair, his wet snouts flaring between the gaps of its rotten Foul Weather Stripping.

Principal Bubb rose from her chair, smoothing her new genuine Heckifino skirt.

"Fine, my bitter sweetums," she said as she walked from her corn chowder–colored Barfolounger toward her desk. "Mommy's not feeling her beast either. There's something afoot, and it stinks."

The principal sat down behind her imposing mahogany desk strewn with an assortment of official documents, less-than-official documents, definitely unofficial documents, and bags of empty Assaulted Unicorn chips. She sighed as she reread her Notice of Double-Secret Probation.

EMPLOYEE NAME: Bea "Elsa" Bubb
DEPARTMENT: Heck
DATE OF NOTICE: As you are in Limbo, Today, Right Now

You are hereby, as of this writing, put on Double-Secret Probation regarding your significant role in the unfortunately named BOWEL (Blimpo: Overweight With Erroneous Laws) Movement uprising. Your colossal lapse in judgment, when you saw fit to deputize most every demon guard in Blimpo to aid you in your crusade against Milton Fauster, left the circle uncharacteristically lean in terms of disciplinary personnel.

The above-mentioned misconduct constitutes adequate grounds to terminate your employment. We—the Powers That Be Evil—however, wish to give you another opportunity to prove your value to our company, and are therefore placing you on Double-Secret Probation, a probation that is initially kept secret to spare you any undue humiliation yet, due to the secret being kept a secret, your probation is thus rendered unsecret, or double-secret—for a period of six months, which, considering your base of operations is in Limbo, where time has no meaning, is another way of saying "until we see fit."

In the event there is a repeat incident, we shall have no choice but to terminate your employment without further notice. You will be notified if we decide to terminate your employment without notice.

Sincerely,
THE POWERS THAT BE EVIL

Multiple copies sent to: The Department of Unendurable Redundancy, Bureaucracy, and Redundancy

Principal Bubb crushed the paper in her talons, yet—due to the notice being printed on special uncrumpleable paper—it infuriatingly smoothed back to its original, mocking state.

You would think that capturing Milton Fauster would count for something, the principal seethed to herself. *Sure, I was capturing him because he escaped . . .* twice. *But at least I was showing initiative.*

Principal Bubb scooped up several puzzling financial statements that had come to her attention. Apparently, a flux of mysterious funds had been funneled to Fibble and the Furafter. Though the untraceable transactions had bypassed her authority due to her current probation—and the fact that the Furafter was not her purview—the Department of Unendurable Redundancy, Bureaucracy, and Redundancy had sent her multiple copies, in triplicate, several times over.

She would normally find this only mildly irritating, but considering that not only had P. T. Barnum, Fibble's vice principal, failed to return any of her calls, *but* Milton Fauster—the procedural snag at which her career had begun to unravel—had also just been transferred there, she was a touch concerned.

Plus, Satan had seemed so distracted lately, so immersed in the devilish details of his own diversions that he had left much of the Netherworld to its own devices—*never* a good idea considering some of the nefarious devices that could be found down here.

Principal Bubb sighed, leaned back in her chair, and put her hooves up on her desk. She stared up at a patch of sick some child had projectile vomited on the ceiling long ago.

Many of the devil's decrees were monkey business as usual, like cutting corners by downgrading Heck's toilet paper quality, she thought, squirming in her chair. But a few of his actions didn't seem like him at all, such as pouring money into some new TV network—as if any world, whether under, above, or in between, *needed* another TV network. It would be one thing if h-e-double-hockey-sticks was showing a profit, but the Netherworld was in the red—a *deep* red hemorrhaging of funds impossible to ignore even in this predominantly red place. Shifting his focus to some vanity project was inexcusable.

Instead of wasting my afterlife mooning over the devil, I should be looking out for myself, the principal seethed as she uncrossed her haunches.

Something rapped upon the principal's door. She rose from her chair.

"What is it?" she called out.

The door to her lair opened.

"Excuse me, Principal Bubb," a thin, ropy demon resembling a twisted pepperoni stick said, peering inside the not-so-secret lair. "It's time for your Swedish Mass Age treatment—oww!!"

Cerberus had sunk all three sets of his mercilessly sharp teeth into the demon guard's leg before bolting past him into the hallway.

"Cerberus!" Bea "Elsa" Bubb shrieked. "My widdle boopsy bottom! Come back!"

For perhaps the first time in his monstrous life, the three-headed dog failed to heed his master. His claws scrabbled along the slick floor of the hallways, shooting sparks behind him.

"Don't just stand there, you ridiculous, once-living rawhide!" the principal screeched at the demon guard. "Go wave yourself in front of my schmoopy cuddle snugglet and get him back this instant!"

The demonic meat-stick-of-a-man bowed and trundled after Cerberus, who, at this point, was just a fuzzy, panting, clattering blur. Demons, teachers, and assorted dead boys and girls dove out of the creature's determined way.

Principal Bubb darted out of her office and hoofed it into the hallway.

"Oh my badness!" she gasped. "My li'l wuv devil! I *knew* I shouldn't have switched to that new Impurina Hound Chow!"

The corridor was a carnival of confusion.

"Calling all demon guards!" the principal bellowed as an oily tear seeped out of her pus-yellow goat eye. "Drop what you are pretending to be doing at once and bring me back my *precious moopie lumkin chunkalunks!*"

But it was too late. Cerberus was running like a wingless bat out of Heck.

7 · DÉJÀ VOODOO

"DO YOU KNOW why you cry when you cut an onion?" Colby asked in that way that isn't a question, more like an announcement that your time is about to be hijacked at tongue-point.

Marlo cinched the telephone-wire suspenders that held up her flaming pants. They weren't literally on fire like those of her vice principal—fortunately, as she never *did* have the legs for hot pants, now even less so as her brother—but emblazoned with lapping flames poorly embroidered with red and orange thread.

"No, but I have a feeling I'm about to find out," she said as they walked to their first class.

"They used to think it was because of some chemical in the onions," Colby said as he scratched at his lice-infested shirt. "But . . . it's really because you—

everybody—craves onions right when they are about to cry."

Marlo smirked despite herself.

"Well, I'm about to cry from boredom . . . does that count?"

She noticed that, right after Colby told a whopper of a lie, he stopped scratching. *The little white lice are hungry,* Barnum had said, *and want to be fed with fibs.* Marlo fumbled for her brother's puked-up pendant that she kept in her pocket. For whatever reason, it seemed to keep the little white lice comatose, like some kind of repellant.

The class bell tolled as Marlo and Colby stepped into a room resounding with crazy drumming and chanting. There, in front of a circle of students with conga drums for desks, were three old men wearing neckties and grass skirts. Marlo recognized Mr. Nixon but didn't recognize the other two men, though they all wore a similar expression of assumed importance and, unfortunately, not much else.

"Ah, the late, hardly great Mr. Fauster and some anonymous shifty-eyed ragamuffin," Mr. Nixon replied with a deep rattle. "To your drums . . . *if it's not too much trouble.*"

Marlo brushed past the chalkboard by the door, which—scrawled across it in fancy cursive letters—read: "Voodoo Economics, taught by dead presidents Fillmore and Pierce with special guest Mr. Nixon."

Marlo made her way to an empty drum in the back

of the room. Next to it, a boy was stooped over, scratching his calf.

"Excuse me, Itchy McScab, but is this drum taken?" Marlo asked the boy's back.

With deep brown eyes daubed onto a stark white canvas of a face, the boy looked up at Marlo with sullen charisma.

"Zane!" Marlo yelped girlishly.

Zane Covington, the cool British exchange student she had met back in Rapacia! While the particulars of Marlo's Infernship were still just vague smears finger-painted across her memory, Zane's brief appearance had had a profound effect upon her psyche. Even in his flame-print pants and writhing, lice-encrusted shirt, he was still a "smashing bloke."

Impulsively, Marlo bent down to give him a hug. Zane recoiled.

"Whoa, mate," he replied with a look of sour shock. "I'm a Brit. We don't do that."

As the boys on either side of Zane snickered, the full awfulness of her situation drizzled foully down upon Marlo, as if incontinent pigeons had suddenly flocked overhead.

I'm Milton, she thought sadly. *I'm finally next to a boy that doesn't make me want to dry heave, and I'm my brother. My skinny, gross* boy *of a brother.*

Marlo tried to pull herself together.

"I, um, am Milton," Marlo managed as she sat down

behind the conga drum. "You saved me from becoming a big gold statue back in Mallvana—you know, the Grabbit's big ceremony?—when King Midas tried to grab me . . . he actually grabbed this big sort of centipede demon guard thing—yuck, huh?!—that had grabbed *me*, really, but . . ."

Zane's eyes became faraway, as if his mind had booked a flight to an exotic locale. Marlo sighed.

"I'm Marlo's brother . . . *Marlo Fauster.*"

Zane's eyes returned home, suddenly, from their short vacation, not even taking time to flip through the mail.

"Marlo?" he said in his faintly posh accent. Zane examined Milton's face. "Yeah, I suppose there *is* a resemblance."

Marlo shut her eyes.

I do not look like my hideous, mutant, goody-goody, sci-fi convention–going, comic book–collecting geek of a brother! Marlo screamed in her head.

"Have you heard from her?" Zane asked. Marlo was filled with a sort of full-body nausea. It was weird. She was queasy all over but didn't want it to go away. It was like being on a roller coaster that only went down.

"Not in a while," Marlo replied, opening her eyes. "But last time I saw her, she seemed great. And she looked really good, too! You know . . . for a sister . . ."

Suddenly, someone thwacked Marlo's drum, nearly causing her to jump out of her brother's skin.

"Mr. Fauster," the overweight, piggish-looking man said as he leaned into Marlo. "Do you have any idea who I am?"

Marlo looked the shirtless geezer up and down.

"No, but let me guess," she replied crisply. "You used to be really important, or so you thought, and—in the end—that didn't really matter. Now you're down here in a grass skirt with two other bygone bozos forced to deal with brats like me—a fate you can't stand, but there you go. You were famous, though no one here knows who you are, and—to you—I'm nothing, but here we are in the same room. It's kind of funny, but no one is laughing."

The man's torso flushed crimson with rage.

"I'm Millard Fillmore," he hissed, "the thirteenth president of the United States of America!"

"That's what I meant," Marlo said, sharing a sideways smirk with Zane.

Mr. Fillmore lunged at Marlo across the drum, before being restrained by a skinny, nervous old man with wavy salt-and-pepper hair.

"Millard," the man said in a quavering voice. "You know what Principal Bubb said about strangling students."

Mr. Fillmore composed himself as much as a half-naked senior citizen can.

"Yes, Franklin, that it should never be done during class. What we do on our own time is our own business."

"*Benjamin* Franklin?" Colby said, peeking through a gap in his hair. "Like the guy that discovered kites?"

Mr. Nixon smacked his drum impatiently. "Franklin *Pierce*," he clarified. "The fourteenth president of the United States, and can we all please get back to the subject at hand?" he said, his jowls hula dancing with outrage as he and the other two teachers trudged back to the chalkboard.

Zane leaned in close to Marlo.

"You've got your sister's nerve," he whispered.

Marlo slid back in her chair with a dopey grin smeared across her brother's dopey face.

"You don't know the half of it," she murmured.

Mr. Nixon scratched a series of short, seemingly contradictory phrases on the chalkboard: "Spending saves money. Tax cuts increase tax revenue. More for the rich means more for the poor. Increased supply equals increased demand."

He beamed at the words on the board.

"That's our lesson, in a nutshell," he said, the ex-president's face threatening to slide into his grinning mouth. "Therein lies the beauty of Voodoo Economics, its simplicity and eerie ability to solve every financial problem at once."

The African American boy with the ski beanie raised his hand. Mr. Fillmore glanced down at the student roster on the teachers' desk.

"Yes, Mr. . . . . Cummings?"

"Yeah, *Darnell Cummings,*" the boy said as he folded his arms and sat back in his chair. "I used to work after school as a janitor at MIT and had a gift for math, despite my blue-collar roots. But achieving my dream of being a math wiz meant turning my back on my working-class neighbor and best friend—"

"Sounds like something out of a movie," Mr. Nixon said dubiously. "Your point?"

"My point," Darnell continued, "is that nothing on the chalkboard makes any sense."

Mr. Nixon pounded his fists on his drum.

"That's because it's magic!" he shrieked. "That voodoo that we do that's so swell! It's not supposed to make *sense* . . . it's supposed to make *dollars*! Lots of them!"

Mr. Pierce hiked up the sagging grass skirt that kept drifting below his blinding white belly.

"Maybe if they saw it in action, Mr. Nixon," he offered.

"Of course," Mr. Nixon said as he turned to erase the chalkboard. "Let's start with a clean slate." He stooped down to retrieve a piece of fallen chalk.

"And no more wisecracks," Mr. Nixon said, giving the students an entirely new and unwelcome view of the thirty-seventh president of the United States.

He scratched the words "trickle down" on the chalkboard.

Mr. Pierce let loose a salvo of conga slaps. "Now,

students, chant after us," he hollered. *"Trickle down to make profits go up! Shine the crown to fill the beggar's cup!"*

As the students apathetically smacked their drums and mumbled along with the three half-naked politicians, the PA speakers in the classroom's ceiling squealed and squawked.

"This is ARGH—Ahoy Rogues, Guerillas, and Hearties!—your pirate radio station!" a gruff, salty voice thundered through the speakers. "I'm yer marnin' DJ, Calico Jack, broadcasting live—or as live as could be expected, considerin'—from the corner of None of Yer Beeswax and Wouldn't You Like to Know?!"

The dead presidents clapped their ears.

"What is that infernal racket?" Mr. Fillmore spat.

Pirates? Marlo thought as the students around her sat up straight, roused awake by the salty spray of chaos. *Taking over a classroom through a PA system?*

"In our roving ramshackle studio," Calico Jack continued, "we've got the one and only Truthador here to play for us one of his puzzling yet catchy-as-a-wet-hacking-cough-below-deck musical yarns. So, without any more of me bilge," Calico Jack said, punctuating the word "bilge" with the prerecorded sound of a toilet flushing, "here be the Truthador!"

"He's walked infinite miles down a higher-than highway. This slick creature of wiles . . . will never see things my way," the Truthador sang in a grating yet oddly compelling wheeze, like a rusty old harmonica against a steady

strum of harp. *"Now he's a-itchin' to sell us all out, and max out our species' charge card. But it's a hard, it's a hard, it's a hard . . . truth's a-gonna fall."*

The boys began scratching themselves beneath their lice-infested shirts.

Despite the itching, there was something about the Truthador that Marlo sort of liked. Even though the song reminded her of the music her dad used to listen to in his den when he felt sad or old or sad that he was old, there was something about it that struck a chord with her. It felt *real*. The music also made Milton's pendant warm and cool at the same time, a strange sensation of confidence that spread out throughout her body—or Milton's body if you wanted to get technical.

"Though his lies can blind and twist tongues till they're broken, I'm here to tell mankind, from down here to Hoboken," the Truthador sang. *"That he won't kick us out, to some lame-o space junkyard. 'Cuz it's a hard, it's a hard, it's a hard . . . truth's a-gonna fall."*

The class bell tolled and the boys flew out of their chairs. Marlo hung back, pretending she was having trouble with her weird shoe—pinched sneakers with heels so that they were always on their toes.

"So, how come you're in Fibble?" she asked Zane. "I mean, last time I saw you, you were in Rapacia."

Zane looked at Marlo quizzically.

"Rapacia?" he asked, puzzled. "I don't remember you in Rapacia."

Marlo blushed. *Of course he doesn't remember me,* she thought. *I was me then; now I'm not.*

"Right. I meant Mallvana. Marlo was in Rapacia. We're so close that sometimes it's hard to figure out where I end and she begins!"

Zane shot Marlo a peculiar sideways glance, like how a psychiatrist views a patient right before deciding to up their dosage.

"Okay . . . sure . . . um, anyway, I was all twitchy back there with wanting to take things—"

Marlo's stomach felt like a halfway house for recovering squirrels.

"Yeah," she replied. "I know what you . . . I mean, *Marlo* would tell me how that felt. That weird, allover itchiness that begins deep in the stomach then branches out through your arms and fingers, that itch that only snatching something can scratch."

Zane stared at Marlo, startled, as they headed toward the door.

"Something like that," he said. "*Spot on,* actually."

Mr. Pierce grabbed Zane's hand at the doorway.

"I hope I can count on your vote," he said, pumping Zane's and Marlo's hands.

Zane and Marlo walked down the hallway of ramshackle, crumbling plaster columns and flickering projections of ornate lamps and wall sconces, all painted—Marlo realized—as if with clown makeup.

"So you were talking about how you got here," Marlo continued. "To Fibble."

"Right," Zane said. "Anyway, I started, um, *collecting* chalk. *Loads* of it. After a while, it was getting hard to hide it and—one day—I got caught white-handed. But I still wouldn't bobby to it, no matter how darning the evidence was. For some reason I just couldn't admit that I was a chalk stealer. Frightful embarrassing! Finally, after talking with headmistress O'Malley—"

"She's awesome . . . I hear."

"Yeah, all that great, flowing red hair," Zane said with a faraway smile.

Marlo prickled with jealousy.

"*Anyway,* go on."

"Right, so we both agreed that my urge to porky, that is *lie,* about stealing was a little stronger than my urge to nick, that is *steal*—at least in this case—so Grace, um . . . headmistress O'Malley, transferred me here."

"Well, it's nice to have you—I mean, *a friend*—here," Marlo said, gazing into Zane's soft brown eyes that stared back like twin chocolate pudding cups. And even though her confession had caused an outbreak of squirming lice bites over her heart, it was worth it.

8 · GETTiNG DOWN TO SHOW BUSiNESS

INT. SMALL CAVELIKE DWELLING—NIGHT
A simple, one-room home made of stone,
circa AD 16. MARY, a young woman with
large, kind eyes and a hood holding back
her long dark hair, chases after her
agitated ADOLESCENT SON.

                    MARY
Son! What has gotten into you?

                ADOLESCENT SON
You wouldn't understand. No one
understands!

An older, shrewish woman, the boy's
AUNTIE, hovers over MARY.

                    AUNTIE
Bah! The boy will never amount to anything!
He's brought you nothing but trouble since
he was born. All those weirdos dropping by
at all hours, hanging on his every word!

                ADOLESCENT SON
Those "weirdos" are my friends!

AUNTIE turns her nose up and leaves. MARY
tries to put her hands on the ADOLESCENT
SON's shoulders, but he shrugs them off.
She sighs.

                    MARY
Why don't you go to the temple? Aren't
they having a dance today? Maybe that
girl you like will be there. What's her
name . . . Magda?

The ADOLESCENT SON blushes, embarrassed.

                ADOLESCENT SON
Ah, Mom!

JOSEPH, a bearded man in a brown robe and head wrap, enters through the primitive wooden door.

> JOSEPH

I'm home! Phew . . . what a day at the salt mines!

JOSEPH senses the tension in the room.

> JOSEPH

What gives?

The ADOLESCENT SON rolls his eyes and tries to leave. JOSEPH grabs him by the wrist.

> JOSEPH

Oh no you don't. You're staying right here and we're talking this out.

> ADOLESCENT SON

She tells me to leave, you tell me to stay . . . you're both tearing me apart!!

MARY begins to cry. JOSEPH scowls, angry.

JOSEPH

Now look. You've made your mother cry.
Apologize to her!

The ADOLESCENT SON breaks free of
JOSEPH's grip and storms out the door,
stopping short to address the man.

ADOLESCENT SON

You can't tell me what to do! Besides . . .

The ADOLESCENT SON's eyes dart back and
forth between JOSEPH and MARY.

ADOLESCENT SON

. . . you're not even my real father!!

The ADOLESCENT SON slams the door. MARY
sobs in JOSEPH's arms.
FADE OUT
CUT TO TITLE:

TEENAGE JESUS

Milton flipped through the rest of the script, made a
few suggestions—such as trimming the shoving match
between Jesus and Pontius Pilate, the Judean governor's
spoiled-brat son, in the Nazareth High cafeteria scene

(the whole thing was a little overwrought)—and tossed it into the "Yes" pile.

Though the scripts Milton had been asked to review as part of Marlo's new role as production assistant had, for the most part, been derivative, cliché, and blasphemous even by h-e-double-hockey-sticks standards, they *did* have a certain energy to them. The shows themselves certainly weren't any worse than the desperately-aimed-at-tweens-and-teens shows that plagued the Surface. In fact, Milton had only put one script in the "No" pile so far: *The Rabid Rabbi,* a show about a Jewish scholar who, after being bitten by a mad bandicoot on a religious camping retreat, develops treatment-resistant hydrophobia, which prevents him from administering Jewish water rituals such as the tevilah.

Two things perplexed Milton—and, thankfully, distracted him from the creepy tingle of wearing leggings. The first was the strange videocassette he had watched of *The Man Who Soldeth the World.* Who or *what* had sent it? How much of it—if any—was real? What did it mean? Milton wasn't sure, but it cost nothing to produce, and he had a lot of slots to fill.

The second thing that perplexed Milton was T.H.E.E.N.D.'s content and scheduling strategy. All of the shows catered to specific religions and faiths, which was fine and surprisingly all-inclusive considering that the head of the network was the devil. But these shows were all set to air *at the same time* in the most coveted prime-time slot: Sunday at 8 p.m. It didn't make any sense. Satan had enough decent shows to launch a successful network with a full and diverse lineup. Why would he create a network of networks, pitting his shows against one another and not even allowing people to watch them on DVR? It would create a sort of religious ratings war. . . .

Hmm . . . Milton thought. *Maybe that's what the devil is up to. Creating fundamentalist friction up on the Surface, rubbing different beliefs against each other like a Cub Scout trying to earn his fire badge . . .*

Milton's nostrils were suddenly filled with a noxious odor, as if someone had wrapped old sneaker tongues in seaweed and set them aflame.

"Hello . . . Miss . . . Fauster," Mr. Welles panted, standing in the doorway of the cramped Boob Tube chomping down on a cigar. "Elevator's . . . *out.*"

Breathing hard in that way that only the morbidly obese do, Mr. Welles looked like a big bomb with a stinky, smoking fuse, his cigar flaring with every wheeze.

"I don't think the elevator has ever been *in*," Milton replied.

Mr. Welles wiped his sweaty forehead with a handkerchief.

"Well, this building has more flights than a commuter airline," he gasped before noticing Milton's "Yes" and "No" piles.

"You didn't like *The Rabid Rabbi?*"

Milton shrugged his shoulders.

"I wasn't mad about it."

Mr. Welles flipped through the script.

"Perhaps you're right," he murmured. "The production values on the temple flood scene alone would have laid waste to our entire budget . . . it's odd, Miss Fauster. I heard that you were an impudent young lady, but you actually seem respectful and forthright."

Uh-oh, Milton thought.

"Whatever, Mr. Well-fed. I just *looooove* my new job," Milton replied quickly, feigning his sister's insincerity.

Mr. Welles leveled his penetrating stare at the *Man Who Soldeth the World* video sticking out of the VCR like a petulant toddler's tongue.

"Did you have the opportunity of screening that mysterious submission?" he asked, his eyebrow arching like a suspicious scalene triangle.

Milton gulped. He wanted to keep an ace up his sleeve, and *The Man Who Soldeth the World* was the only card he had to keep. Whether it could beat whatever a jack-of-all-trades like Mr. Welles was holding, or even the hand Satan, the King of the Bottomless Pit, had been dealt, he had no clue.

"Miss Fauster?" Mr. Welles coughed. "Are you having an internal conversation? The audience can't follow along unless there's a voice-over track. . . ."

"Oh, right . . . sorry," Milton replied. "The tape. Yes,

it was . . . kind of weird. But I . . . well . . . I'll need to see where it's going to be sure."

Mr. Welles nodded.

"Fine. I'll add it to the roster anyway. It might achieve cult status . . . especially with viewers who happen to be in cults."

He picked up the *Teenage Jesus* script and grinned.

"This, however, is pure ratings *gold,*" Mr. Welles said.

Milton caught his reflection, *Marlo's* reflection, in one of the video monitors, noticing that—once again—he had gotten lipstick on his teeth.

"It's a great story," Milton said, brushing his tooth with his index finger. "One of the greatest stories ever told. But that puts a lot of pressure on the lead. He needs to be, like, *Jesus* perfect."

Mr. Welles tilted back his head and expelled a great cloud of cigar smoke. He looked like a carcinogenic PEZ dispenser.

"And I have found the *perfect* Jesus," he replied with a smirk.

Mr. Welles scooped up the "Yes" scripts and cinched them under his arm.

"Come with me, Miss Fauster. Son-of-God speed."

Milton picked up his purse, missing his trusty backpack. He couldn't fit *nearly* as much stuff in it, and missed the reassuring pressure of it between his shoulder blades. He slipped the videotape inside the bag.

"What about the Boob Tube?" he asked, hesitant to wean himself from his multimedia sanctuary.

"We have a Vidiot Box all set up for you at our next destination," Mr. Welles replied.

"But why do you need me?" Milton said as he rose and straightened his skirt. "Don't I just read scripts and make notes?"

Mr. Welles held the door open for Milton. It was nice to know that chivalry wasn't dead, even if everything else here was.

"Satan wants you to edit the scripts . . . on the fly," Mr. Welles panted as they rushed across the production office to the stairs. "To ensure that . . . the shows speak to their intended demographic. And to keep . . . the talent . . . pacified."

"Pacified?" Milton replied, clutching the handrail to avoid tumbling down the stairs in his clearly-designed-by-a-sadistic-misogynist heels.

Mr. Welles stopped on the stairwell between the mezzanine and the main floor. The portly director was huffing and puffing harder than the Big Bad Wolf during Crafty Pig Awareness Week.

"As you mentioned yourself . . . an actor cast as the son of God must surely exude, if anything, a sense of suffering and perfection," Mr. Welles said. "And, that said, I'm sure you will find the star of *Teenage Jesus* perfectly insufferable."

They pushed open the double doors to the parking

lot, where, waiting for them, was a ruby-red, over-the-top, ultraelegant, four-wheeled SUV mansion.

"A Cadillac? A Lincoln?" Milton said, gawking at the luxury car that sneered back at him with its chrome-accented grille.

"Wrong and wrong," Mr. Welles replied as he blotted his forehead with his hanky. "A Badillac, by Wilkes Booth motors."

The door opened, the limousine exhaling a breath of rich leather, oiled wood, and polished aluminum. Milton slid across the cool-despite-the-heat bucket seats. Behind the wheel was a chauffeur demon that, with his pleated leather skin, blended perfectly with its seat. A third arm sprouted from the creature's chest with a round, over-sized hand boasting twenty fingers, each of which curled perfectly around the leather-wrapped steering wheel. He turned to address Mr. Welles as the large man struggled to get inside the limousine.

"Where to, sir?" he asked in a smooth, snooty tone, like freshly ironed silk. Milton noticed the chauffeur had a bony ridge fused across his brow that jutted out of his forehead like the calcified brim of a cap.

"The Hellywood Hole," Mr. Welles answered. "With a pickup at the Four Treasons Hotel."

"Yes, sir," the demon replied as the glass panel separating the passengers' and driver's areas closed. The limousine pulled out noiselessly onto a potholed street, shaking and shimmying, before barreling down an emptied aqueduct. Milton stared out the window at the bleak, barren terrain that limped by, block after block of burned-out homes surrounded by chain-link fences—whether to keep people out or in, Milton couldn't tell.

"So what's at the Hellywood Hole?" Milton asked as the charred skeletons of dilapidated buildings streamed by.

Mr. Welles lit a fresh stale cigar.

"That's our base of operations," he rumbled. "T.H.E.E.N.D. Headquarters, where we weave our dark dreams and unleash them upon the Surface."

Milton's stomach churned like a washing machine full of marbles and rancid buttermilk. He opened the window to clear his head and his lungs of cigar smoke. Outside, however, rows of chemical plants spewed noxious plumes of smoke that swirled together to form an oppressive, deep brown haze, like a radioactive milk shake of pollution.

"Why the Surface?" Milton asked as he quickly rolled up his window.

"Satan has his reasons, and I have mine." Mr. Welles shrugged. "I suppose the devil just wants to make a statement, as do I. We both have something to prove. Me, that I can produce several network lineups on one stage in less than a month. Satan? He's more than likely just thumbing his snout at the Big Guy Upstairs."

He tapped on the chauffeur's glass window. "Turn here."

The demon nodded his head and swerved the car up

and out of the aqueduct toward a gleaming skyscraper that reflected the smog-smothered blight surrounding it. Illuminated in black light above the portico entrance was a fluorescent green-and-orange sign: THE FOUR TREASONS HOTEL.

Milton noticed a lone figure standing outside the hotel's lavish foyer, a tanned young man with long blond hair, expensive sunglasses, and pouty lips, wearing a cream-colored robe, sandals, and a look of supreme self-possession.

"That guy looks familiar," Milton said as the limo drove up to the entrance.

Mr. Welles laughed.

"Yes, I'm sure he looks familiar to every girl your age."

Milton rolled his sister's eyes.

"Okay, I'll play your little game, Miss Fauster," Mr. Welles continued. "The charismatic vampire-wolf in *Crashing Daybreak*? The young rookie cop who must de-activate a runaway hovercraft in *Fastness*? The amnesiac secret agent in *Bourne Yesterday*? The young rapper who joins the army to help pay for his mother's tummy tuck in *Hip-Hop Hup Two Three*?"

The limousine stopped. The chauffeur bounded out of the vehicle and placed the young man's luggage in the trunk. The man took off his glasses to glare at the demon with his squinty, steely blue eyes.

He looks familiar, Milton thought, *but I still can't place his smug face.*

"Miss Fauster," Mr. Welles said as the chauffeur demon opened the limousine door, "meet the heartthrob of every girl, whether their heart still throbs or not. Van Glorious: action hero, rapper, clothing line, cologne, and poster boy for *not* doing your own stunts."

Van Glorious scooted into the limousine, seemingly taking up every spacious square inch of the luxury vehicle with his sheer *over*-presence.

"But you can call him . . . *Teenage Jesus.*" Mr. Welles smirked around his smoldering cigar.

Van looked Milton up and down and sneered.

"Wow, drop-dead gorgeous . . . *hold the gorgeous,*" he said. "I'm just joking, honey," he said, putting his hand on Milton's. "Besides, beautiful women make *terrible* assistants!" Van added with a condescending wink.

Milton's whole body grew white-hot with rage and revulsion as he tried to, molecule by molecule, creep away from the smarmy, arrogant actor.

"Assistant?!" Milton said, turning to Mr. Welles. "I thought I was *Satan's* production assistant?"

Mr. Welles stared out the window as the Badillac drove away from the hotel, merging onto a crowded highway.

"You are, dear, you are," he replied. "Since T.H.E.E.N.D. is Satan's production, you must, therefore, *assist* with it. And, as Mr. Glorious here is so crucial to the network-of-network's appeal, he definitely falls under your nebulous job description."

"Blast it," Mr. Welles muttered, looking out the window at the busted-fender-to-busted-fender traffic jam. "Crush hour is especially bad today."

Van took out his copy of the *Teenage Jesus* script. The text itself was nearly obscured by hundreds of sticky notes and comments scribbled in the margins.

"Good," Van said as he scooched closer to Milton. "That will give us a chance to go over my suggestions. And by suggestions, I mean mandatory changes. Let's start with my first line: 'You wouldn't understand.' That sounds so passive. And if there's one thing that the Messiah *isn't*—especially one on the cusp of manhood—is passive. So if we switch it to . . ."

Milton sighed and slunk back in the overly upholstered seat. He had a feeling that his eternity had just gotten a little longer.

9 · SEEING iS DECEiViNG

THE CADAVEROUS TEACHER looked like a withered wizard straight from Central Casting. He scrawled Milton's name on the chalkboard in just a few squeaky strokes with his creepy chalk manicure, which allowed the teacher to write using all of his bony fingers at once.

Marlo's hand shot up.

The teacher, with his back facing the class, let out a dry, mirthless chuckle.

"Because of the wad of paper you throw at me," the teacher continued, scratching beneath his poofy black velvet beret.

"But I haven't—" Marlo shot back.

"You will," the teacher said as he scraped the chalkboard like a large, literate cat sharpening its claws. After a split-second symphony of wince-inducing screeches, the teacher had finished:

"Soothsaying and World Hysteria 101 with Mr. Nostradamus"

Marlo was furious.

How dare *some phony-baloney wannabe warlock act like he knows what* I'm *going to do!* she fumed as she ripped out a piece of paper from her binder, wadded it up in her fist, and—without thinking—tossed it at Mr. Nostradamus. *If Marlo Fauster is anything at all, she's—*

The ball of paper knocked the teacher's velvet beret to his desk, knocking over a small container of milk.

—unpredictable? Marlo thought, puzzled, as Mr. Nostradamus knelt down over his desk, righting his box of milk and retrieving his ridiculous cap.

"Told you so," he croaked, screwing his cap back onto his head.

Colby raised his hand.

"Soothsaying is the art and practice of foretelling events," the thin, drawn man said, his back still to the class. "And World Hysteria is the study of global panic and how it can be stoked through targeted prophecy."

Spooked, Colby lowered his hand. Darnell scowled and raised his.

"And, Mr. Cummings, I knew what Mr. Hayden was going to ask because I'm a certified seer, and a certified seer sees everything with certainty," Mr. Nostradamus answered before any question was formally posed. "My credentials speak for themselves. . . ."

He turned, took off his large, dark glasses, and

gestured to a wall of framed certificates: a B.S. in augury from the University of Phoenicia and a degree in second sight from the Learning Annex. Mr. Nostradamus set his glasses on his desk beside a crystal ball that held down a stack of parchment paper. Marlo noticed that the edges of his glasses were extra reflective on the inside, just like those cheap novelty spy glasses she saw advertised in the back of Milton's comic books.

So that's *how he saw Colby and Darnell raise their hands,* she thought. *But how did he . . .*

Marlo stared at the angry remnants of the torn sheet from her binder.

Certified seer, my brother's foot. Nostradumbus knew that telling me what I was going to do would make me mad, and that I would do the first thing that popped into my head, which just so happened to be the last thing he said. . . .

"Let me tell you something about myself and the prognostic arts," Mr. Nostradamus said as he rustled around his desk in his flowing, velvet robes. "In 1555 I wrote my first collection of prophecies, which, in a fit of inspiration, I decided to call *The Prophecies*. It's one of the bestselling books of all time, somewhere between *The Very Hungry Caterpillar* and *Who Moved My Cheese?*"

Colby raised his hand, then, self-consciously, put it down.

"Some of my more famous predictions, Mr. Hayden, include: 'The young lion will overcome the older one, on the field of combat in a single battle . . . ,' which, obviously, foretold the death of Henry II. 'Pau, Nay, Loron will be more of fire than of blood . . .' plainly speaks to the reign of French emperor Napoleon, with 'PAU, NAY, LORON' an anagram for NAPAULON ROY. You know: 'Roy' as in French for 'king.' And then there was perhaps my most unsettling prognostication: 'In the year 1999 from the sky will come the great King of Terror,' which is an indisputable reference to George Lucas's release of *The Phantom Menace*."

A pudgy boy with a mop of stringy brown curls raised his hand.

"Prophecy involves a number of complex methodologies, Mr. Stawinski," Nostradamus replied as the boy sheepishly lowered his hand. "There's scrying, for one—"

Zane raised his hand.

"—which is the act of predicting the future using a crystal ball, Mr. Covington."

Zane lowered his hand, baffled, as Mr. Nostradamus peered into a snow globe submerged in a small pool of milk on his cluttered desk.

"Hmm . . . the future is clouded," the ancient man mumbled. "Well, one should never scry over spilt milk. . . . In any case, prophecy can also involve comparative horoscopy, where the planetary configurations corresponding with past historical events are used to predict similar events based on equivalent celestial arrangements. Also helpful are—"

Marlo raised her hand. Mr. Nostradamus studied her with unease.

"I . . . you . . . Mr. Fauster," he faltered. "You . . . want to . . . know what sign I am—"

"Actually, I didn't want to ask a question at all but to share a story," Marlo said with a knowing smirk. "But nice job anticipating everybody's questions based on the last thing you said, not quite explaining something so someone naturally has a question. It's like when a lawyer leads the witless."

"You mean *witness*," the teacher interjected, his nostrils flared with outrage.

"Wrong again, Mr. Nostradamus," she replied. "I meant what I said. *Anyway,* my mom went through a spooky phase when I was little. Numerology, horoscopes, hypnosis to stop smoking, which—in a way—worked because, after all those sessions, we were so broke that she couldn't afford cigarettes. All in all, she was flakier than an apple turnover with psoriasis. When her favorite psychic, Yuri Null, predicted the end of the world, my mom wrote the date on our family calendar that hung on the refrigerator. *The date that we were all supposed to die.* The day came and, of course, nothing happened. At that point, I decided that life was just too short to worry about how short life was and that all that psychic friends network junk was bunk."

Zane bit his lower lip to hold back his laughter. "Brilliant," he snickered under his breath.

Marlo's chest swelled with pride. Mr. Nostradamus, however, swelled with bristling irritation, like an anaconda that had just swallowed a porcupine. "While I have, with eerie precision, pinpointed the most significant events in history, I cannot pin down *your* point, Mr. Fauster," the teacher spat through thin, foam-flecked lips in desperate need of Atomic Cherry Balm.

"Well . . . um . . . let me show you," Marlo said as she sat up, scooted her desk back, and walked over to Colby's desk.

"Hey, Colby. How's it going?" she asked.

"Fine, I guess," Colby replied, "though, as the *real* Dalai Lama, I find the air here super thick, not like back home in Tibet—"

Marlo punched Colby in the arm, then returned to her seat.

"Now watch," Marlo said as she again rose from her desk and walked over to Colby, who was rubbing his aching shoulder. "Hello, Dalai. How's it going?"

Colby flinched.

"Why'd you hit me, psycho?!" he replied, shrinking back in his seat.

Marlo smiled and returned to her seat.

"See?" she said as she crossed her brother's legs.

Mr. Nostradamus scratched his wooly gray beard.

"Well, of course I *knew* you were going to do that," he replied in a voice like a wheezy pair of bellows. "But perhaps you could explain to the students exactly *why.*"

Marlo looped her thumbs beneath her telephone-wire suspenders.

"See, Colby didn't see the first blow coming, and he was totally *fine* with that," she explained. "But the *second time,* he thought something was going to happen and was all stressed out about it, even though nothing ultimately *did* happen. What's more, his worrying about getting punched was sort of . . . irritating. Like a little dog that's all scared of you and you end up wanting to kick it, even though you had no intention of kicking it in the first place. It's like your soothsaying or whatever. It makes people freak that something is going to happen that *wouldn't* to the point where they make it happen, probably because they can't stand worrying about it anymore—"

The room was suddenly filled with the sound of sizzling pants. In the doorway stood Vice Principal Barnum. Marlo noticed that his hair seemed to . . . *sputter.* One second he had a full, sleek mane, the next it was gone, leaving Mr. Barnum's head looking like a gleaming cue ball. The vice principal tapped his brass belt buckle, and his hair regained its thickness and luster.

"Good day, Mr. Nostradamus," he stated, gazing at the boys as if they were an assembly of crash-test dummies. "Class, we have a special treat for you. You are all hereby invited to partake in Focus Group."

The stout, chinless man waddled over to Mr. Nostradamus—how the vice principal's fine, tailored waistcoat wasn't even *singed* by his burning britches was beyond Marlo—and set a brass briefcase on the teacher's desk.

Zane raised his hand.

"Focus Group, Mr. Covington, is where you and members of your highly sought-after demographic chime in on a host of proposed products," Mr. Nostradamus replied.

P. T. Barnum flipped open the briefcase. It crackled, hummed, and exuded a faint scent of smoke and ozone.

"Enjoy, students, and I look forward to your opinions," the vice principal said as he turned to leave. "Mr. Nostradamus, I will be in the usual place."

The teacher nodded, his eyes darting to a large mirror on the side of the classroom wall.

The mirror is set into *the wall,* Marlo thought, her mind going back to countless department store reconnaissance missions. *Like a two-way mirror.*

"Class, please move your chairs closer," Mr. Nostradamus said as he spun the briefcase forward, revealing a selection of strangely glimmering products tucked inside the velvet-lined attaché.

The boys obliged, while Marlo took the scenic route. She sashayed past the mirror, grazing her fingernail against it.

Yep, no gap between my nail and the reflection, she observed. *There's* definitely *a room on the other side of this thing, with somebody inside . . . watching.*

Mr. Nostradamus curled his long chalk nails around a strangely glimmering, cellophane-wrapped pastry sporting a black label with neon green, Gothic letters:

DOOMSDANISH®. The pastry itself was shaped like a mushroom cloud and was iced in fiery reds and yellows.

"Cool," the chubby boy with the curly brown hair said as he reached for the danish. Mr. Nostradamus pulled it away.

"This is a prototype, Mr. Stawinski," the wizened teacher scolded. "Not for consumption, but for discussion. So you were obviously drawn to it."

The Stawinski boy nodded.

"It's actually just *Stawinski*," the boy replied with a flip of his curly hair. "Anyway, it looks like it would be rad to eat, or even just cool to have packed in your lunch!"

Mr. Nostradamus gave a sideways glance to the mirror.

"*Excellent.* Just the kind of feedback we're looking for. What if Doomsdanish were available in a variety of 'extreme' shapes and colors? Say, flaming skulls with prunes for eye sockets, horsemen wielding banana-cream swords, sweeping scenes of civil unrest studded with Red Hots, and angry angels armored with almond slivers? Are these options that you and your specific age group would be interested in?"

Colby bobbed his head.

"Yeah!" he replied enthusiastically. "I'd probably trade them with my friends at school or collect them. That's sort of what I was thinking when I invented Poké-mon cards—"

"Thank you, Mr. Hayden," the teacher interrupted. "Now, are there any potential taglines that spring to your young minds?"

"Bite me," Marlo offered, her arms crossed, leaning against the mirror.

Mr. Nostradamus fumed at Marlo.

"I will not tolerate your insolence!" he roared.

"Insolence?" Marlo replied. "Isn't that for diabetics? I meant 'Bite Me' as in a tagline."

The teacher straightened his poofy velvet beret.

"Of course," he replied stiffly. "Any others?"

"A Taste to Die For?" Zane offered.

"That's good," Marlo whispered, trying desperately to train her puppy love to not yap and make a mess everywhere.

"Doomsdanish, for when you're *filling* bad?" Darnell said. "See, danishes have fillings, and 'filling' sounds like—"

"Let's move along," Mr. Nostradamus said as he put the odd pastry back in the case and removed another faintly glimmering product: a tube glazed in a weird, swirling paint that actually moved like smoke and fire. Printed on the side of the tube, in flaming letters, was the word APOCALYPSTICK®.

"Now, even though you are boys," Mr. Nostradamus continued, "perhaps you could share your impressions—"

"Let me see!" Marlo blurted before the stares of her fellow classmates dampened her overenthusiasm. "I mean, it looks cool. Is it, um, a game controller or USB drive or something?"

The teacher rubbed his smoky gray beard.

"It's a tube of lipstick, Mr. Fauster," he said slowly. "Apocalypstick, to be precise." Mr. Nostradamus tapped the bottom of the tube with his finger. The lipstick uncoiled, revealing not just one color, but a churning collage of complementary colors in progressively incendiary shades of neon.

"Cosmetics in Explosive Colors?" Colby interjected.

"Look Great and Devastate?" Marlo suggested. "Stop, Drop, and Roll It On? Apocalypse *Wow*?"

Mr. Nostradamus snickered, a creepy laugh that sounded like a baby hyena in a vacuum cleaner bag.

"You certainly are in touch with your feminine side, Mr. Fauster," he said.

Marlo's face grew hot.

"Well, my sister and I are . . . close," Marlo murmured. "She's really cool," she added, her eyes darting toward Zane. "Like one of the guys, but, you know, totally a girl. *Totally.*"

"Right," the teacher said, distracted, as he put the lipstick away—much to Marlo's disappointment—and removed a gray tombstone-shaped tin marked FINAL JUDGMINTS®. "Now, this product is in a very experimental stage, and the staff of Fibble are not responsible for any ill effects incurred. . . . I'll consider your silence as implied consent. Now give me your hands. . . ."

The boys held out their palms as Mr. Nostradamus sprinkled tiny, sparkling mints into their waiting mitts.

"Final Judgmints," Colby said before popping the mint in his mouth, "Make Your Last Breath Your Best . . . oww!"

The mint felt like a drop of stinging electricity on Marlo's tongue. Smokey, sharp, shocking, and totally without substance. Then, after the initial wave of tingly pinpricks, she was gripped with the sensation of burning spearmint, hot peppermint, and nuclear winter mint. They weren't flavors, exactly, but swarms of impressions that buzzed in her brain like locusts before abruptly flitting away.

"Twern Yer Mowf into a Toxic Twaste Doomp?" Darnell attempted to say despite his electrocuted tongue.

"What?" Mr. Nostradamus asked.

"Gwound Zewo fo Yer Twaste Buds?" Colby managed through his short-circuited mouth as the class bell tolled.

Mr. Nostradamus sighed as he put the tin of Final Judgmints back in the humming briefcase. "We'll try again tomorrow, class," he muttered.

Vice Principal Barnum appeared in the doorway as Marlo and the other students filed past him into the hallway.

A few yards out of the classroom, Marlo noticed a door masquerading as a not-door, which is to say, it was almost imperceptible to the naked eye. Yet, luckily, Marlo's eyes were always dressed for mischief, even when they were her brother's. She gently pressed her palm to the door. It opened inward to a dark, *L*-shaped room. At the end, just beyond the turn, was a large window looking into Mr. Nostradamus's classroom. The room smelled faintly of burning pants.

"Score," she giggled as she sat down in a folding metal chair set in front of it. Her giggle, though, soon became a subaudible *"eewww"* upon feeling, first-hind, how uncomfortably warm Barnum had left the seat.

Through a speaker mounted off to the side of the mirror, Marlo could hear the vice principal and her pathetic, prophetic teacher talking.

"Without advertising, something terrible happens, Mr. Nostradamus," the vice principal said bitterly. *"Nothing!* It's like that campaign for scented underwear—*Gee, Your Farts Smell Terrific!*—all over again! I have half a mind to cram those students in the box!"

"That seems a touch extreme. While some of the students' marketing suggestions may not seem like much to us," the teacher replied, "they may resonate with the intended demographic."

Mr. Barnum nodded and sat down on Mr. Nostradamus's desk, his flaming pants igniting a stack of ungraded tests.

"The children *did* seem to respond to the test products, even though they weren't real," Mr. Barnum said, flipping open the buzzing briefcase. "The Humbugger is an amazing machine—projecting the most realistic illusions ever—though it is still having trouble simulating flavor."

It's kind of like electric tofu, Marlo thought as she swished her prickly tongue around in her mouth.

"So we're fine-tuning our product messaging and—with the Big Guy Downstairs's help—securing media saturation," he continued with a wicked snicker. "And now that I've got Dr. Brinkley toiling away in the R & D lab, we're poised to bring our little marketing sideshow all the way up to the Surface."

"The Surface!" Marlo gasped, her hands rushing to cover her mouth as Mr. Nostradamus gave a suspicious darting glance to the mirror.

"Advertising as theater . . . as shameless *spectacle*," Barnum murmured, nestled deep in his unfathomable thoughts. "And, in the end—*the very end*—no one will be able to tell the difference."

He flipped a toggle switch on the inside of the briefcase. All of the products in the briefcase winked out of existence.

Dr. Brinkley is helping them peddle this junk to the Surface? Marlo thought with alarm. *I've got to find a way into that lab!*

10 · SEARCH PARTY POOPER

THE PRINCIPAL'S ELECTRO-TORCH beam sliced through the darkness like shears through black velvet. Unfortunately, the pitch-black velvet had been graciously concealing miles of poop-encrusted pipe and fresh pools of fetid sewage.

Bea "Elsa" Bubb crouched down, skittering sideways into the murk like an Alaskan queen crab clad in lime-green spandex. "Sweetums?" she called out in an uncharacteristically quavery voice. "Moopsie Sugar Britches? My Whiddle Honey Bunches of Goats?"

Principal Bubb's snout wrinkled as a somehow even more disagreeable odor elbowed its way to the front of the disagreeable odor line. She turned sharply and screeched. Caught in her flickering torch beam was Limbo's Metaphysical Education teacher, Blackbeard, sheepishly tugging at one of the dozen or so ribbons tied into his fittingly black beard.

"Argh, Miss Principal, forgive me if I a-startled ya," the pirate apologized.

"Mr. Beard—"

"Call me Black," the pirate smiled, exposing two teeth, both of which were capped with gold.

"*Mr. Beard,*" the principal repeated. "What are you doing here?"

"Excuse the intrusion, ma'am," he said with a voice like a blast of swamp gas. "I saw yer flyer—"

He held out a soiled handbill.

HAVE YOU SEEN ME?
MISSING:
Almost-unendurably adorable three-headed hound of Heck
Pomeranian/Shih Tzu/Chimera mix
AGE:
Approximately 13 millennia
Answers to Cerberus, Sweetums, Mr. Fancy Puddles, or the sound
of struggling prey (go online to www.houndbgone.hck for a
complete list of nicknames and endearments)
IDENTIFYING MARKS:
Three heads up front, small rash in back
REWARD:
Your freedom*
*Heck staff not eligible

"Ah, I see," Bea "Elsa" Bubb replied. "I must ask you, though, did you read the fine print?"

The burly pirate rubbed one of several long scars on his weathered cheek.

"I can't say I've had an eye fer the finer things, Miss Principal. But with the right woman to help trim me ragged jib . . ."

The principal held her torch to the bottom of the flyer, highlighting the fine print: *"Heck staff not eligible."*

The realization was, to Blackbeard's spirits, like a cannonball tearing through a damp paper dinghy: a swift, deadly assault for which there was no counter-maneuver.

The principal looked down the subterranean conduit of caca that shuttles every last plop and tinkle of waste down the River Styx to h-e-double-hockey-sticks. She sighed with the enormity of the task ahead.

"So I understand if you'd prefer to shiver your timbers elsewhere," she said.

Blackbeard hoisted his thick black belt over his grog-fattened belly.

"Nah, I'll help ya find yer salty sea dog," he replied with a sigh.

Principal Bubb's face trembled and quaked until it finally pushed out something approximating a smile.

"I don't know how to thank you," Bea "Elsa" Bubb responded. "Really. It's been so long since I've thanked anyone for anything, I'm truly at a loss."

Blackbeard rubbed his bearded, braided chin.

"Well, ya could always—"

"And I'm perfectly fine with *not* knowing how to thank you, thank you," the principal replied, turning back to face the stinky blackness up ahead.

The two splashed along the dark, cramped pipeline that smelled like the distilled essence of every neglected rest stop bathroom, everywhere.

"My Pookie Snuggle Bottom, er, *Cerberus,* is so sensitive," Principal Bubb fretted. "I worry he won't be able to smell his way back into my arms."

"I doubt if that'll be a problem, Miss Principal," the pirate offered.

The principal's electro-torch cast the River Styx with a sickly orange flicker, creating a dance troupe of nasty, prancing shadows.

"Do ye mind if I listen to me *iPood*?" Blackbeard blurted, his voice slapping against the sides of the sewer pipe like a doctor's hand on a newborn's bottom.

The principal shuddered.

"I certainly hope that last word was a victim of your accent," she grumbled. "In any case, go ahead."

Blackbeard grinned and plucked a brown MP3 player from the pocket of his bullet-ridden, gash-ventilated frock coat.

"Yo ho!" the pirate shouted as he wedged his earbuds into the nests of dark hair sprouting from his ear canals. "It's time fer me favorite ARGH show!"

Unfortunately for Principal Bubb, a lifetime of drunken bellowing, cannon fire, and macaws squawking on his shoulder had rendered Blackbeard virtually deaf, so the strains of ARGH blared as loud as a conch shell blast. High-energy, techno-pirate pop with bubblegum buccanette vocals throbbed through Blackbeard's earbuds.

> "I'm a wench who wants a boy,
>   to weigh anchor in my heart.
>   And make me shout and scream 'ahoy!'
>   And sail me off the chart!"

The DJ blew a bosun whistle and howled.

"Blow me down!" he roared. "This is Calico Jack here and *that* was Me Hearties, those scurvy and curvy pop sensations, with 'Looking for My Jolly Roger.' Next up, we've another ditty from that crafter of tuneful tales, the Truthador, with a splash of refreshing sea foam for yer ears, 'Swan Song from the False Power.' "

The Truthador slashed power chords from his harp.

" '*We must get these monkeys out of here,*' said the E.T. to *the thief,*" the Truthador sang in his strained, raspy voice. "'*They're infesting our new home, and we need some relief.*'"

Principal Bubb rolled her curdled yellow goat eyes.

"*I* need some relief . . . from this awful music," she said as her hooves slipped in a sludgy pile of dung. "Mr. Beard . . ."

The pirate crooned tunelessly along with the music, barking like a sea lion choking on a broken toy trumpet.

"'But me and my fiends, we'll move them to a duller, sadder fate,'" Blackbeard sang on. "'We'll use the power of falsity now, and their Last Judgment create.'"

The power of falsity? Principal Bubb thought. *As in . . .* fibbing?

She extended her thumb and foreclaw, activating the thimbles of her No-Fee Hi-Fi Faux-Phone.

Mr. Nixon sat in an overstuffed, rust-colored Sleazy Chair in Fibble's Lie-Brary reading a book: *Abraham Lincoln: Was Honesty Really His Policy?*

The Truthador's music squawked through Fibble's PA speakers.

> *"Monkeymen, they moan and whine.*
> *They just don't dig the Earth.*
> *None of them would know the diff,*
> *if we sent them somewhere worse."*

A slender, twisted demon—rather like a leather curly fry with a face—peeked into the room.

"Telephone, Mr. Nixon," he rasped as he entered the Lie-Brary, carrying a silver tray holding two thimbles atop a white lace doily.

Mr. Nixon picked up the thimbles and scowled at the

tightly coiled demon as he struggled to affix them to his fingers.

"Hello?"

"Mr. Nixon . . . ," Principal Bubb answered as she waded in gallons of castaway human filth.

" 'So let's show them the exit,' the thief he slyly spoke," the Truthador sang, eerily through both her phone and Blackbeard's earbuds. " 'There is no one here among them that would know it was a hoax.' "

"Are you listening to that awful singer too?" she asked.

"Unfortunately, yes," Mr. Nixon replied. "He's squawking through every PA down here. It's a blasted nuisance."

"Speaking of nuisances I'd like *blasted*," the principal continued, "*Milton Fauster.* He's the reason I'm calling. I have a hunch—actually, a little throb *in* my hunch—whenever that little creep is about to pull something—"

"Don't worry your petty little head about him," Mr. Nixon interrupted, tapping his arthritic fingers on the coffee-ringed coffee table next to his chair. "I'm keeping Mr. Fauster, like all enemies, close. You have my promise as a disgraced career politician that Milton Fauster is snoring away in his bunk, beaten down and dispirited, posing no trouble to anybody."

★　　★　　★

Marlo crept down the deserted hallway in her hair pajamas, cradling two balloons—surgical gloves swiped from the infirmary—filled with a thick mixture of powdered milk, little white lice, Elmer's glue . . . basically whatever bright, white substance she could find. She turned her head around the corner and saw—*just barely*—three black chameleon demons marching in front of Fibble's darkened R & D lab.

The hallway was still but far from quiet. ARGH radio was very much on the air.

"Swan song from the false power," sang the Truthador in his distinctive nasal twang. *"The Salesman, he skews the view. Every last man, woman, and child will bid their home world adieu."*

Not much for the merry melodies, Marlo thought as she waited for a clear shot of the wall behind the marching chameleon guards. *But his lyrics loiter around in your head, like some kind of puzzle aching to be solved.*

Marlo *had* to find out what P. T. Barnum was cooking up in his viral marketing laboratory. Suddenly, she saw her chance. Hefting the balloons in her hands, Marlo screwed up her brother's eyes as she gauged her trajectory, then lobbed both balloons at the R & D wall. The balloons splashed in wet, milky explosions, turning the dark, dirty walls brilliant, uncompromising white. The guards swiveled about and eyed the glaring, dripping wall with their protruding peepers. After a moment of paralyzed silence, the three black chameleons trembled and fell to the ground—screaming as their chameleon skin struggled to process the abrupt, total change in color—before turning pale white and passing out.

Marlo trotted toward the lab and tried the door, which was—unsurprisingly—locked. She knelt down by one of the unconscious guards and yanked a wad of keys from his belt. After a few tries, Marlo found the right key, gave it a twist, and opened the door slowly, stepping into the dark.

"The truth is our weapon," the Truthador sang. *"With it, we'll lead the attack."*

Marlo felt along the wall as she padded softly into the laboratory.

"And beat every swindler, impostor, and—"

The fluorescent lights flicked on.

"Quack?"

11 · iF THE SHOW HiTS, BEWARE iT

Van Glorious, dressed in character as Teenage Jesus, walked across the Nazareth High gymnasium set to join some of his adolescent disciples—Simon, Andrew, James, John, Philip, Bartholomew, and Judas—at the refreshments table at the Annual Purim Dance and Social. He ladled dark, lumpy juice into wooden cups for his friends. Bartholomew took a sip and grimaced.

"Ugh," the tanned boy grumbled. "*Fig* juice. It's not even strained. *Nasty.*"

Judas, a curly-haired boy with peach fuzz on his upper lip, leaned into Jesus.

"*Brock, brock.*"

"Shut up," Teenage Jesus replied. "I'm not doing it."

"*Whatever,*" Judas shrugged. "If I could make this

dance less than lame, I'd *totally* do it. But that's just me. . . ."

"What are you guys talking about?" Simon interjected, flipping back his feathered hair as the band played a slow-dance number on lute, harp, and rattled sistrum.

Teenage Jesus sighed and glared at Judas.

"Well, since you all *must* know," he explained, "I was getting a bucket of well water for my mom the other day and noticed it had all sorts of crud in it. So I was fishing out olive leaves and junk because Mom would totally freak if the water wasn't clean . . . she has a thing about purity . . . and, well, the water turned into . . . um, *wine.*"

Andrew gave Teenage Jesus a shove.

"Get out!" he exclaimed.

"Dude, my hand's stamped, so if I get out I'll just come back in," Teenage Jesus joked.

"Do it!" James and John chanted in unison.

"Shhh!" Teenage Jesus said, looking over his shoulder at his aunt, patrolling the perimeter of the dance floor with a scowl. "My auntie's here as a chaperone. She'll totally bust me if she finds out. . . ."

"Brock, brock," Judas taunted.

Teenage Jesus sighed, succumbing to the ceaseless erosion of will that is peer pressure.

"Fine," he said, sticking his finger in the punch. "With friends like you, Judas, who needs enemies?"

Judas smirked as the punch darkened.

"I have no idea what kind of wine I make," Teenage Jesus explained. "With the fig juice it'll probably be gross and sweet anyway."

"That's very unhygienic, nephew," Teenage Jesus's auntie interjected from behind him as he ladled punch to his friends. With a start, he spilled some on the woven straw tablecloth.

"So jumpy," she continued. "Now pour your auntie a cup before you splash it all over the place."

"Um," Teenage Jesus replied. "It might be a little sweet for you."

"I like it sweet."

"And it seems like it might have . . . fermented. A bit."

"Just pour me a flippin' cup of punch!" she shouted. "My mouth tastes like the Dead Sea."

The boy sighed and handed his aunt her drink. She took a sip. Her beady eyes squinted and sparkled with the gift of confirmed suspicions.

"I knew it," she replied, more delighted than angry. *"You spiked the punch."*

"I didn't!" Teenage Jesus exclaimed. "Not really, any-way. Search me! I don't have a jug or cask or anything!"

She grabbed him by the ear and dragged him away from the table.

"I don't care how you did it," the bitter old woman

said. "But you did, and you're done. No more cavorting with your long-haired friends."

Teenage Jesus blushed with embarrassment as the crowd of dancing teens gawked.

"You have it out for me . . . you always have!" he exclaimed. "Why do you always do this to me?"

"Because I'm Auntie Christ!" she replied between gritted teeth. "And it's my job to make sure you lead a normal, respectable, and ordinary life! Not go off gallivanting across Judea, filling people's heads with this peace and love nonsense!"

A look of conviction crept onto the teenager's face. The kind of certitude that comes when you hear your calling ringing loud and true in your ears, and you can't help but answer it.

"You haven't seen anything yet," he said, his blue eyes sparkling like the Sea of Galilee.

"And cut!" Mr. Welles bellowed offstage in his canvas chair by the camera. "Superb! Truly inspired."

Van shuffled offstage.

"I don't know . . . I was perfect, but I think the scene could've had more . . . *intensity,*" he said with an actor's blend of arrogance and neediness. A short demoness with large goo-goo eyes and two pig's tails sticking out of her head handed him a bottled water. Van turned and shrieked at the creature. "The water tastes terrible when you bring it to me! Have Marlo give me the bottle!"

The pig-tailed demon hid her weeping face in her claws and ran out of the makeshift studio at the center of the Hellywood Hole, a cavernous, subterranean amphitheater housing dozens of demon stagehands, extras, and actors. With its scarlet fiberglass shell of concentric arches, the Hellywood Hole—to Milton—resembled the inflamed ear of the Unjolly Red Giant.

Milton sighed, knowing firsthand through Van's explosive tantrums of the last forty-eight hours that it was far easier for everyone—Milton included—to instantly succumb to Van's irrational demands. He picked up another bottle of H2No, the trendy anti-water that Van drank, and handed it to the temperamental star.

"Thanks, doll," he said with a demeaning wink.

Milton, irritated, walked back to Mr. Welles as he flipped through the day's scripts.

"Mr. Glorious," Mr. Welles intoned, "As the director of *Citizen Kane*, *Macbeth*, *Touch of Evil*, and countless other films you've never heard of, I assure you that your performance made the scene utterly *Van-tastic*."

Van tucked a tuft of blond hair behind his ear and nodded, his ego temporarily sated.

"Maybe you're right," he murmured, taking a swig of water, rinsing his mouth, and spitting it out on an extra's shoes. "I'll save my energy for the Sermon on the Mountain Bike scene."

Mr. Welles wiped his brow with a white hankie as Van strutted back to his dressing room.

"Dealing with young superstars is like trying to defuse a bomb," Mr. Welles muttered to Milton. "You're never sure if you're going to snip the right wire. Anyway, Miss Fauster, what did *you* think of the scene?"

"Um," Milton replied hesitantly, "well, the scene had energy and the acting was decent, but . . ."

"But *what*, Miss Fauster?" Mr. Welles pressed as he scrutinized Milton with his glassy, red-rimmed eyes.

"It's just that Jesus is such a crucial figure in the lives of so many," Milton continued. "And his turning water into wine was a miracle, not some teenage prank. So I guess I'm kind of worried that we're taking too many liberties with, you know, the central figure of Christianity."

Mr. Welles smirked, as if the criticism were an old friend that kept reappearing unannounced at odd hours.

"Ah, yes. I heard the same concerns when adapting Shakespeare," he said, rubbing his dense beard. "Sure, every great story loses something in the translation to the screen, but—in the hands of a genius like myself—the story gains something even greater. It gains a new audience. If I was faithful to someone's faith, I would be merely preaching to the converted. But by getting to the dramaturgical pith, the very *marrow* of Teenage Jesus, I release the timeless intensity of emotion—the passion of Christ—that will grab today's young people where they live!"

Mr. Welles makes a good point, Milton thought, reluctantly. *But I still think his ego is eclipsing whatever is* really *going on here. . . .*

Offstage, Milton could see Van and his costar Inga Hootz—aka Auntie Christ—engaging in a heated argument.

"You're in *my* chair!" Inga screeched.

Van crossed his legs casually as he tilted back in the canvas chair, reading *Acting Up: Scrupulously Preparing for Improvisation.*

"It's not like it has your name on it," he replied without looking up.

"Actually, it *does*," Inga replied, pointing to her name clearly inscribed upon the back of the chair.

Van smirked.

"Squatter's rights," he said with a shrug.

Mr. Welles waved his cigar at a thick-featured demon stagehand wearing a rotten sombrero.

"Sancho, we're ready for the next set."

The demon nodded and—with a full-body yank—pulled a large metal lever offstage. The round, thirty-foot stage shuddered and revolved like a massive lazy Susan. Mounted on top of the rotating stage were wedged, triangular sets to several T.H.E.E.N.D. shows, each shaped like a theatrical slice of pie. The gymnasium of Nazareth High spun away as a living room scene clicked into place in front of Mr. Welles and the demon camera crew.

"Miss Fauster," Mr. Welles said as he pushed the one-eyed cinematographer away from the camera to peek through the lens. "The next script, please?"

Milton skimmed through the stack and handed Mr. Welles the script for the sitcom *Allah in the Family*. A middle-aged, Middle Eastern man with a bulging middle galumphed out to sit on his shabby wing chair. As the man nestled his butt into the well-worn cushion, it took on the dignity of a throne. A woman in a black, full-length burka and veil waddled out onto the stage and sat in a less-padded chair next to his.

"Arshad, Edibe," Mr. Welles said, addressing his two actors, "as you know, you're playing Arshad and Edibe Buainain, two fundamentalist Muslims who view the changing world around them as a direct assault against their values. Unfortunately, *Teenage Jesus* ran a little long—"

"Figures," grumbled Arshad as he crossed his arms with irritation.

"—so we just have time to do a quick teaser for the show, and a product endorsement," Mr. Welles continued. "Lights . . . camera . . . *action!*"

Arshad leafed through an Islamic newspaper.

"Aw, look at this, will you?" he complained. "An article from the Western imperialist media on how the economy is so bad that women may have to work to help bring home the bacon!"

Edibe, working a small loom with her hands and feet, shakes her head.

"And we can't even *eat* bacon!" she replied, shaking her head as she wove together strands of brightly colored yarn.

Arshad rolled his eyes heavenward.

"Allah, give me strength," he murmured. "My wife is a few goats short of a herd!"

Their teenage daughter, Galiah, strode into the living room, wearing a hot-pink Juicy Couture burka and a sheer, rhinestone-encrusted veil.

"Where do you think you are going, young lady, dressed like some shameless jezebel!" Arshad yelled, throwing down his paper. "I can practically see your knees and nostrils!"

Galiah turned to face her father as she opened the door to leave.

"Oh, Father!" she replied in a shrill, sassy tone. "*All* the girls dress like this!"

"Yes . . . *all the girls in the harem*!" Arshad spat.

Galiah sobbed and ran out the door. "You are totally incomprehensible!"

Arshad shook his head.

"Maybe so," he mumbled. "But I make a lot of sense."

Edibe held out a tray of pastries to Arshad.

"Something *else* that makes sense," Arshad continued, "is the delicious, portentous taste of *Doomsdanish*®."

He unwrapped the mushroom cloud–shaped pastry, and took a big bite.

"Mmm . . . a taste to die for!" Arshad said with a wink. Just then, Galiah reentered the room, strutting to the tray, and scooped up several Doomsdanishes.

"Be sure to collect them all!" she said with a mischievous smile. "Like me and all of my totally cool friends do!"

Galiah ripped off the cellophane, lifted her veil, and sunk her teeth into the flaming skull-shaped pastry.

"Oh, and Father," she added with a smirk, "bite me!"

The family laughed good-naturedly as the stage lights dimmed.

"And . . . *cut!*" Mr. Welles shouted as the stagehands shuffled props around to prepare for the next shot. Milton sidled close to him as he handed the rotund director the next script.

"*Doomsdanish?*" Milton commented. "That's kind of creepy."

Mr. Welles nodded while he flipped through the pages of the script.

"Yes, I have to concur, Miss Fauster," he replied. "But show business is indeed a *business*—and these disturbing products from Fibble are paying for my comeback."

"Fibble?" Milton croaked. "But that's where they send kids who lie." *Like my sister disguised as* me, he thought.

"It's ingenious, really," Mr. Welles said, distracted, as

he framed the set with his hands. "Who better to devise ways of marketing to kids than kids themselves? I probably would have thought of that myself, had I thought of it."

Just then, a stooped demon pushed a cart of mail next to Milton.

"Delivery for Mr. Welles," the ancient creature wheezed, holding out a bulging manila envelope with no return address.

The writing, Milton noticed as he studied the envelope, was precise yet florid and very distinctive.

The Man Who Soldeth the World! Milton thought. *It must be the next episode!*

"I'll take that," Milton chirped as he snatched the envelope quickly from the demon's leathery hands and signed for it. "Mr. Welles is really busy."

The wrinkled demon shrugged its bony shoulders and pushed its overflowing mail cart away. Mr. Welles chewed on his cigar like a tobacco-filled pacifier, deep in thought as he perused his script.

"So, Mr. Welles, you—um—mentioned that there was a place where I could watch dailies of the latest shows and review submissions—"

"The Vidiot Box," he grunted, gesturing to the back of the bowl-shaped band shell behind the rotating stage.

Milton nodded and clutched the envelope tightly underneath his sister's alabaster arm.

I know that television is bad for you, he thought as he

stomped toward a large wooden crate sprouting dozens of cables, *but I have a feeling it's going to get a lot worse unless I do something. What that something is, I'm not quite sure . . . but I have a feeling this freaky show will show me the freaky way. . . .*

12 · REIGNING CATS AND DOGS

ANNUBIS PADDED ONWARD in the dark. The tall, slender jackal-of-all-trades who had extracted and appraised the souls of the darned for time immemorial (before impulsively eating his gelatinous associate Ammit) had no idea how long he had been walking. His extended tour of duty in Limbo's Assessment Chamber had permanently hampered his concept of time.

Despite this setback, Annubis was certain he was traveling in the right direction. His love for his family—his lovely Weimaraner wife Anput and young daughter Kebauet—was like a compass inside him, leading the deposed dog god straight to the Kennels: the howling, mewling basement of the Furafter, where the cries of the caged echoed, unheeded, off cold concrete.

As Annubis staggered forward, the ground beneath his hind paws began to crinkle. *Newspaper,* he thought. *I must be close.* Annubis sniffed the air. Mingled musks, sour-sweet breath, the corn-chip smell of paws, and the ever-present undercurrent of ammonia. *Closer than I thought.*

Suddenly, the darkness surrounding him was blasted away as a bank of blinding bright lights exploded up ahead. Annubis winced and shielded his sensitive eyes from the harsh light. Through his paw-hands he saw a guard tower topped with a cluster of piercing klieg lights.

"Stay!" a human voice commanded. Annubis found the urge to sit, paralyzed, almost impossible to resist. The voice repeated, never changing in timbre or volume. As his eyes became accustomed to the glare, he could see that the guard tower was empty. *"Stay!"* the voice squawked from a pair of rusty speakers beneath the abandoned guard station.

An automated intruder response, Annubis gauged. *Nothing but a recording designed to give programmed commands, though I would assume that most of the passed-on pets here failed basic obedience. . . .*

A crowd of slinking shadows emerged from the edges of Annubis's sight. They crept, low to the ground, separate yet working together as one. Their gait was slow, deliberate, and cunning.

Cats, Annubis realized as the fur on the back of his neck instinctually raised.

The creatures circled around him, silent and purposeful. The dog god counted thirteen in all. The cats, like inky shadows spilled across the newspapered landscape, stalked nearer, crossing his path on all sides. Their ebony fur rippled with sly, predatory instinct as they tightened their circle, a black velvet noose cinching snug and deadly.

A ragged chorus of bays, howls, and yaps discharged from beyond the rim of brutal light. The cats froze, sniffing the air—stock-still—while their tails jerked about like angry black snakes. Suddenly, above them, sailing over the guard station, were a dozen whizzing balls of yarn. The cats exchanged quick, edgy glances before abruptly bounding away, yielding to their uncontrollable urges. They gamboled past the guard station to intercept the brightly colored balls.

A chaotic jumble of shapes emerged from the murky shadows. A pack of dogs. The first was a terrier, next an Italian greyhound, followed by a beagle, a Chihuahua, and a French bulldog with a limp. Each had a red plastic Speak & Spell strapped to its side and a stylus tied around its neck, all save for the Italian greyhound, who had a round, plastic wheel with farm animal pictures belted to its shaggy side. The beagle was fitted with a pneumatic toy cannon atop its sloping back.

The terrier approached, alert, taking in Annubis with its open, white-and-tan face.

"Um, *good doggie*," Annubis said, crouching, holding

out the back of his paw-hand for the little dog to sniff. "Thank you for—"

The dog snatched the dangling stylus in its mouth and tapped the Speak & Spell's keypad.

"Name is Virginia Woof," the box squawked in a computerized monotone. "You are in Stay! . . . receiving area for Furafter. We saved you from cats."

Annubis, realizing that he wasn't dealing with your average "good doggie," withdrew his paw-hand and rose.

"The yarn was a clever diversion," he replied. "Lucky for me you had it with you."

Virginia Woof nudged the sack lashed to her back with her nose, before typing another message.

"We are pack animals," the flat voice explained. "Prepared for anything."

"And resourceful," Annubis said, gesturing to Virginia Woof's Speak & Spell. "Why do you choose to communicate in such a way?"

The spry terrier jabbed the toy.

"Old caretaker, Mr. Noah, taught us years ago. Now habit."

The other dogs joined Virginia Woof. First, the beagle.

"This is Poochiano Pawvarotti," Virginia Woof said, expertly tapping the Speak & Spell with her stylus. The beagle nodded as the Chihuahua sprang forth, quivering as it tapped its name.

"Hola," it relayed through the red plastic box on its

side. "I'm Chi-chi LaRue." The French bulldog limped past the Chihuahua. Annubis noted that the dog had an artificial foreleg. "This is Faux Paw," Chi-chi explained as the French bulldog let loose a tremendous fart. "Pardonnez-moi," the three-legged dog apologized via Speak & Spell. The Italian greyhound bounded toward Annubis and leapt up on him with its bony, impulse-control-challenged limbs. "This is Napoleon Bone-apart," Virginia Woof explained, concluding her introductions. The Italian greyhound, not having a Speak & Spell, nudged the round plastic toy strapped to its side.

"The cow says . . . *mooooooooo!*" the See 'n Say said cheerfully. Virginia Woof tapped out her explanation. "All that was left. He'd probably say same thing even if he could speak, though."

Annubis, proud and dignified, willed his tail to wag in canine camaraderie. Through years of working alongside humans, he had learned to restrain the flagrant expression of emotion so common with his species. Most humans—especially those in the aggravated bowels of Heck—had a way of holding something like that against you.

"My name is Annubis," the dog god said, "and I am here to retrieve my wife and daughter, in addition to a friend's ferret. I know that they are in the Furafter, yet I know not where."

Poochiano Pawvarotti shook his droopy flews, then tapped a response.

"Ferrets," he replied in a halting monotone. "Fun

chase, no fun catch. Probably in Kennels. Where they put pets don't know what to do with. As for wife and child—"

The klieg lights—obviously set on some timer, Annubis thought—winked off, submerging the dogs in darkness. Almost immediately, the faint, guttural sound of malicious feline boredom pricked Annubis's ears.

"Best be moving," Virginia Woof suggested. "Place is regular Katmandu when lights out."

The dogs' home resembled a dank, wood-paneled rubbish heap composed of all the castaway junk that remained unsold at the worst garage sale *ever*. The stiff, orange shag carpet—a horizontal work of abstract expressionism made of oil stains, cigarette burns, and what Annubis prayed was fossilized spaghetti—was, to Annubis's eyes, perhaps the most pleasing aspect of this caved-in rumpus room on the haunches of the Furafter.

The dogs led their guest to a clutch of gutted beanbag chairs.

Annubis sat, cross-legged, beneath a black velvet picture of a group of dogs huddled around a table engaged in a game of poker. The painting seemed, by its gilded frame and position at the intersection of two beams of track lighting, to hold some importance to the dogs.

"*A Bold Bluff*," Virginia Woof commented through the flat tone of her Speak & Spell.

Annubis cocked his head. It was amazing how all of these old habits came flooding back when surrounded by your own species.

"Excuse me?"

"Name of painting," Chi-chi LaRue clarified, trembling on a burned-out chesterfield that appeared to have not quite survived a fire sale. "Masterpiece."

Annubis turned back to Virginia Woof as she cleaned her back foot.

"This is all very . . . cozy, but I need to find my family, who I assume are suffering in the Kennels. Now this caretaker, this Mr. Noah . . ."

"He greet every new arrival in Stay! before leading to either Really Big Farm, pet Heaven, or—in extreme cases—Kennels: pet *you know where*," Virginia Woof said, tapping the red plastic toy strapped to her side. "But haven't seen him for weeks. Without Noah, cats treat place like scratching post."

"In any case," Annubis pressed, "I need to go to the Kennels. As soon as possible. I don't care if the cats play—"

"*Ruff* . . . the dog says . . . *ruff*!" Napoleon Bone-apart, tongue lolling out of his mouth with happiness, communicated with a nudge of his See 'n Say.

Virginia Woof rubbed her face against Annubis's leg reassuringly before tapping out another message.

"It's okay," she said through the toy's flat, digitized voice. "We take you there when cats nap in Catacombs."

Annubis bared his teeth in a half-dog, half-human smile.

"Thank you," he said, patting Virginia Woof on the head. "It is a pleasure to know again the loyalty of my kind."

He rose from the floor and walked to the broken window of the dogs' house. Annubis stared off across the grim newspapered wasteland toward the maddening stillness of Stay!

"And, perhaps, tomorrow, I will be reunited with my beloved wife and daughter. . . ."

Annubis tasted the stale air with his elegant nose, sifting through the complex clot of odors that settled at the back of his throat. They seemed far more intricate than he would expect in a dominion of once-domesticated pets, more redolent of the ambiguity of humans. . . .

Annubis felt a cold nose poking his ankle. At his sandaled feet, Napoleon Bone-apart nibbled at a mound of dry dog food that Annubis had been unwittingly standing in.

With a bleary half-smile, the exhausted dog god sensed that his journey to locate his family and Milton Fauster's ferret had only just begun, and that he had trod in some very deep kibble indeed.

13 · DUCK UNCOVER

THE FEATHERS SPROUTING from the neck of Dr. Brinkley's white laboratory smock stood on end.

"Quack!" he quacked again. "I mean, what are you doing here, young man?!"

"I, um," Marlo quavered in shock, gazing down at the gleaming linoleum floor, as if for an easy answer, "got up early. That Truthador—gosh—who can sleep with all that, all that . . . *truth* blaring down the halls!"

Dr. Brinkley waddled to the door. He peered out the chain-link reinforced window, his bright orange bill tapping against the glass, and noticed the sickly white chamelcon demons splayed out, unconscious, on the ground.

He turned and glared down his bill at Marlo through his spectacles. Marlo backed away until she was up against a brushed platinum counter covered with gurgling beakers. She clutched a glass vial in her hand and held it behind her back. The odd duck demon scratched the rim of his goat horns as he goose-stepped toward Marlo.

"I'm on to your little secret," he seethed, drawling slightly like a talking duck in a balmy South Carolina pond. Marlo tightened her hand around the neck of the glass cylinder.

"My secret?" she said as she prepared to smash the beaker across the doctor's beak.

Dr. Brinkley stopped before her, scowling, his wing-arms akimbo. "Yes . . . that Vice Principal Barnum sent you here to spy upon me."

Marlo loosened her grip on the beaker.

"Uh . . . okay," she said. "But if I'm Mr. Barnum's spy, then why did I knock out the guards?"

Dr. Brinkley rubbed the silver-gray goatee surrounding his bill.

"To make me believe you were working alone," he surmised. "But I know better . . . I didn't die yesterday."

Marlo smirked as she stepped away from the counter and took in the laboratory. It resembled a game of Mouse Trap, only constructed with glass tubes, glittering vials, Bunsen burners, sizzling electric coils, and jars of glimmering smoke instead of bright plastic boots and bathtubs.

"Since you found me out," Marlo said, carefully feeding the doctor words as if luring a cat into its crate with

Fancy Feast, "perhaps you can give me an overview, and I'll spill to Mr. Barnum, omitting whatever you don't want me to pass along. That way, we both come out smelling like . . . whatever flower they have down here that doesn't stink."

The doctor nodded and smiled as he passed his hand through the thinning down on his head.

"I find that arrangement most agreeable: spreading flimflam to a flimflam man," he responded with a nasal pseudo-quack. "Well, since the tragedy that befell my beloved team of Night Mares, the vice principal has had me working in indentured servitude here in his laboratory."

Like the laboratory of a mad scientist who got some serious *grant money,* Marlo noted as her brother's hazel eyes darted about the room. *Wow . . . it's like Toys 'R' Nuts in here. An Evil Genius Superstore . . .*

Marlo had to squint Milton's myopic peepers nearly shut to force the smudgy blobs around her to submit to full clarity. She followed a thick, double-barreled pipe leading from the floor connecting to a large brass water heater thingie that was, itself, connected to several glass domes full of glittering smoke. The brass cylinder branched out into thinner pipes that led out of the room in a variety of directions. The pipes were fastened to the unusual beams Marlo had seen throughout Fibble, made out of that creepy wood that seemed almost flesh-stained, with knotholes every yard or so, that resembled anguished faces, knotted in pain.

"What's this all about?" Marlo queried, gesturing to the tangle of plumbing. "Not like I don't know, but just so I can tell Mr. Hot Pants that I asked."

Dr. Brinkley rubbed his spectacles clean with his subtly webbed hands.

"I'm game," he said, before clearing his throat and motioning to the wall. "This main pipe on the left arrives from Fibble's Boiler Room, supplying ample hot air to the facility, while the one on the right feeds all of the vice principal's lies into the prevarication system."

"His lies?" Marlo asked. "What do you mean?"

"The brass buckle he wears collects lies, fibs, falsehoods . . . all manner of malarkey," Dr. Brinkley said before perching on a metal stool.

"You see, young man," he continued, "lies are composed of a certain energy, a negative charge that repels them from the truth. This is how lies push us away from who we really are. Deep inside, on a molecular level, we recognize the honest truth, even when our minds are muddled by skillful falsifications. This is why advertising has, historically, had to try so hard to sway our decision-making processes. To its credit, it has done so with flying colors. Yet Mr. Barnum believes that flimflammery can be made even *more* deceiving with far *less* effort. Which is why he has commandeered my services to help aid in his experiments, due to my past history with both questionable, leading-edge chemistry and unorthodox marketing campaigns."

This was a lot to take in, thought Marlo, especially for someone who hadn't bothered to finish her school counselor's attention deficit disorder test. But if Milton's body was designed for anything, it was prolonged mental focus. Plus, as a gifted liar herself, Marlo noticed that Dr. Brinkley was actually making eye contact, something almost impossible to do when trying to pawn off a whopper.

Marlo's skittish attention was captured by a bubbling beaker of silver liquid. A rubber tube snaked from its stoppered top to a small aquarium filled with little white lice. Every few seconds, a drop of the liquid fell on a wriggling mound of the tiny parasites. The liquid, at first, made the lice intensely agitated, biting each other and thrashing about. But after these brief, angry spasms, they smoldered and died. Marlo fingered the pendant hanging from her neck beneath her hair pajamas. It quivered, as if with excitement.

"This weird liquid," Marlo said. "I've seen it before." She pulled the pendant out from beneath her pajama top. Though Marlo didn't completely trust the untrustworthy doctor, he was at least no friend to the vice principal. Dr. Brinkley's beady, bespectacled eyes widened at the sight of the gurgling pendant.

"Where did you ever procure this?" he said. "It's so pure."

Marlo shook her head.

"To tell you the truth, I really don't know."

The pendant hanging from Marlo's hand began to, almost magnetically, gravitate toward the beaker of shimmering fluid until it touched the glass, as if to kiss a reunited friend.

"The truth," she muttered. "That's it, isn't it?" she continued, igniting her brother's eyes with the spark of realization. *"This stuff is truth.* And the little white lice. They feed on fibs and can't stomach the truth. It gives them full-on, full-body indigestion. Right?"

Dr. Brinkley rubbed his goatee and nodded.

"Exactly, Mr. Fauster," he replied with a smirk. "Distilled truth. The scarcest substance in the Underworld. Which is why Mr. Barnum has me trapped here, perfecting his personal formula. He calls it *liedocaine.*"

"Why would you use pure truth to make something called *lie*docaine?"

"There is always a grain of truth in the most effective lies," Dr. Brinkley explained. "After all, what is a lie if not measured against the truth? It's how an expertly crafted distortion makes it past the gateway of your frontal lobe. So liedocaine is a delicate and potentially volatile mixture of lies with trace amounts of truth. Just a *touch* so that it can be swallowed whole yet not *too* much or else it rips itself apart on a molecular level . . ."

Dr. Brinkley considered Marlo, probing her eyes so deeply that it made Marlo swallow with nervousness. He grabbed one of the beakers of liquid truth and held it to Marlo's face.

"I seem to be explaining an awful lot of Mr. Barnum's work to someone who is supposedly acting on his behalf," the doctor said. "I suspect, perhaps, that you are not being completely up-front with me, so I am going to ask you a simple question. . . ."

Please don't ask me if I am really me *hiding out inside of my brother's body,* Marlo fretted as she squinched up her eyes, hoping to avoid detection.

"Are you *truly* working for the vice principal?" the fowl doctor posed.

"Of course I am—" Marlo blurted out as the liquid within the beaker roiled with distress. Marlo eyed the gurgling liquid and sighed. "—not," she added. The liquid truth settled, resuming its usual calm, billowing motion.

Satisfied, Dr. Brinkley set the beaker back atop the counter.

"Out with it then, young man," he said, crossing his legs.

Marlo scowled at the beaker as if it were a friend that had betrayed her. She'd have to come clean, or at least splash some water on the truth.

"I overheard the vice principal talking," Marlo said, trying to push the cuticles back on her brother's nails, "and he mentioned something about a Humdinger—"

"Hum*bugger,*" the duck demon corrected. "It's the machine that allows him to create, distort, amplify, and transmit illusions—such as his guard clown outside the gates."

"The point is, he's figured out some way of beaming his illusions to the Surface."

"The Surface?!" Dr. Brinkley quacked. "That's impossible! The Transdimensional Power Grid doesn't grant access back up, unless cleared by the Galactic Order Department in cases of birth, rebirth, possession, and the occasional April Fool's prank."

"Well, my brother . . . I mean, *oh brother,*" Marlo faltered, her eyes darting to the beaker of truth as it birthed a herd of confused bubbles. "*I was able to do it . . . some-how.*"

"True," the doctor said with a nod.

"The thing is, you are—whether you know it or not—helping him to spread some nasty viral marketing thingie up on the Surface. Something he said would seem real . . . and, I'm guessing—considering the source—real *bad.*"

Dr. Brinkley's feathers ruffled as his head hung low.

"He would have told me," the doctor said sadly. "After my team of Night Mares were . . . were"—the doctor sniffed back a tear—"*flattened* by Fibble, he offered me a position as a partner."

Marlo scooted her chair closer to the doctor until they were almost knee-to-knee.

"*And you believed him?*" she asked. "A man who made his living, and apparently his dying, too, telling the biggest, most fantastic lies imaginable?"

Dr. Brinkley absentmindedly picked at the webbing

between his fingers as he stared at beakers of burbling liquid truth.

"*My Night Mares,*" he muttered.

Marlo heard stirring outside the door. She padded across the floor and peered out the window. The chameleon guards, though still unconscious, were coming to. Their luminous white skin gradually emulated the grimy yellow-orange sawdust strewn across the floor.

"Your Night Mares," Marlo repeated as her mind chewed on a faint idea that suddenly burst in her head like a Blow Pop. She turned to face the doleful duck.

"We can't believe anything around here," she said. "So let's check out the Big Top to see for *ourselves* if your horsies really *are* today's special at the International House of Pony Pancakes . . . and maybe I-hop the next stagecoach out of Fibble."

Dr. Brinkley fluttered to the door as Marlo crept out into the empty-save-for-several-semiconcious-lizards hallway. The two snuck down the dim, smoky corridor, hugging the drywalled walls, until they reached the Big Top.

Marlo scanned the less-than-grandstands, shrouded in clots of shadow, and grabbed the doctor's hand.

"C'mon," she said before taking her hand back and grimacing. "*Eww* . . . clammy."

"Shhh!" Dr. Brinkley said as he pointed to the Feejee Mermaid hung on the wall, asleep, sucking in air through its dried-up sliver of a nose and snoring out through its gills. Scattered across the seats were sleeping shrimp demons and Tom Thumb—his tiny top hat covering his eyes.

Marlo nodded. She crouched down and scooted toward the center of the ring, where a large hoop framing a sheet of paper painted like a bull's-eye lay on the ground. She waved the doctor over. They slunk down at the target's edge, then crawled to the center on their bellies. Marlo began pounding the thick paper.

"Are you insane?" Dr. Brinkley hissed. Marlo, on her stomach in the middle of a darkened circus talking to a duck, had to admit that this was a valid question. "We'll tear right through and join my flat little foals," the doctor explained.

Marlo swallowed as she contemplated plummeting several hundred feet to the frozen Falla Sea.

"Understood," she whispered as she carefully pressed her fingers into the paper. Unfortunately, Milton's nails weren't chewed into sharp points like hers, but—by twisting her fingers—Marlo was able to drill two holes into the bull's-eye. She peered through the ragged punctures. Marlo gasped at the distance between her and the rugged ground below.

The two demon guards, wearing their scary brass metal masks, sat inside the Gates of Fibble at the center of the brightly colored concentric rings. Marlo strained to see beyond the gates until there, at the edge of sight, she saw a pair of gleaming black horses, snorting and stomping their hooves in the cold.

"Guess what?" Marlo smiled. "Mr. Pants-on-fire is a total liar. See for yourself."

She rolled away to let Dr. Brinkley take a gander.

"Shuck and Jive!" he exclaimed. "My Night Mares are alive!"

The Feejee Mermaid stirred, giving its hurdy-gurdy a sharp squeeze before returning back to sleep. Marlo crept close to the doctor.

"That means if we can get *down,* we can get *out,*" she whispered. "It's just a question of . . . um, *down-and-out.* But before we vamoose-and-squirrel out of here, we do a number on the vice principal's lab so he can't spread his junky ads and freaky-deeky products up on the Surface— as if there's even any *room* for more junky ads and freaky-deeky products up there. So . . . are you with me?"

The edges of Dr. Brinkley's bill curled up into a smile as he tore his gaze away from the eye holes.

"If I was found out by Mr. Barnum, I'm afraid I'd be one dead duck," he whispered. "We must work in stealth, and be extra careful not to draw attention to ourselves."

With that, a thundering bell tolled and the Big Top flooded with light.

"Quack!"

"Quick!" Marlo yelped.

"Quack?"

"The morning bell!" Marlo clarified as the sleeping shrimps awoke. "Let's go!"

Marlo and Dr. Brinkley raced out of the Big Top, leaving an incriminating cloud of sawdust behind them, and entered the main Classroom and Boarding tent. Above them on the exposed second level, grumbling boys emerged sleepily from their bunks.

"You should get back to the lab," Marlo panted as fresh glitter-smoke—otherwise known as, Marlo now knew, *liedocaine*—wafted down upon them. "I'll drop by tonight."

Dr. Brinkley skipped down the hallway, delighted at the prospect of being free as a bird, even if that meant running a-waterfowl of Barnum. Marlo dashed to the ladder leading to the bunks.

"*What do you think* you're *doing this morning?*" boomed the vice principal from behind her. "Actually, save your excuses . . . I know where you've been, what you've done—" He stopped suddenly, then added with a wretched cackle, "and *where you're going!*"

14 · EVERYBODY WANTS TO FOOL THE WORLD

THE MAN WHO SOLDETH THE WORLD

PART TWO: THE TEAM

MILTON COULD ONLY catch brief glimpses of the man behind the camera—fleeting, garbled reflections caught in a crystal mug brimming with some steaming elixir. The mysterious figure sat at an immaculate marble table cluttered with manila envelopes and videocassettes.

"The perfect crime requireth the perfect team," the man said, his flawless voice burning like ice-cold fire. "And I am, humbly, as neareth to perfection as one can be. *Nearethly*. But all that may change if I can zingest a fast one past He Who Apparently Knoweth All and start *my own* heaven. And—who knoweth?—perhaps by swindling a supposedly omniscient entity, I could one day lay claim to His tarnished kingdom as well . . . but I digress . . ."

In the man's white-gloved hand was what looked like a contact lens. He affixed it to one of the envelopes, where it was virtually invisible.

Milton, nestled inside the cramped, multiscreened tomb of the Vidiot Box, examined the manila envelope in which this latest videocassette had arrived. There, just above the address, was a tiny, nearly imperceptible lens. Milton looked back up at the screen.

The image of the marble table, stacks of handwritten notes, envelopes, and swaying tendrils of burning incense blinked.

A contact lens camera! Milton thought. *Like the one Principal Bubb put in Cerberus's eye back in Limbo to track us! That's how he's able to record everything he does.*

"It taketh teamwork for a team to work," the man continued as he folded several impeccably inscribed parchment notes into an envelope. "But when your team is composed of charlatans, frauds, and career criminals, you suddenly find yourself with an abundance of self-serving *I*s in the word "team." Which is why each member of my team haveth no idea that they are actually *on* my team . . . or anyone else's, for that matter. Brilliant, of course, though blowing one's trumpet is a sin, so I'll leave it for history to decide . . . that is, before history *itself* is history. . . ."

The man wrote a name on an envelope with a white quill dipped in ink. Milton blew away his sister's irritating blue hair that was always getting in her face. The name was Elmyr de Hory. Address: The Furafter.

"Let us meet them now!" the man declared in a voice as cool and unyielding as marble. The image spasmed with bursts of static before settling on the suspicious face of an old man with refined features and a pink-and-green paisley ascot cinched to his neck. "Firstly is master forger Elmyr de Hory."

The elegant man, Mr. de Hory, arched his eyebrow to the camera quizzically as he set it down—apparently a contact lens camera attached to an envelope, Milton surmised—and squinted at the almost too-florid-to-be-deciphered handwriting of the notes within. Behind Mr. de Hory were rows and rows of cages.

"Ridding the earth of human infestation without actually . . . *K-I-L-L-I-N-G* them—or arousing undue suspicion—is a thorny endeavor, which is why I must forgeth a billion or so makeshift souls and transfer them to the afterlife at the *exact* moment of relocation," the man explained off-camera as the image fast-forwarded to Mr. de Hory sculpting a shimmering hologram of globs and sparkles with a pen laser. "Mr. De Hory, as the world's greatest art forger, is deftly fashioning a mold approximating the human soul that—after the souls of forgotten, forlorn animals trapped in the Kennels are melted down—will be used to cast as many convincing knockoffs as needed."

The image flickered again, now showing Mr. Welles raising his eyebrow as he opened the envelope containing the first *The Man Who Soldeth the World* episode. Milton—as Marlo—joined the portly director.

"Second is master of dramatic illusion Mr. Orson Welles," the man continued in his eerily smooth voice. "He who-eth perpetrated one of the most ambitious hoaxes of all time: an ingenious radio adaptation of *The War of the Worlds.* By presenting fantasy as fact, he convinced listeners that the Earth was under Martian invasion."

The image on the monitor crackled back to the man scribbling notes with his quill on what looked like, to Milton, a script.

"This time I will helpeth him to effectuate another brilliant Wellesian ruse, only this time presenting fact as fantasy."

The man lifted his crystal mug from a white lace doily to take a sip of his steaming, almost luminous beverage. Written on the doily in fussy cursive calligraphy was REVELATION 12:7.

The image, after a brief seizure of static, resolved to another hidden-contact-lens view of a froggish fop of a man, roasting marshmallows over what looked like a pair of flaming trousers.

"Third is P. T. Barnum," the man continued, "the famous showman and charlatan who turned his wily frauds

into wild applause. His celebrated hoaxes were spectacles that even the most jaded human couldn't—"

"Miss Fauster?" Mr. Welles said suddenly from behind Milton.

Milton's nervous system blew a fuse. Startled, he instinctively slapped off the VCR.

"What are . . . *were* you watching?" the director rumbled from the doorway of the Vidiot Box. Luckily, Milton thought with relief, Mr. Welles was an enormous
round man who couldn't fit through the box's square-
shaped hole.

"*The Man Who Soldeth the World,*" Milton blurted out,
lacking Marlo's ability to instantly prevaricate. He warily
eyed Mr. Welles's reflection in the darkened television
monitor.

"Oh . . . how was this latest installment?"

Milton was at a loss at how to proceed. He still didn't
know what to make of the disturbing show. If it *was* all
true, why would the mysterious man confess his crime
in the making? Did he believe that, if you made the truth
so convoluted and ridiculous, no one would believe it?
Should he confide in Mr. Welles—an unwitting costar in
the show—or would that only make things *worse,* leaving
Milton without any possible bargaining chip later on if
he *had* actually uncovered some kind of conspiracy. . . .

"Miss Fauster, you're doing it again . . . too much internal dialogue and not enough action. *Show,* don't tell. . . ."

"Right," Milton answered as he swiveled to face Mr. Welles. "It's just that—"

Mr. Welles cleared his spacious throat, breaking up a family of phlegm globs.

"In any case, I need you to run an errand for me," he said as he turned and walked away through a humming hive of technical assistants.

Milton tucked the videocassette into his bag and followed Mr. Welles to the Hellywood Hole stage. The first episode of *The Man Who Soldeth the World* had been cleared for broadcast, but Milton decided to hold on to the second episode for the time being. *A mindless errand will give me time to sort out what to do,* he thought, as he joined Mr. Welles at the edge of the stage, which had been transformed into a suburban New Jersey synagogue.

Mr. Welles scanned the tacky set, his sagging eyes shining with disgust.

"This is not a synagogue, but a sin of gawdy-awfulness!"

A nervous demon slicked back his seaweed-like hair. Mr. Welles yanked away the creature's clipboard.

"Looks like we'll have to reshoot *Queen of the She-brews,* where Newark's most stylish superheroine, Bat Mitzvah, is revealed by her archenemy, the Jersey Jokester," he grumbled as he flipped through the production notes. "Did you manage to shoot *The Ethel Mormon Show?*"

"J-just the 'When the Latter-Day Saints Come Marching In' musical number," the twitchy demon gurgled back, licking his pencil-thin mustache.

The hunched mail delivery demon chose that inopportune moment to push his cart to the side of the stage.

"Delivery for Mr. Welles—"

"Miss Fauster!" the director shouted.

Milton grabbed the familiar manila envelope: another episode of *The Man Who Soldeth the World*!

Mr. Welles sighed, his chest collapsing like a gargantuan soufflé at a heavy metal concert.

"Do what you can to make this set worthy of the Chosen People!" he barked, thrusting the clipboard back to his slimy, kelp-haired assistant director. "Sancho!" Mr. Welles yelled, raising his arm with a flourish. "Stage switch, *por favor.*"

Sancho nodded his sombreroed head and yanked the massive lever.

The immense rotating stage shifted, settling on a set with a grim backdrop of smoke, fire, and epic desolation. Four glamorous teenage girls on small prancing ponies clopped onto the stage, each wearing a unique glittery T-shirt: "Pestilence," "War," "Famine," and "Death." The girl on a sickly Camarillo pony, Pestilence, carried a buzzing jar in one hand. War, on a red-spotted apocalyptic Appaloosa, carried a sword. Famine, riding atop an emaciated horse a few cents short of a quarter pony, held a scale in one hand, while the skeletal Death held a tin of something labeled FINAL JUDGMINTS® as she steadied her deathly pale Shetland.

Mr. Welles stooped down to grab a stack of scripts from a messenger bag leaning against the stage.

"Miss Fauster," he grunted as he handed Milton the pile of scripts. Each was lacerated with so much red ink that it appeared to be bleeding.

"The Big Guy Downstairs had a lot of changes for the series finales. Especially the endings, which seem pretty . . . *final,* if you ask me. Have the writers make the changes, immediately."

Mr. Welles stalked over to the camera.

"This will just take a moment, ladies," he told the actresses as he squinted through the viewfinder. "I've got to rescue *The Queen of the Shebrews,* so we'll have to do this in one take . . . but I'd expect nothing less from the Four Pretty Ponies of the Apocalypse."

Milton flipped through the scripts. As Mr. Welles had said, each of the cliff-hanger endings had been scribbled out and replaced with new conclusions, each one more dark, abrupt, and calamitous than the last. *Teenage Jesus,* for instance, was to have ended with the title character bailing on college and going on a European road trip to "find himself" instead. Now the devil wanted Teenage Jesus to be believed dead, only to return three days later to confront his malevolent Auntie Christ, bringing about the end of the world: a sweeping wave of destruction, led by four young divas releasing pestilence, war, famine, death, and . . .

Milton waved away a buzzing insect.

Locusts.

"The Revelation will be televised," Mr. Welles chuckled. *"Action!"*

Milton looked up at the stage, swarming with ravenous flying locusts streaming out of Pestilence's jar.

"Make your last breath your *best!*" Pestilence said with a grinning mouth full of rotten teeth.

"Because when we come to judge *you,*" War added, "don't you want your breath to be minty fresh?"

"Right before we take it away!" Famine laughed.

Death flipped open the tin of mints and popped one into her mouth. Unfortunately, her head was nothing more than a grinning skull smeared with makeup, and the mint fell through her jaw. Her fellow pony princesses laughed.

"Oh, Death," Pestilence clucked. "Go take a holiday . . . but be back soon. We've got a lot of work to do!"

A surge of dread flooded Milton's borrowed body. He sat down at the edge of the stage.

Satan and—

Milton looked down at the manila envelope containing the latest episode of *The Man Who Soldeth the World.*

—whoever are not only plotting the biggest reality TV event the world has ever seen, Milton thought with a shiver, *but I get a creepy feeling they want it to be the last.*

15 · ALL THE NEWS
THAT'S FiT TO BE TiED

"I KNOW WHERE you've been, what you've done, and where you're going . . . ," P. T. Barnum bellowed. "So what do you have to say for yourself?!"

The vice principal's words were tranquilizer darts paralyzing Marlo, inside and out. Somehow P. T. Barnum had found her out, but how?

The boys filed out of the Totally Bunks above her on the second floor of the boarding tent, oblivious to Marlo's predicament.

"Can't he keep it down?" Colby whined as he changed out of his hair pajamas into his Fibble uniform. "I have sensitive ears, ever since I had that bat-blood transfusion. . . ."

Marlo drew in a deep breath and turned to face her tormenter.

"I can explain," she said in her brother's unsteady voice. "It's really—".

Marlo stared dumbfounded as, expecting the blustering bulk and flared trousers of the vice principal, she instead found herself face to face with emptiness.

"Nothing?"

"These are just some of the difficult questions we must ask a brand when developing a meaningful marketing campaign," P. T. Barnum declared through the PA speakers in the ceiling.

He sounded like he was right there behind me, Marlo thought, shivering, as her eye caught a plume of heavy, glittering vapor drifting down from the ceiling. "Liedocaine," she muttered. *It must be messing with my head.*

"And when the right questions are asked, the answers rub against one another and create a shower of sparks!" the vice principal continued. "A shower of ideas! But just having an idea is not enough . . . it must be released into the world in the best way possible, able to leap over customer objections in a single bound! Think hard upon this today, young *marketeers*! Good day and good fibbing!"

Marlo slowly regained the use of her limbs as the numbing fear of being found out fled her system.

"D'you know what that nutter Barnum loves more

than the sound of his own voice?" Zane asked Marlo, startling her, as he descended the ladder.

"Um . . . n-no . . . wh-what?" she stammered. *Man, he's even dreamy when he's just woken up after a night in hair pajamas,* she thought, both tormented and giddy.

"Beats me," he said with a shrug and smile. Marlo squealed with the weird disproportionate laughter symptomatic of a girl smitten.

"That's good," she replied, pinching herself hard on the thigh to help stop her deranged giggling. Zane cocked his eyebrow at her before staring at Marlo's rumpled hair pajamas and overall bleary, up-all-night appearance. How Milton's hair managed to contract chronic bed-head without ever making contact with a pillow baffled Marlo.

"Did you get up early or something?" Zane asked with his faint British lilt.

Marlo absentmindedly tried to smooth the split ends from her hair shirt.

"Just, you know, getting a little bit of early morning exercise. There's nothing I—but especially my sister, Marlo—like more than to be fit and healthy. But not *too* fit and healthy, you know? Not in that irritating obsessive gym-rat or carry-my-yoga-mat-wherever-I-go way, but—"

The class bell tolled, a mixed blessing for Marlo in that, while it brought her runaway rant to a merciful end, it also meant that she had sixty seconds to get into her uniform and to her next class.

"Flip a chip in old onion dip!" Marlo muttered through gritted teeth as she scaled the ladder, peeled off her itchy pajamas, pulled up her red, blaze-emblazoned uniform by its telephone-wire suspenders, then slid back down the ladder and dashed to her class.

Marlo broke the imaginary tape of the classroom's doorway just as the last bell tolled. Her prize was a reeking blast of ink fumes.

"Mr. . . . *Fauster,*" the teacher croaked in an unexpectedly high voice. The man's head was shaped like a hard-boiled egg, with wrinkled folds of speckled flesh serving as its shell. His eyes were cold and bright with dark purple circles blotched beneath as if two tiny sports cars had spent the entire night spinning doughnuts under them. "Sit down or else I'll force you to write your own post-mortem obituary for Heck's prestigious newspaper, *GYP:* The news that leaves a bruise!"

Marlo found an empty seat in the back, something of a rarity in Heck, next to a row of machines, each with a large drum in the middle and a hand crank on the side. As soon as Marlo settled, she realized why she had been able to secure this primo classroom real estate: the old contraptions were the source of the horrid chemical stench. Each desk in the class held a bulky old Underwood typewriter.

The teacher rose from his seat as most old people do—slowly, painfully, and under protest—and wrote his name in yellow chalk on the yellow chalkboard. Luckily for the students, the glare on the slate made the teacher's scratches somewhat legible: "Yellow Journalism. Mr. Hearst."

The teacher set his chalk down, leaned over his desk, and glared at the boys with his abandoned-lighthouse eyes. Colby tucked a strand of stringy hair behind his ear and raised his hand. Mr. Hearst stared at the boy's arm until it drooped under the weight of his stony gaze.

"Journalism is something that somebody doesn't want printed; all else is advertising," he declared with a shrill wheeze. "And yellow journalism is just like regular journalism, only slathered with a bright coat of paint so that it's lively, feisty, and unencumbered by fact. Yellow journalism is information that never fills you up and leaves you hungry for more."

Mr. Hearst stooped down to open his lower drawer, his brittle back popping like a tap dancer on a sheet of Bubble Wrap. He pulled out a stack of yellow legal pads and a half-dozen yellow highlighter pens.

"I was an American success story, the epitome of a self-made man," he squeaked as he passed out the pens and paper.

"I don't think I'd want to accept responsibility for making *that*," Marlo whispered to Zane as the decrepit, broken man shambled down the aisle.

Mr. Hearst gave Marlo a stink-eye so pungent that it nearly overpowered the reek of toxic ink. The teacher returned to his desk and yanked a handkerchief from his double-breasted suit.

"Since I've always been an advocate of teaching by *doing*," he muttered while mopping his damp brow, "I'm going to have you do all of the work. *My* work. As editor-in-chief of *GYP*—Heck's Golden Youth Periodical."

He stooped down and removed a stack of yellow file folders from another drawer.

"As a class you will write, edit, proofread, lay out, and print the next issue of *GYP*," Mr. Hearst said while slapping folders down on each boy's desk. "By tomorrow."

Colby flipped open his folder.

"The Op-Dead section?" he asked as the teacher passed out the students' assignments.

"*GYP*'s Deaditorial page," Mr. Hearst muttered, "where you write your opinions on the hot topics of the day, of which there are many down here. In your folder you'll find Principal Bubb's opinions on what your opinions should be. Mr. Cummings, you have the Spoiled Sports section beat."

Darnell scratched beneath his stocking cap.

"An exposé on Sadia's boys' German dodgeball team?"

"After their crushing loss to Sadia's *girls*' German dodgeball team, the team is suffering from some bruised egos . . . bruised *everything*, actually," the teacher explained as he shuffled his old bones down the aisle. "Plus there are those pernicious steroid rumors, that they aren't using nearly enough. . . ."

He handed Zane and Stawinski their folders.

"Mr. Covington, you have Nether News and the Chronic Strips section . . . simply rewrite the press releases and do what you can to make Mr. Van Gogh's *Ear Today, Gone Tomorrow* strip a little less . . . disturbing. And Mr. Stawinski—"

"It's actually just *Stawinski*," the tubby boy replied with a flip of his curly hair. "Like Cher."

Mr. Hearst's wrinkled face scrunched up like an old paper bag.

"I didn't know Cher's last name was Stawinski," he replied. "In any case, your beats are the None of Your Business and the Weather or Not? sections."

"Weather or Not?" Stawinski asked.

Mr. Hearst threw Marlo her folder.

"In Heck, in case you haven't noticed, Mr. Stawinski—"

"It's just—"

"—the weather is fixed . . . unless it's broken . . . which is often the case with the wind. So it's always a question of whether there will be weather or not."

Marlo leafed through her folders.

"Crassified Ads and Inhuman Interest?" she muttered.

Mr. Hearst turned and headed back to his desk.

"Ads are the lifeblood of every newspaper, and *GYP* is

no exception," the elderly teacher said as he settled painfully into his chair. "They are also an endless source of story ideas, often becoming Inhuman Interest stories; stories that are too inconsequential to fit in any other section . . . which is really saying something!"

Stawinski raised his hand. Mr. Hearst attempted to glare it back down, but the boy's sturdy arm was a worthy opponent to the teacher's withering gaze. Mr. Hearst sighed.

"Yes, Mr. Stawinski?"

The boy frowned.

"It's not . . . never mind," Stawinski replied, rubbing his droopy eyes with his fist. "I just want to know what you're going to be doing while we do all of this work."

Mr. Hearst guffawed like a crazed balloon animal full of laughing gas.

"I, like many newspapers, have circulation troubles," he answered as he set his feet on his desk. "So while you deliver the news, I will enjoy a snooze."

Marlo looked through her Crassified folder. Inside was a flyer for a missing pet: *Cerberus.*

Marlo smirked. *So Bubb's creepy lapdog has gone missing,* she thought. *Good riddance. That dog is bad news . . . perfect for* GYP.

She looked through her second folder, Inhuman Interest. Inside was a press release:

FOR IMMEDIATE RELEASE

Contact: Ruth Harrison
REPEAT (Recently Expired People for Ethical Animal Treatment)

THE FURAFTER—This morning, REPEAT dispatched a group of activists to the Furafter, the realm of the afterlife for domesticated and semidomesticated pets, to protest the beastly treatment of animals caged in the Kennels, the joyless jail reserved for pets deemed "bad" by the Galactic Order Department's thoughtless, incomprehensible knee-jerk arbitration mechanisms.

REPEAT's action comes in the wake of rumors that animals incarcerated in the Kennels are to be undone— energetically nullified. Caretaker Noah was not available for comment.

"We will cross the line, because the Powers That Be have crossed the line," says REPEAT founder Brigid Brophy. "That's why we are going down to the Furafter, to get our hands dirty and raise an unholy stink as only we animal-lovers can. It's the only way we can realize our vision for a cruelty-free realm of eternal condemnation."

Behind the press release was a small stack of grainy photographs, taken—according to the stamps on the back—from the Kennels' insecurity cameras. The photographs captured towering rows of cramped cages, each occupied by a howling, miserable animal. Thousands of them, perhaps millions. Just as Marlo was about to close the folder in disgust, her eye was caught by one particular animal caged in the upper left-hand corner of the last photograph. A thin, white ferret with burning red eyes, hissing at the camera.

"Lucky!" Marlo yelped.

Zane looked over from his work.

"I'm glad *someone* likes their assignment," he grumbled as Marlo raised her hand.

"Mr. Hearst, I have a question!" she exclaimed.

The old man bolted awake, nearly falling off his chair.

"Mr. Fauster," Mr. Hearst said, wiping the drool from his thin lips with the back of his hand, "how dare you ask a question in class."

"But it's about *GYP*," she responded. "I want to make my Inhuman Interest story as interesting to inhumans as possible. So I thought I should go down to the Furafter and cover the REPEAT protest myself."

"REPEAT?"

"*I said that I should go down to the Furafter and—*"

"I heard you!" Mr. Hearst spat. "It's just that what you are proposing reeks of"—Mr. Hearst shivered—"*reporting*! And I will *not* have students make a mockery of yellow journalism by engaging in unbiased investigation and thoughtful inquiry!"

Marlo clenched her fists and fumed silently to herself.

It was worth a try, Marlo thought as she stared at her

brother's ferret, Lucky, gaping back at her in wide-eyed terror from the photograph. *If Mr. Hearst wants sensation, I'll give it to him, with interest. I'll make this protest sound like the biggest, most controversial thing to hit the Underworld since they banned not-smoking.*

Around her, typewriters began to slowly click and clack, like a flock of robotic chickens pecking listlessly at rusty worms.

Lucky is *a sign, and he'll be a sign for Milton, too,* Marlo thought as she turned the humble REPEAT protest into a seething hotbed of frenzied hullabaloo, something that would surely get the Nether media jumping through hooplas to cover it. *Milton and I are better together. We can meet in the Furafter to switch back our bods and rescue Lucky from nulli-whatever, figure out what Barnum's up to, save the Surface from an outbreak of viral marketing, and find a way out of this mess!*

16 · WRITING WRONGS

DALE E. BASYE, middle-aged and muddling through the middle of his latest book, *The Breath-taking, Wind-breaking Fartisimo Family,* chewed the tip of the pipe he pretended to smoke as he stared at the blinking message light of his answering machine.

It's probably that creepy kid again, he mused. *The one that cornered me at that reading in Topeka during my tour of Midwestern rec centers last month.* Dale shivered. *All those big kids on little bikes . . . and the chlorine . . .*

He pulled out a black notebook and jotted down "Big kids on little bikes . . . over-chlorinated pools" on a crowded page labeled "Irrational fears."

Dale sighed and set down his pipe. His series about the exploits of a family who, when sufficiently gassy, perform the cheekiest, most exquisite choral music ever heard—that is, when they aren't breaking up illegal bean cartels and catching international cheese-slicer smugglers—had hit a rough patch, creatively. And after fifteen minutes of writing—or at least thoughtful staring—he was due for a break anyway.

Dale hit the playback button of his answering machine.

"Hello, Mr. Bass . . . *Baze* . . . *Bayzee*," the young voice squawked through the speaker.

No one ever gets my name right, Dale reflected as he drained his tea cup and set it on the coaster just like his wife had asked him to.

"This is Damian Ruffino . . . *again*," the voice continued. "We met at the Topeka Community Rec Center, Play Pool, and Assisted Living Facility last month. You must think I'm stalking you, which is ridiculous, because if I was, you'd be really, really scared right now. *Believe* me. Anyway, I have a business proposition to make to you. A collaboration. A ghostwriting project."

Ooh, I've always wanted to write about ghosts, Dale mused.

"Not writing about ghosts," Damian continued, "but *you writing something for me.* Only it's sort of the opposite of ghostwriting, I guess, because it would be *your* book. I have the concept and basic story worked out, I just need someone to write it down. I tried, but my, um, editor wasn't happy with it. Said it focused too much on the ant agonist or whatever. I can't help that he is totally *awesome.* The character sort of wrote himself. . . ."

The boy snickered, a dark, secret laugh, like that of a maniac who knows *exactly* where someone is buried.

Dale stared at the twin red lights of his answering machine, the ones that always reminded him of a demon's eyes. *I need to make some* real *money if I'm ever going to quit my JiffyAds job—*

"And you would make some *real* money with this," Damian added. "So give me a call. I'm at 555-727-6765 . . . that's 555-PAR-NRML. Don't ask. . . ."

A click and the swarming wasp buzz of a dial tone filled Dale's small home office. He snatched up the phone before the usual chorus of doubt and apprehension could clog his head.

"What?" Damian said brusquely as he picked up the phone. Dale could hear the sounds of struggle, and a man protesting in the background.

"It's my phone, man!" the voice wheezed. "This is totally uncool . . . like, *Altamont* uncool!"

"Whatever, Cherry Garcia," Damian barked. "*I'm* the one holding the phone now, and that's all that matters. I paid your rent, so just peace out somewhere else . . . *who is it?*" Damian barked.

Dale swallowed.

"I . . . this is Dale E. Basye. *The author.* You called me just—"

"Yeah, I know I called you," Damian interrupted. "Thanks for *finally* getting back to me. Those Fartisimo Family books can't take *that* much time to write!"

"Um, you see, I have to do them on weekends," Dale explained, flustered. "I have a day job as a copywriter, to pay the bills and—"

"Well, tell your boss to take a hike," Damian blustered. "*I'm* your new boss now."

Dale shivered uncontrollably as if someone had poured a scoop of crushed ice down the back of his boxers, which his son hadn't done for months.

"We still haven't even discussed—"

"You have no idea how hard it's been to track down someone to write my story," Damian interrupted. "I called a bunch of other people first, then I saw your book in the Books This Library Shouldn't Carry section of the Generica Central Library. You're a hard guy to get ahold of, since no one knows who you are . . . and your weird name. Are you sure it's spelled B-A-S-Y . . . ?"

"Yes, I'm sure. So what's the book you want me to write?" Dale blurted out, shoving as many words as he could through the slight breach in Damian's one-sided conversation. He could hear a shuffle and crash through the receiver.

"Watch out for Bigfoot . . . you almost smashed his big toe!" the wheezing man shouted in the background. "Move all your boxes to *your* side of the Paranor Mall . . . you're not paying me enough to break all of my exhibits!"

Damian sighed.

"Never mind our landlord," he explained, "he's so crazy that even the voices in his *head* think he's crazy. But we won't be here for long, especially when my . . . *our* book becomes a big hit."

"Yes, *the book*," Dale asserted as he chewed the tip of his pipe with frustration. "And it's called . . . ?"

"*Heck: Where the Bad Kids Go,*" Damian offered.

Dale smiled to himself—literally, as there was a framed picture of himself on his desk.

"That's clever . . . kind of corny, but clever," he replied. "Plus there's a lot of interest in the afterlife lately, with those new shows *Teenage Jesus, Allah in the Family,* and *Queen of the Shebrews* being such big hits on TV—"

"With my connections, we can turn this into one *hot* property," Damian interrupted, before adding a deep, unsettling snicker to his comment: the cherry bomb on the cake. "So I'm guessing you're on board. I'll send you a plane ticket for Kansas. Be sure that *you're* on board and we can seal the deal."

"Plane ticket?" Dale replied before realizing Damian had hung up on him. He cradled the phone for a moment longer, hoping to save face with the accusatory mob of *Star Trek* (original series) action figures staring back at him from his desk. "That will be just . . . fine."

Dale put the phone back in its cradle, opened his journal, and added "sudden plane flights," "bossy kids," "ghostwriting," and "Kansas" to his ever-expanding list of irrational fears.

His hasty deal with Damian reminded Dale of

Christopher Marlowe's classic play *The Tragical History of Doctor Faustus,* in which a man sells his soul to the devil for power and knowledge.

Hmm, Dale contemplated as he scribbled the names Marlowe and Faustus in his journal, *maybe Damian's right—this book practically writes itself.*

MIDDLEWORD

It could be said, or written, or even dictated (though there are plenty of dictators in the underworld, no-thank-you-very-much) that lying isn't just human nature: it's Mother Nature.

Nature is, when you get right down to it, a big fat liar, full of cheaters (and cheetahs). Take the blenny: a spiny, blunt-headed/sharp-witted tropical fish that is one of the marine kingdom's most spurious con men (or women . . . it's hard to tell with fish). The blenny impersonates fish known as cleaners, who dutifully remove parasites from the bodies of larger fish out of the goodness of their little fish hearts. The true cleaner and the host fish have an arrangement that's been working just swimmingly for millions of years. That is, until the blenny. This conniving impostor crashes the party of mutual advantage by adopting the cleaner's vivid stripes, then lurks in the crevices of rocks, waiting. Suddenly, it sets itself upon the unsuspecting host fish, who—expecting a morning session of gentle hygiene—instead gets its flesh ripped off in savage strips and chunks.

This is all to say that humans—and even creatures who believe that they are more than human—are not immune to nature's predisposition toward prevarication. It's hot-wired into humanity as a means of survival. Every shade of lie is told by billions of humans each second as they simply try to make it (or fake it) through their day, much like the blenny. But humans have this nagging little accessory called a conscience. To some, it is like an appendix*: a small, unused organ of no known function. To others, it's an opportunity to grow and evolve, to realize their true humanity.

So why do humans go to such lengths to disguise who they really are by playing dress-up with the truth? Perhaps it's because while lies take a hundred thousand forms, the truth itself has but one face. And rarely does anyone—fish, fowl, demon, or deity—have the courage to look that face in the mirror, for fear of what might be peering back. . . .

*An appendix is also supplemental information included in a book that distracts while adding nothing.

17 · RIDING OUT THE BRAINSTORM

HAVING TROTTED STEALTHILY through the mind-warping haze of liedocaine all the way from the Totally Bunks to the R & D lab, Marlo bent over—her palms wedged on the front of her thighs—and panted.

"Man . . . Milton sure is . . . out of shape," she puffed. After a short breather, Marlo edged her way along the Sheetrock walls toward the lab. The entire third tent was benumbed by a thick, late-night hush.

I hope Dr. Brinkley was able to drug the guards with those full-spectrum kaleidoscopic color pills he was talking about, Marlo pondered. *If not, I don't know—*

"What are you doing out of bed?" Vice Principal Barnum's voice boomed from behind her.

Marlo's heart was suddenly "it" in a game of neuro-biological Freeze Tag.

Wow, I don't know if it's the sleep deprivation or the liedo-caine that's slow-leaking out of the ceiling, but that sounded like he really was right behind me, Marlo thought as she fought back the asthma that so often called Milton's lungs home.

"Plug your blowhole, you blabbering blowhard," she muttered, Marlo thought, to herself as she turned to face the furious face of her vice principal, his pants sizzling angrily.

". . . is an excellent example of something you would never say to a respected authority figure," Marlo continued, holding her brother's arms to prevent them from trembling loose from their sockets.

Vice Principal Barnum tapped his hard-leather shoes against the floor in time with his own irritation.

"Imagine my surprise, Mr. Fauster, when I entered the Boys' Totally Bunks with the intent of arousing my students from slumber to instigate an impromptu mid-night brainstorm and, shock of shocks, one Milton Fauster is not in his assigned bunk."

Marlo fingered the bauble of truth dangling from inside her white lice–infested hair pajamas. It burbled angrily at the fib poised to take off from Marlo's tongue.

"To tell you the truth," Marlo lied as the vice princi-pal shuddered at the mere mention of the word, "I found out about the brainstorm and was taking a late-night stroll to hatch some great ideas to impress the flaming *pants* off you, since you've always been such a role model for me. Truly inspiring. I found out from Scampi . . . but don't blame him, I grilled the little guy. I mean, I just *love* grilled shrimp!"

Perplexed yet appeased by his ego's midnight snack, the vice principal's temper—and pants—relaxed to a rankled crackle.

"If I catch you wandering my halls after hours again, I will damage your perceived brand value so completely that no campaign, however ingenious, will ever hope to resuscitate it," the vice principal said as he grabbed Marlo by the scruff of the neck and led him down the hallway. "Do I make myself clear?"

"Crystal Light," Marlo murmured as she was dragged into the Big Top. Vice Principal Barnum threw her to the sawdust floor as he lumbered toward the center of the ring.

"Take your place in the stands with the other hunks of fresh gray matter," he ordered as he yanked down the microphone suspended from the ceiling and held it to his face. Marlo, naturally, climbed up the stands to sit next to Zane, who—even crumpled, yawning, and bleary-eyed— made her heart, or Milton's, feel like it was jumping a game of double Dutch.

"Judging from the results generated in class, it seems as if we've thought ourselves into a corner," Vice Principal Barnum barked into the dangling microphone, scowling as he gazed upon the glazed faces in the stands. "And my latest campaign is so sweeping in scope, so epic in grandeur, so groundbreaking in its artful dodginess that I felt it necessary to pluck you from slumber— where the creative mind is at its most fertile—and assemble you here for a spontaneous late-night brainstorming session." He looked over at Tom Thumb, who was twiddling his surname at the base of the bleachers.

The dapper, diminutive man nodded, then marched up through the stands, passing out pads of paper and pencils. Vice Principal Barnum walked over to the Feejee Mermaid—the disgusting semiliving amalgam of kelp and bone mounted to the wall—and transferred it to the middle of a large whiteboard, wedging a marker to its withered flipper.

"Now, the only rule with brainstorms is that there *are* no rules," the vice principal relayed. "And that there is no such thing as a bad idea. Now I would like your young noggins to chew upon a purely hypothetical advertising scenario, pretending that if the afterlife were, say, a brand, what would it need to communicate in order to connect with your demographic?"

P. T. Barnum crossed his fingers behind his back.

"Please, be free with your thoughts, as I value your opinions most highly."

Marlo heard a peculiar creaking noise behind her. She turned and noticed the creepy wooden beams framing the tent tremble and . . . *stretch*. Subtly, but enough to cause the canvas to grow taut. The boys around her were oblivious as they rubbed the sleep out of their eyes. Colby stretched and yawned.

"Yes, Mr. Hayden?" the vice principal said.

"Uh, me? Well, what if the afterlife was like some awesome amusement park, where you got your hand stamped and could leave whenever you want and come back?"

The Feejee Mermaid's marker squeaked across the whiteboard.

"That's a terrible idea," Vice Principal Barnum declared flatly.

"But I thought there *weren't* any bad ideas in a brainstorm?" Marlo replied.

"I lied," the vice principal said with growing irritation. Zane raised his hand.

"What if it was some super exclusive, totally brilliant club?" he posed in his crisp London accent. "With perks and rewards, you know? Not some naff church club, but something really posh?"

The vice principal, having contracted a contagious yawn from Colby, opened his mouth wide as the mermaid wrote down Zane's idea. "Congratulations, Mr. Covington," he said with a dismissive stretch, "you've just reinvented the Paradisco: Heaven's after-hours never-quite-nightclub. *Next!*"

Marlo seethed at the dissing her not-quite boyfriend received. Her hand shot up.

"What if the afterlife were like some awful circus run by an arrogant madman?" she said.

The vice principal's face flushed red.

"This is to be the high point of my career! To deploy the most shamelessly ambitious marketing campaign ever devised!"

The vice principal shot a loaded, sideways glance to his team of shrimp demons. Scampi and Annette nodded, their creepy feeler eyes bobbing with comprehension, and disappeared underneath the bleachers. Barnum shuffled in tense circles across the sawdust floor.

"My entire life has been spent attempting to dupe the masses with spectacle. Now, by removing all of the typical restraints that confine even the most successful marketing campaigns, I can permanently blur the line between reality and advertising, giving people both what they want and what they fear the most. . . ."

The shrimp demons emerged from the grandstands lugging behind them a wooden crate crisscrossed on the outside by a network of brass tubes.

"Speaking of which," P. T. Barnum said with a smirk, tilted drastically to one side as if his lips were surreptitiously pouring poison into someone's glass, "I have a little surprise. Since I can't seem to get you to think outside the box, maybe it's time I put one of you *in* the box . . . the Box of Bitter"—an expression of sour distaste darted across the vice principal's face—"*Truth*. Mr. Fauster, since you seem so eager to participate, I'd like you to be the first pupil to climb inside."

Marlo shivered as she eyed the splintered, unvarnished crate.

"That's okay, I'm good," she replied just as Tom Thumb, swirling a loop of rope above his top-hatted head, lassoed Marlo and tugged her off her seat and down to the ring.

"*Ugh,*" Marlo grunted. "You're pretty strong for a pygmy!" she groaned as she struggled against the midget's surprising might. The vice principal sneered.

"My generous attempts to reward you children by involving you in the campaign of a lifetime—*and then some*—seem to have failed," he said as Marlo—with a little help from the swarming shrimp demons—was pushed into the claustrophobic crate. "So you've forced me to motivate you all with another, baser advertising tactic: the threat of shame and punishment."

Tom Thumb shut the lid of the Box of Bitter Truth, sealing Marlo in darkness. She could hear a beam of wood falling into place, bracing the door from the outside, and the squeal of a metal spigot being turned. The box vibrated as something gurgled through the lattice of pipes girding the crate. At first, Marlo was filled with a pleasant sense of clarity—her head unburdened by the noise of doubt and worry—but then this feeling of naked insight became raw and painful.

"A truth that's told with bad intent," the vice principal said, his voice piercing the hiss and rattle of the pipes, "beats all the lies you can invent."

Rolling waves of barbwire anguish scratched at Marlo's insides, scraping away at her thoughts and feelings like electrified cheese graters. The little white lice infesting her clothes wriggled in pain before drying up and dying. Marlo's mind was rubbed raw and tender by a caustic Brillo pad parade of bitter, painfully amplified realization.

I'm . . . an awful person. . . . I've hurt so many people. . . . I deserve to be down here in Heck. And I'm not even—

Suddenly, Marlo could feel her soul wriggling inside of her body—struggling in fear and agony—as if it were being torn away.

—me! I'm a lie!

With that, Marlo's consciousness—like a guttering candle—was snuffed out.

Moments later, the sound of booming voices roused Marlo from unconsciousness.

"Yo ho ho!" two female voices squawked. "It's ARGH: dropping anchor in yer eardrums once again. I'm Scurvacious Dee—"

"And I'm Shabby Bloomers," a salty-throated woman chimed in.

"And she ain't kidding, folks. . . . Next up, we have another smash hit from the Truthador that'll surely get you rockin' the plank! Here he is with 'Terranean Eviction Blues'!"

The door of the Box of Bitter Truth opened. Marlo shielded her tear-swollen eyes from the glare. Zane scooped her up and dragged her out onto the sawdust.

The Big Top resounded with the sound of crackling static.

"Can't someone do something about that?!" Vice Principal Barnum yelled as Tom Thumb and the shrimp demons milled around in confusion, clapping their ears. Marlo took in the scene with groggy detachment, as if Fibble's Big Top was a ginormous dryer and everyone in it simply articles of brightly colored clothing just spinning and spinning and spinning. . . .

Marlo heard a weird woody scream, a muffled wail coming from all around her. She noticed the wooden supports of the Big Top tent contracting, causing the canvas to scrunch and crinkle. Barnum, his face slick with the oily sheen of worry, began whispering to the major support beams bracing the tent. The posts moaned as they returned to their original length.

"Someone's in the basement, mixing up malarkey.
Humans on the pavement, chattering like monkeys . . ."

Marlo shivered and tilted her aching head, still sore on the inside from her blunt truth bludgeoning.

On the side of the box was a pressure meter, with the red needle hovering between Honesty and Cold, Bitter Truth.

"Milton," Zane whispered, "let's sneak you to the back of the grandstands before Barnum gets wise."

Marlo smiled faintly.

"That should take a while," she murmured as Zane slung his arm around her and led her up the bleachers.

Vice Principal Barnum scanned the ring, his bulging eyes settling on a small, red cannon.

"Okay, put some shrimp demons in the cannon and aim them at the speakers. . . ."

"Look out kid, it's all under their lid.
Let out the truth until every lie is undid . . ."

Marlo and Zane climbed to the top of the grand-stands. The wooden beams behind the benches creaked violently. Marlo leaned against the back of the Big Top as Barnum wedged wriggling shrimp demons into the cannon. Marlo examined the contracting wood, stained with splotches resembling screaming faces. At the bottom of each beam, Marlo noted a name burned into the wood. She knelt down to read it.

"Geppetto Lumber Company?" Marlo murmured as she read the branded inscription. "Geppetto, as in Pinocchio's dad?"

"You don't need a feather, man, to take you where the
crow flies.
Don't follow cheaters, honesty's your leader . . ."

With each word the Truthador sang, the wooden
beams strained, contracting smaller and smaller.

"The Truthador," Marlo mumbled. "The Truth!"

And in that instant, Marlo knew *exactly* how to escape from Fibble to—hopefully—rescue Lucky from the
Kennels. Grinning madly, she teetered back to Zane and
tapped him on the shoulder.

"How would you like to get out of this place?" she
said, her brother's fingers reflexively pushing nonexistent glasses up his nose. *"Honest."*

18 · CAWS FOR ALARM

ANNUBIS AND THE dogs padded across the crinkling newspapered no-man's-land of Stay! toward the low-lying fortress in the distance. The structure was a massive, nine-sided pen reinforced with heavy-duty steel bars. Atop the nine-foot walls was a parapet of scaffolding, broken up every nine feet by a pair of bronzed pets: a house cat and a watchdog. Inside the enclosure were two spherical portals that shimmered and crackled like great balls of invisible fire. These rounded, energetic doorways, according to the dogs, allowed a creature entry from any side to cross through to their specific destination.

If Annubis squinted his eyes just right, he could make out blurry images inside the humming, sputtering spheres. The doorway on the left held a muddled view of crates—thousands and thousands of them—stacked willy-nilly into towering walls set upon acres of cracked, stained concrete.

"The Kennels," Annubis muttered with dread as he fixed his gaze upon the doorway on the right, revealing warped, wavering images of a gorgeous, expansive ranch drenched in sun-soaked splendor.

"The Really Big Farm!" he said with an uncontrollable grin. "Now it's just a question of opening the gates—"

An explosive chorus of caws rent the air. The unmistakable sound of liquid splashing on newspaper followed shortly thereafter.

"*Pardonnez-moi,*" Faux Paw apologized through his Speak & Spell.

Annubis could now see, perched atop the walls, nine oversized crows peering out across Stay! with their beady, incomprehensibly black eyes. Annubis turned to Virginia Woof, who was panting anxiously by his side.

"*Crows,*" Annubis said with irritation. "How come none of you thought it important to mention the presence of nine freakishly large crows?"

Virginia Woof sat down on her haunches, her back legs splayed ladylike to one side. She grabbed the stylus dangling from her collar and jabbed a message into her Speak & Spell.

"*Scarecrows,*" she replied in the toy's flat, digitized voice. "To be honest, never thought cats let us get this far."

"Scarecrows?"

"Guard Globeways. Many-sided portals, ideal for

transport struggling animals. Ever try herd cats? Globe-ways make easier for Scarecrows, virtually scratch-free."

The imposing crows spread out their wings until they formed a wall of gleaming black feathers.

"Caw!"

Annubis's eyes grew wet as he stared longingly into the rotating spheres beyond the fence, one of which led to his wife and daughter.

"Well, we stand no chance vanquishing them through force . . . especially since none of us are bird dogs," Annubis commented with resignation. "So I suppose I'll just have to reason with them."

Annubis smoothed out his shimmering white tunic. Virginia Woof whined and gently nipped at his ankle.

"Careful," the terrier tapped. "Crows be murder."

Annubis nodded and approached the fortress. The Scarecrows paced along the parapet nervously, hunching their shoulders and puffing their crest feathers, and turned their backs. He stood at the front by the latched gate, took in a deep breath, and addressed the birds.

"Good day, good crows . . . *Scarecrows,* forgive me," Annubis declared in a smooth, diplomatic tone. "Might I speak with—"

The dog god was barraged by a hot salvo of viscous white crow droppings, accompanied by a cacophony of caws. The crows shuffled about their roosts with their tail feathers quivering in satisfaction.

Annubis, stiff with mortification, smeared clumps of

thick, oily excrement from his face. The dog god at least had got his answer: there would be no reasoning with these sometimes predatory, sometimes scavenging, all-the-time intimidating birds. He saw the pack of dogs retreat behind a wall of old yellowed newspaper stacks.

A muffled clutter of mews filled the stale, still air around them. In the distance, a roving mass of cats came, their tails twitching in their maddening, secret cat language.

The dog god shook himself alert, as one should never have a fuzzy head *inside* when dealing with cats. He trotted stealthily to the newspaper wall.

"Chairman Meow, Claude Yereyesout, Hannibal Lickter, Felonious Mouse-de-meaner, and . . . *Lulu*," Virginia Woof said as she scrutinized the front line of shabby, filthy, snaggletoothed felines. "Those are some bad, bad kitties."

Suddenly, parting the sinewy sea of cats with his three noses, came Cerberus, who pranced to the front of the ragged team of felines, and drank in the feast of smells around him.

Annubis's jaw dropped.

"Cerberus!" he gasped in shock. He rubbed the crown of his sleek head. "Where that hound of Heck goes, Bubb is sure to follow," he added miserably. "Figures that treacherous, disloyal lapdog would side with the cats."

Napoleon Bone-apart scratched and barked.

"Shhh!" Annubis scolded.

The Italian greyhound whimpered and scratched at the newspapers beneath him. Virginia Woof cocked her ears as she tentatively pawed the hole Napoleon Bone-apart had started. The ground beneath the shredded newspaper was softer than she had expected, a mixture of sawdust clumps and cedar shavings.

Annubis's tail waggled beneath his tunic as he examined the terrier's freshly dug hole—already a foot deep—then followed with his eyes to the inside of the fortress.

"You are in no way obliged to help me further," Annubis said. "I don't wish to put you and the pack in harm's way."

Virginia Woof stopped digging, her muzzle clumped with sawdust.

"In Noah's absence, you closest thing to a master," she said, working the Speak & Spell with difficulty in the cramped space. "We no roll over, lie down, and play dead while one of own in need."

As it is physically impossible to not crave cheese puffs at the sight of someone eating cheese puffs, the other dogs were incapable of standing idly by as one of their pack joyously dug fresh earth. Together, the dogs made quick work of the hole, soon an expansive tunnel. Even the noble dog god could not resist the lure of soil sifting and tickling between his claws. Annubis just hoped, as he dug his way in the dark, moist soil beneath Stay! that he and his adopted pack would strike pay dirt.

★　　★　　★

Loose clumps of compressed cedar shavings fell down the dog god's back. He could see faint light trickling through the ceiling of the tunnel. Annubis stuck his slender nose up through a small opening and inhaled deeply. The sharp tang of crow droppings was powerful. Peeking through the odor were faint traces of dog, cat, and other domestic mammal musks, along with the occasional canine crazy-making scent of squirrel. Annubis cautiously peered past the lip of the newly dug hole.

The energetic portals leading to the Kennels and the Really Big Farm were only a few yards away. Beyond, up on the parapets, the crows were perched, facing out with agitated interest at the cats languidly swarmed outside the fortress.

Annubis hoisted himself out of the hole and sprinted on all fours toward the sputtering, spherical portal leading to the Kennels. Virginia Woof hopped out and trotted at his heels.

The sensation of passing through the Globeway was, to Annubis, like running through an electric, full-body flea comb. Annubis skidded across the concrete floor and slammed against a wall of metal crates that stretched above, nearly touching the ceiling of flickering fluorescent tubes. The pungent odor of animal despair and the harsh, relentless din of whines, meows, and barks knocked the wind out of Annubis as he crumpled to the floor.

"No creature . . . no matter how they behaved while living . . . deserves to be treated . . . like this!" he snarled in between labored breaths. "Forgotten . . . *furever* . . ."

Annubis's long, droopy ears pricked at a sound poking through the wall of miserable noise. A yap. And this yap held with it a special timbre to Annubis, a precise flavor unique in all the universe.

"Kebauet!" Annubis yelped as he sprung to his feet.

The yapping gained in urgency and intensity.

Annubis cocked his ears, separating yelps from bays, until he isolated his daughter's plea for help.

"Paw-paw," she whimpered from twenty crates above.

"Nub-nub?" a weak, crumpled velvet voice queried from a nearby crate. "Am I . . . dreaming? My legs aren't twitching. . . ."

"Anput!" Annubis howled with longing. "I'm coming." The dog god darted his head from side to side, searching for some way to reach his family.

"I apologize, my fellow creatures," he said as he began assembling stray crates into a sort of stairway, leading him as close as possible to his wife and daughter.

Virginia Woof bit into the wire mesh of the cages and dragged them to Annubis, one by one, with feisty heaves and jerks.

"Thank you, my friend," Annubis said gratefully as he hoisted the cage of a hissing tabby to the top of the ad hoc stairwell. The dog god clambered up the steep, gently swaying tower of crates until he could just touch, by fully extending his long, graceful limbs, the cage of his beloved daughter. He felt the pink tickle of her tongue.

"We knew you'd come!" yapped the odd-looking girl, with her glossy gray coat and dark pointed ears. Annubis wiped the tears from his eyes with the back of his paw-hand.

"Of course, my pup," he said as he strained to lift her latch. He unclasped the rusty cage door and Kebauet leapt into her father's arms. Annubis hugged her close before, reluctantly, lowering her down to a ledge of crates five feet above the floor.

Annubis scrambled to rearrange the crates to reach his wife, imprisoned across the cramped channel separating the wall of cages. Anput was several stories higher than Kebauet had been, so Annubis climbed upward using a series of meager footholds until he made his way to his wife's cage.

"My dear," he said as he took in the shocking image of his wife, a Weimaraner, her pelt a once-lustrous charcoal-blue storm cloud of fur now worn in patches.

The light behind Anput's amber eyes flared at the sight of her husband.

"I had . . . nearly given up hope," she replied, her short tail wagging feebly. Though emaciated, Anput still radiated elegance and nobility. Annubis tucked his paws around her frail form and pulled her to his chest.

"You have lost so much weight," he said as he draped

his wife across his back and, with great care, inched his way toward his pile of cages.

Anput clutched tightly around Annubis's neck.

"I would flick whatever stale kibble bit the auto-feeders deigned to give toward our daughter," she replied with effort. They arrived at the crate tower, with Annubis folding his fragile wife in his arms and climbing down to the concrete floor. He set her beside his daughter, the two gripping each other tightly.

A pungent, curry-dusted musk caught the attention of Annubis's nostrils, cutting through the sour wash of urine and feces.

"A ferret," Annubis said as he attempted to zero in on the odor's source with his keen nose. "Lucky!"

A fierce scrabbling rattled a cage stacked twenty feet high in the corner by the glimmering Globeway entrance.

"You rest there, my treasures," he said as he dragged crates toward the source of the sound. "I made a promise to a friend."

Virginia Woof tapped her displeasure into her Speak & Spell.

"Must hurry," she relayed through the plastic box. "Can't rescue every creature."

Annubis doggedly constructed another tower of cages by the Kennels' entrance. "We'll see about that," he panted as he hauled the heavy crates into a jumbled yet sturdy-enough heap. Annubis scaled the pile nimbly until he was greeted by a pair of glowing red eyes and a blast of anchovy-hiss.

"You must be Lucky," Annubis said as he noted the pair of dice hanging from the ferret's collar. "Or as lucky as a creature can be in the Kennels." Lucky spun about frantically in his cramped cage, a white whir of restlessness. Annubis unlatched the cage, and the ferret spilled out onto his back like a living fur stole.

"Don't . . . worry," Annubis said between clenched teeth as Lucky buried his claws in the dog god's back, "we'll be out of here soon, and no one will be the—"

Annubis froze as he turned to descend the jumble of crates, staring straight into a security camera mounted in the corner.

"—wiser."

The red light blinked mockingly, as if to say "gotcha." Annubis hurried down to Anput, Kebauet, and Virginia Woof waiting obediently for his return.

"You're right, Virginia," he said with haste as he scooped up his family in his arms. "We must make haste, before the Scarecrows come to—"

"Caw!!"

Through the electric blur of the spherical portal, Lucky and the petrified dogs saw three giant crows, their gleaming black wings flapping with menace. At the base of their cruel black talons sat Cerberus, his three mouths panting smugly.

19 · JOiNED AT THE HYPE

"HEY, GIRLY," THE faceless, chain-smoking writer said to Milton the second he walked into Hack: Where the Bad Writers Go. "Do you want to hear a joke?"

The office roared with the incessant clacking of bulky tripewriters and the occasional carriage return and bell.

Milton looked around and noticed that all of the writers, stooped over their desks, looked as if they were wearing sheer pantyhose over their heads, their features dull and nondescript.

"Actually," Milton replied, cradling a stack of edited scripts, "I just came to drop these—"

"What blood type is deadly to proofreaders?" the writer posed.

Milton shrugged.

"Type O!" the writer blurted out. "Get it? Like a *typo* . . . a mistake!"

Milton scratched at the waist of his dress, which he had put on backward, accustomed as he was to zippers up front.

"That's not bad," he replied nervously as he set the stack of T.H.E.E.N.D. season finale scripts on the writer's desk. "So, here are Satan's edits. Mr. Welles wanted them back right away, so if you guys can just smooth out what he wrote and messenger them back—"

The writer flipped through the scripts, examining them closely.

"Wait a second," he said as he pulled out a large electric magnifying glass that cast a vivid blue-white glow upon the pages. "Just what I thought," he pronounced, setting the instrument down on his desk. "Not all of these are *his* edits. Some are, but the ones at the end . . . someone wrote over them in red ink."

Milton gulped and glanced down at his sister's ink-stained fingers. He quickly clasped the incriminating digits behind his back, not wanting to be caught red-handed.

"Hmm . . . are you sure?" he asked, staring down at his sister's painful black shoes.

The writer smirked, which simply creased his beige, creepy-smooth face.

"Yeah, girly. I'm sure. Look, we were given specific instructions to only make edits where we saw this distinctive writing . . . inscribed in blood with a quill."

That writing, Milton thought as he tried to wipe his

hands on his sides. *Those fussy loops and swirls. It looks so familiar.*

The writer got a glimpse of Milton's red-tipped fingers.

"Everybody wants to break into this business," the man said, gesturing at his fellow execrable scribes bent over their tripewriters. "And, while I appreciate a plucky bobby-soxer trying to get her foot in the door, I ain't going to let your chicken scratch through and incur the wrath of *Old* Scratch, dig?"

Milton did not *dig,* exactly, but gathered that his attempts at softening the apocalyptic endings to all of the T.H.E.E.N.D. finales had been thwarted.

"So you cool your heels, Little Red Writing Hood," the man croaked as he lifted his bones from his hard metal office chair. "I'll get the boys to make the *real* edits for you," he added with a wink—a quick wrinkle where his eye should have been—as he trundled down the row, tossing scripts to the faceless hacks.

Milton hobbled over to the Waiting and Waiting Area. He plopped down on the couch and anxiously bit his sister's fingernails, listening to the writers grumble and grouse at their latest deadline.

Figures the devil would edit manuscripts in blood, Milton fumed as he flipped through a copy of *The Helly-wood Reporter* left out on the coffee table. *He's probably type O, too.*

Milton stopped at a full-page article, topped with a

photograph of Satan, leering at the camera with a mouthful of capped fangs.

DEVIL GETS DUE WITH BOFFO IDIOT-BOX OFFICE!

Satan's new T.H.E.E.N.D.-eavor racks up major aud up on Surface! This slate of niche chucklers and dramedies with unrepentantly religious themes are a resounding click with the demo. Critics wonder why all these hot shows are up against each other—their own worst competish—but with Orson Welles lensing, and Satan himself at the helm, who are we to judge this socko sked? The hit of hits of this—and only, if sources prove correct— season is *Teenage Jesus,* starring heartthrob Van Glorious, with *Allah in the Family* a close second, both of them chugging toward fiery finales.

Satan has been strangely silent about T.H.E.E.N.D., only commenting on the hullabaloo brewing upstairs with this cryptic announcement: "I am honored to be at the center of this religious ratings war, and I can assure all of my fans that, yes, T.H.E.E.N.D. is closer than you think!"

Milton reread the phrase again and again.

T.H.E.E.N.D. is closer than you think. . . .

What is Satan's deal? Milton wondered. *What's in it for him?*

Milton crumpled inside, like an empty soda can crushed by sucky circumstance. The whole point of switching bodies with his sister had been to protect her, especially considering the weird brainwashed state she had been in as the devil's Girl Friday the Thirteenth. He had also hoped to use Marlo's status as an Infern to get to the bottom of whatever the devil was cooking up.

But Milton was realizing, as he held *The Hellywood Reporter* in his sister's trembling hands, that he was entrenched in a system devised by adults who had centuries of experience working their own system. Milton was just a kid learning the ropes of eternity, and the only thing Milton knew for sure was that he was in over his head, and his head was halfway across the underworld in Fibble. He needed his sister, as much as that pained him to admit. They were like some pop group that squabbled all the time, broke up, and then put out solo albums that no one liked. They were, somehow, better together. And if Milton was to unplug whatever Satan had getting "boffo idiot-box office" on the Surface, he'd need his sister's help.

He threw *The Hellywood Reporter* on the table. Next to it was the latest copy of *GYP.* The grainy photograph on the cover caught his eye: a grim wall of cages each housing a miserable, dispirited animal. A dog, a cat, a ferret . . .

A FERRET.

"Lucky!" Milton yelped as he seized the newspaper and guzzled the cover story with his eyes.

MILITANT ANIMAL RIGHTS GROUP WAGES WAR ON FURAFTER:
Founder Vows That Fur Will Fly if Passed-on Pets Are Put Down
By Milton Fauster

The vigilantes of REPEAT (Recently Expired People for Ethical Animal Treatment) had their fur rubbed the wrong way at reports that animals were to be energetically "nullified" in the Kennels, the pitiless pet prison of the Furafter where the bad animals go down, boy, down. And these courageous cat and canine crusaders weren't going to just roll over and play dead.

"I and a crack team of armed animal activists are mounting a massive assault against the Kennels and all it stands for," said REPEAT founder Brigid Brophy, as she and her team of ex-supermodels prepared leaflets, signs, and badges—their so-called weapons of mass instruction. "We will cross the line—between the Hereafter and the Furafter, between wrong and right, between protest and combat—because the Powers That Be have crossed the line!"

No word on how REPEAT's offensive will be greeted, but it can only be assumed that this band of angry Amazons will be the center of a raging media storm as all eyes fix on the untamed, anything-goes jungle that is the Furafter.

"We're going to raise an unholy stink as only we voluptuous, unpredictable animal-liberators can!" Brophy said, sneering, as she slipped into her sleek catsuit and flak jacket. "And woe be to those who stand in our way, 'cuz these kitties scratch!"

Milton smiled. It was weird to read a message from yourself *to* yourself, but that's exactly what this was, he was sure: a message from Marlo, telling him that Lucky was in the Kennels and to meet him there. She had made this protest seem like a huge, must-see media event to make sure he found out, and also—Milton speculated—to create chaos, a diversion to help them to sneak in, meet up with Annubis, rescue Lucky, and slip away . . . *somewhere.*

But I have two big problems, Milton reflected. *One, how to get to the Furafter without arousing suspicions, and two, how to stop whatever Satan or the Man Who Soldeth the World has brewing. . . .*

Milton giggled out loud, despite himself, as he—instantly—solved both problems with one risky, long shot of a solution.

He bolted from the Waiting and Waiting Area toward a writer lingering by the sulfur water cooler.

"Excuse me," Milton said, "but—"

"Hey, girly," the faceless hack said with a smile that split his face in two, "would you like to hear a joke?"

"I don't have time," Milton continued. "I really need to use the phone."

The hack shrugged his shoulders.

"Your loss . . . it was a doozy, too."

"The phone?"

"Over there," the hack replied, pointing to an unoccupied desk by the front door.

"Thanks," Milton said as he dashed over to the desk. He snatched up the phone, then, after puzzling over the big dial and the lack of buttons, recalled from an old movie that you stuck your finger in the holes and spun the dial around to make a call.

"Hello, Mr. Welles?" Milton spoke into the cumbersome, salmon-colored handset. "This is Mil—*Marlo*. Listen, I just came up with a great idea for some, um . . . *boffo* publicity for *Teenage Jesus* . . . to hype the heck out of the finale: LIVE! All I need is Van Glorious, a limo, and a camera with a powerful satellite feed!"

"Hey, cyclops," Principal Bubb called out to a boy with an eye patch in Limbo's Cafeterium.

The freckle-faced boy scowled at the principal as he held out his tray of liver and overcooked Brussels sprouts.

"That was insensitive," the boy replied stiffly.

The principal snorted.

"Insensitive?! Here that was the equivalent of a high five and a bear hug!"

She stepped closer to the boy.

"Let me guess . . . BB gun?"

The boy nodded sadly.

"Ouch . . . lucky it wasn't a double-barreled air rifle," the principal said as she wrapped her pudgy arm around the boy, whose face was now—unfortunately for him— at armpit level. "Since I'm not without compassion, I'll let you in on a little secret. See that delicious, triple-cream-filled maple bar with the candied bacon bits on top in the Automat over there?"

The boy nodded as he, with his good eye, examined the delectable treat tucked away in a compartment behind a little glass door. It was surrounded by compartments containing other mouthwatering treats, several of which also held the hands of screaming boys and girls whose purple meat-hooks were ensnared in the booby-trapped doors.

"Well, I know for a *fact* that that particular compartment isn't a trap," Principal Bubb confided. "So go on. Enjoy yourself. You deserve it."

She shoved the boy toward the Automat. Gulping, he shuffled to the compartment, reached out his trembling hand, and then stopped short.

"How do I know this isn't a trick?" the boy asked.

Principal Bubb shrugged her lumpy shoulders.

"Why would I waste my precious time tricking little milksops when there's a big, bad underworld to govern?"

The boy slid open the compartment and stuck his hand inside. The door promptly closed, painfully, on the boy's hand.

"Owwww!!" he screamed. "You said you weren't tricking me!!"

Principal Bubb stalked past the squirming, one-eyed boy as he writhed in pain on the Cafeterium floor.

"No, I simply posed the question 'Why would I?' " she said as she stuck her claw through the small opening the boy's hand made in the compartment door. "And the answer is 'Because I wanted a maple bar.' "

The principal snatched the pastry and clacked away. She cast her imposing shadow on a table filled with terrified girls. One of them was reading the latest copy of *GYP*.

"Girls," Principal Bubb said as she wiped her forked tongue across the part of her mouth usually reserved for lips. "I believe I saw your parents waiting by the gates. This has all been some ghastly mistake."

The girls squealed with delight as they bolted out of the Cafeterium.

The principal sat down in a recently vacated chair and picked up the open newspaper, flipping to the back page. There was the principal's ad for her missing Cerberus.

Principal Bubb wiped away a curdlike tear birthed by her hardly-ever-used tear ducts. She turned to the cover.

MILITANT ANIMAL RIGHTS GROUP WAGES WAR ON FURAFTER:
Founder Vows That Fur Will Fly if Passed-on Pets Are Put Down
By Milton Fauster

The principal nearly choked on a clot of clotted cream as she saw Lucky's grainy image in the corner of the large photograph, hissing just above the headline.

"That foul, albino rat in the Furafter?!" Principal Bubb sputtered as her claws perforated the paper. "And its owner, Milton Fauster, reporting on its possible nullification?!"

The principal's goat eyes settled on the ancient black-and-white television mounted on the wall. Its image rolling vertically in a near blur, Principal Bubb was able to make out a news reporter.

"This is Barbra Seville with URN News—All Over It Like a Cheap Suit," the newswoman said as her crew loaded a van behind her with equipment. "My courageous, award-winning news crew and I are off to cover the brewing brouhaha down in the Furafter, the realm of passed-on pets. No one knows what the savage, unrepentant she-wolves of REPEAT are plotting, so we are prepared for anything and everything. . . ."

Principal Bubb cocked her unruly monobrow so that it resembled a hairy seesaw tilted to one side. She flipped the newspaper over and stared at her precious three-headed hound of Heck, Cerberus.

"Is this why you ran away, my tri-headed prince of pups?" she murmured under her foul breath. "Did you catch a whiff of that awful Fauster ferret, your sworn enemy? Did it drive you mad with vengeance, and force you to take matters into your own paws?"

The principal rose abruptly and shoved the table into a cluster of students, knocking them and their trays of green bean casserole and cod-liver oil to the floor.

"Guards!" she bellowed as she stormed out of the Cafeterium. "I'm rounding up a squad of precision goons for a rescue mission down in the Furafter. We'll go over that putrid petting zoo with a fine-tooth flea comb."

She sneered at the crumpled copy of *GYP* in her claws.

"And, if my suspicions are correct, we may be bringing back some . . . *old friends.*"

Milton met the Badillac in the alleyway behind the Hack offices. The doors of the extravagant ruby-red SUV popped open. Milton popped his head inside.

"Good, that was quick—"

Inside was Van Glorious, his hot-tempered costar, Inga Hootz—otherwise known as Auntie Christ—and a load of video equipment that nearly filled the limo's interior. Van nudged down his Italian sunglasses and gave Milton a wink.

"You can always sit on my lap," he said in his I'm-used-to-getting-everything-I-want purr.

Milton sighed and wedged his sister's body in between Van and Inga.

"So, what are we doing here?" the smug actor asked. "Mr. Welles said something about a PR junket?"

"Yeah," Milton replied, prying himself away from Van with the point of his sister's elbow. "There's a big protest down in the Furafter, with REPEAT—"

"REPEAT?" Van asked.

"I said, *'There's a big protest down in the—'*"

"I heard you," he clarified. "I just meant, is that some animal rights group?"

Milton nodded.

"This is a great opportunity to publicize the show, by presenting yourself as an ardent supporter."

Van snickered.

"You're a smart cookie, Marlo," he replied in his slick, oily way. "Like an Oreo with brains in the middle. I'll have to ditch my leather kicks, but hey, I'm up for it. I like animals . . . especially when my personal chef prepares them properly."

He slapped Milton on the back, knocking him into Inga.

"You bigheaded celebristars, mistaking arrogance for artistry!" Inga spat.

"Whose character happens to be *the name of the freakin' show*?!" Van replied.

"I cannot *wait* to lay into you for the finale, you insufferable brat!"

"Bring it on, *has-been* . . . actually, *never-was!*"

As Van Glorious and Inga Hootz came to blows across Milton, he leaned forward and tapped on the chauffeur's window. The three-armed driving demon turned and rolled down the glass.

"Where to, miss?" he asked.

"To the Furafter," Milton replied anxiously. "And hurry—this is a race against prime time!"

20 · WOOD i LiE TO YOU?

ZANE AND MARLO stepped over the convulsing chameleons as the demons' multicolored skin danced and swirled like a jumbo set of Crayola crayons frying in a skillet.

"What happened to those poor blokes?" Zane asked, still half-awake as he and Marlo tiptoed in the dead of night to the R & D lab.

"One of the side effects of Dr. Brinkley's full-spectrum kaleidoscopic color pills," Marlo replied as she grasped the copper handle to the laboratory. "If symptoms persist—or if you are super allergic to drastic swings in pigment—please consult your quack of a doctor."

Marlo cracked open the door.

"Milton," Zane asked in his smooth as British fog voice, "are you sure this Brinkley gent won't mind me tagging along?"

"Of course not," Marlo assured him as she pressed

open the door, softly, with her palms. "The more, the . . . *escapier.*"

They stepped into the dark, still room. Marlo's nose prickled at a caustic bouquet of chemical odors. Beneath was the reassuring scent of the liquid silver: a mixture of fresh laundry, baked bread, and summer rain.

"Dr. Brinkley?" Marlo called out as quietly as possible. She could hear a faint rustling amidst the clinks and gurgles of the laboratory. Suddenly, the room was filled with the stinging flicker of white-blue fluorescent lights.

"What's *he* doing with you?!" Dr. Brinkley quacked as he waddled out from behind a table loaded with brass funnels, graduated cylinders, an aluminum canister, a pair of bulky metal goggles, and what looked like a beaker full of slugs.

Marlo grabbed Zane by the forearm and pulled him inside the laboratory, then kicked the door shut.

"I invited him along. He's a good guy. He deserves better than this place."

The doctor's white feathers relaxed.

"*Fine, then.* I was able to distill more liquid silver than I had previously anticipated, resulting in a third truth bomb, so we could use another set of hands. *Human* hands."

The doctor ducked down behind the table.

"Truth bomb?" Zane asked nervously. "I don't know about this, Milton. . . ."

Dr. Brinkley emerged with three devices, each like a large roll of foil (if those particular rolls of foil were designed to detonate upon impact with a blast radius of approximately thirty-seven feet, that is).

He set the bombs—steel canisters with copper tubeways, gauges, and red sprinkler handles welded to them—on the table.

"Rapid-fire liquid truth dispersion devices," the doctor drawled cockily, "employing the naturally antagonistic properties of little white lice and liquid silver. When the two are forcibly introduced, an explosion occurs, discharging truth shrapnel in all directions."

"So it's a bomb, right?" clarified Marlo. "It'll help us get out?"

"Yes, young man," Dr. Brinkley said through a gritted orange bill, *"a bomb."*

"Awesome!" Marlo said as she tromped over and grabbed one of the crude-looking devices and tossed it back and forth between her hands.

"Careful!" the doctor sputtered as he took back the bomb and hid it away in his satchel. "I'm still not sure if they will be powerful enough to destroy Fibble's support crutches. And, in the case that they actually *are,* we may be—ourselves—destroyed as we plummet to the ice below."

"Not to worry, doc," Marlo said as she strutted confidently toward the door in her hair pajamas. "I've got it all figured out. We're as 'out' as culottes and wedgie sandals!"

Dr. Brinkley and Zane stared, mute and confounded, at Marlo.

"It's something my, um, way-cool sister told me. Anyway, c'mon! Time's a wastin' and freedom we should be tastin'!"

Marlo stepped out of the door with Zane, nervously, close behind.

"Wait one moment," the doctor said as he swiped the metal goggles Marlo had noticed on the counter and handed them to her.

"What are these?" she asked as she examined the goggles. They reminded her of those old ViewMaster thingies her dad had in his garage, only bronzed, and with two spring-hinged temples to fit over the ears.

The doctor's beak twisted into a smirk.

"Electric Smell-O-Vision goggles," he explained with pride. "To help us find our way to the Furafter."

Dr. Brinkley grabbed an aluminum canister and tucked it in his shoulder bag along with the truth bombs.

"And a can of highly concentrated liedocaine, just in case."

The doctor slung the satchel over his shoulder, then reached for the beaker of slugs.

"What is that, another weapon?" Zane asked with a quizzical squint.

Dr. Brinkley tilted his head back and emptied the beaker of slugs into his gaping bill, after which he replied, rubbing his belly, "Yes, a weapon against hunger. Let us migrate to the Big Top!"

The luxury Badillac sped through the Distressway Tunnel, zooming in the fast lane on the roof of the asphalt passage. Milton swallowed as he looked out the window at the traffic jam below.

"May the centrifugal force be with us," he muttered as he pulled out the videocassette from his purse and slid it into the limo's VCR.

THE MAN WHO SOLDETH THE WORLD

PART THREE: THE EVICTION

The grainy, amateurish video showed a lean, sinewy demon kneeling on a sand dune. It scrutinized the sky with its three protruding, almond eyes, fixing on something light-years away.

"Got it," the creature said—sounding as if he had a raw yolk trapped in his voice box—while tightening the obi of his lava-red kimono. "The Sirius Lelayme system. Perfectly dreadful gated solar community at the other side of the Milky Way, circling a bright beige sun. The third planet is a generic, prefab model—Earth-sized—yet without any of the frills. Flat all over like a bad opera singer standing in a tub of old soda."

The creature's black snake lips coiled into a sad smirk. "Knowing the humans, though," he continued in his wet, gurgling voice, "most of them won't even notice the difference."

Van leaned into Milton and frowned at the screen.

"Terrible production values, wooden acting . . . no wonder it's dead last in the ratings," Van sneered. "Not that anything really has a chance against *Teenage Jesus!*"

Milton rolled his sister's eyes as the camera turned away from the demon on the screen and showed the cover of the *New York Times* splayed out on the sand:

DIE-HARD FANS CLASH AS T.H.E.E.N.D. FINALES DRAW NEAR

By Dexter Filkins

Sporadic incidents of civil unrest continue to plague much of the U.S., Europe, and the Middle East as unruly mobs take to the streets after watching their favorite T.H.E.E.N.D. shows. Whipped into a mass religi-tainment frenzy, zealous fans roam cities seeking to trounce fans of rival shows,

proving that their show—the one true show—
deserves to be renewed, if not in this life, then in
the next. . . .

The wind blew the paper away, revealing an open
copy of *Entertainment Weakly* underneath:

PURE FANDEMONIUM AT PURPORTED SIGHTING OF TABOO TWOSOME

By Jeff Jensen

Hunky son-of-god Teenage Jesus, played by
presumed-dead-yet-hotter-than-ever heartthrob Van
Glorious, was reportedly spotted—according to
unconfirmed innuendo—leaving a tony Beverly
Hills nightspot with perky Muslim muffin Nafeesa
Shabazz of rival hit *Allah in the Family*. News of this
rumor resulted in violent fan-fueled fracases across
the globe as T.H.E.E.N.D. zealots stop at nothing
to prove that their favorite show is 'the one.' . . ."

Van shook his blond head and snickered.

"Do I have a great publicist or what?" he chuckled.
"She has me clubbing *up on the Surface. Classic.*"

Milton shushed Van and wedged his sister's body between the pseudo Son of Man and the limo's TV screen.

This all has to mean something, Milton thought as the

camera trained back upon the robed creature, rubbing a nail file swiftly against his slender fingertips. *It's just too weird to not be real.*

"You hired Goemon, the legendary samurai-thief, for my uncannily sensitive touch," the demon replied, gazing at the camera. "Though you never told me who *you* are . . . or why you keep your identity concealed so . . ."

"Thou art correct," the man behind the camera replied. *"I did not."*

Goemon splayed wide his long, elegant fingers, and carefully touched the air around him.

"It is no matter," the lithe creature murmured as he rose, feeling his way around the desert air with his finger pads, like a blind man hoping to catch a gnat. "Your money is good, even if your intentions are not. Though, I am curious . . . why are you sending the humans so far? And do you really think you can pull this off without the Galactic Order Department getting wise?"

The man behind the camera sighed a weary, ancient breath.

"Ever since the Non-Interventionist Act of AD 33, the Powers That Be hath not overtly interfered with the day-to-day affairs of the humans, something I could never understandeth myself," the man explained bitterly. "Why go through all the bother of creating imperfect creatures only to leave them to their own destructive devices? If the Big Guy Upstairs was so 'rah rah uppeth with humans,' why not provide their maddening species with basic survival skills, such as—oh, I don't know—*the ability to not drive themselves to extinction*?! They are but children, only their toys have outgrown *them*."

Goemon delicately thrummed his fingers on a specific patch of air.

"Konnichiwa . . . the interdimensional seam," he murmured as he carefully squatted down, his outstretched finger never leaving the spot, while scooping up a cloth satchel with his other hand.

"So I am hurrying the inevitable while doing the humans a favor by merely relocating them," the man behind the camera continued while Goemon removed a tiny crystal pick and hammer from the satchel. "The Powers That Be should have seeneth the writing upon the wall—or the writing in sacred books left in hotels—for ages now. It is as if humanity wrote a suicide note thousands of years ago and the Big Guy Upstairs has ignored the classic warning signs: emotional detachment, irrationality, not respecting your home, etc."

Inga yawned loudly into Milton's ear.

"As much as I hate to agree with my costar—"

"Star," Van interrupted. "Just . . . *star*."

"This show is terrible," Inga continued.

She reached to turn the VCR off. Milton batted her hand away.

"I, um, Mr. Welles needed me to preview the show," Milton replied as Inga glared at him. "Besides, it's almost over."

Inga crossed her arms and fumed silently to herself.

On the screen, the samurai-demon drew back his small crystal hammer. "Now it's just a matter of creating the split," he muttered, "and allowing the sacred geometry laced beneath Creation to unfold."

The elegant creature tapped the pick. A rainbow-hued spark materialized out of nowhere.

"So I am sending the humans far beyond His influence, beyond his loving, coddling embrace," the man behind the camera concluded, "so they experience something far worse than death: *life in exile.* And after they hath suffered sufficiently, I will emergeth as their Lord, and get all Old Testament upon them, just like in the Good Old Days: inaugurating the first—unauthorized— heavenly franchise!"

Gossamer cracks of energy sprouted from the tapping point, spreading out across the sky until they formed a shimmering latticework. Goemon put his tools back in his satchel.

"It is done," he stated matter-of-factly. "The humans need to congregate at the specific entry points located at various religious hot spots all over the world. At the exact point of eviction, another tap right *here*," he said, pointing to the dull sparkle throbbing weakly in the air, "should open up the gates to the Sirius Lelayme system. All you need to do is motivate them to pass through at *just* the right time. . . ."

The camera rose as the man behind the camera got to his feet.

" 'Tis simply a magic trick," the man stated in his faultless, resonant voice as he dusted sand off his immaculate white robes. "And, liketh a magic trick, the spectator so wanteth to be fooled that it's just a matter of giving them something that seems *inevitable* and turning that inevitable something into something *spectacular*. But the spectacle that the humans will be watching—in slack-jawed monkey amazement—will be . . . *themselves. Their own demise.*"

The screen went dark.

Van and Inga snored on either side of Milton, like bookends with sleep apnea. He gazed out the window at the Distressway Tunnel whizzing past, feeling completely alone.

If I were Marlo, really *Marlo,* Milton thought as he chewed on his sister's thumbnail, *I'd know what to do, even if it was incredibly reckless and stupid.*

He sighed as a dispiriting, motionless parade of stalled cars and brake lights streaked by beneath the speeding Badillac.

I only hope she really did mean for me to meet her in the Furafter. Whatever's going on is too big for one Fauster to handle alone.

"*Fascinating,*" the duck doctor whispered as he, Marlo, and Zane gathered around one of the wooden support beams bolstering the spacious Big Top, now darkened in the simulated night. "And you're sure you weren't just imagining the effect?"

Marlo shook her head.

"My imagination isn't nearly that vivid," she replied in a hush amidst the gentle wheeze of slumbering shrimp demons and sideshow freaks. "When the Truthador sang, the beam totally contracted. And when Vice Principal Barnum started blathering on about how he valued our opinions, the beam started to stretch out. Then I saw the Geppetto Lumber Company mark and thought—"

"The wooden bones of Pinocchio people," Dr. Brinkley whispered with awe as he touched his webbed finger to the miserable facelike knothole.

"What's up, Doc?" Marlo asked.

"Carlo Collodi, the author of *Pinocchio,* was said to have been inspired by Bavarian folktales of creatures made from enchanted wood that—when exposed to truths and lies—would contract or expand, depending. Like Pinocchio's famous nose—"

A sharp snort from Tom Thumb stopped Dr. Brinkley's story in its tracks.

"We'd better scarper," Zane whispered. They crept down the grandstand aisle as softly as a roving herd of cotton balls pushed along by whispers. Marlo caught a glimpse of the unvarnished Box of Bitter Truth, forgotten beneath the bleachers during the Truthador's last unwelcome broadcast. The sight of it made her dry-heave and shiver, but it also shook loose an idea.

"Help me with this," she whispered to Zane.

"What are you doing?" Dr. Brinkley said as he entered the sawdusted ring.

"A way to amplify your truth bombs," Marlo grunted as she and Zane heaved the box to the edge of the paper-covered bull's-eye floor, "while simultaneously busting up this horrible box."

Dr. Brinkley rubbed sawdust off his spectacles and looked at the box.

"Undiluted honesty . . . bitter, volatile, and nearly impossible to swallow . . ."

Marlo and Zane crawled on their bellies to the center of the ring. Marlo peered through the punctured holes she'd made during her last midnight raid and saw the two ever-vigilant demon guards, seated hundreds of feet below at the center of the Falla Sea, dimly illuminated by the eerie silver glow radiating from beneath the ice.

Zane wriggled next to Marlo and peeked through the perforations.

"Blimey," he gasped. "That's a whopping great drop! And we couldn't just climb down with ropes? We have to take the whole galumphing circus down to get out?"

Dr. Brinkley fiddled with the handle of a truth bomb, scrutinized the gauge, and placed it delicately inside the crate.

"To begin with, I couldn't find a rope anywhere near that length," he explained. "Next, those guards would catch sight of us well before we made it to freedom, unless we *plummeted* down and escaped by splattering ourselves across the ice. Plus, I had hoped that if we sent Fibble smashing to the ground, Barnum's Humbugger machine—wherever he has it hidden—might at least be damaged, thwarting his plan."

Marlo drew a deep, nerve-settling breath and worked her finger into the smallest of the target's concentric circles. She poked a hole every inch until the entire circle was perforated. Marlo rose carefully and, motioning to Zane, grabbed one side of the box. Zane nodded and grabbed the other.

"One . . . two . . . *three*," Marlo muttered as they threw the box onto the perforated circle. The Box of Bitter Truth tore cleanly through the paper. A gust of cold wind blasted from the hole.

The shrimp demons atop the bleachers on the far side of the Big Top stirred. Scampi scratched his rainbow wig and blinked his black eyes awake.

Marlo looked out over the hole, the wind whistling

up her nose. The box tumbled toward the brightly colored rings painted on the ice below. Time itself seemed to telescope—stretching long and smooth like taffy—as the Box of Bitter Truth bombs drifted down as slow as a feather.

Finally, the box smashed against the ice. A small silver "poof" spread out over the target, followed shortly by an audible pop. The demon guards scurried briefly before freezing in their tracks. Marlo turned to the doctor.

"It didn't work!" she yell-whispered. "Now what—"

Fibble lurched violently to one side. Zane skidded across the paper bull's-eye and through the torn hole.

"No!" Marlo screamed as she seized his calf, failing, in that heroic instant, to take into account that Zane was much larger than Milton. Marlo was pulled into the shredded hole, yet, before she could tumble into the abyss, kicked two toeholds in the thick paper and slowed her plunge. The paper began to tear.

"Hold . . . on," Marlo called to Zane through gritted teeth as the wind roared in her face.

"*To what?!*" Zane yelled as he hung upside down.

Upside-down tears spilled out of Marlo's borrowed eyes, rolling over Milton's forehead into his windswept mop of hair. Marlo saw that the truth bomb had damaged only one of the six support beams, which had made Fibble list to one side. Her feet tore closer to the lip of the hole.

I can't let go, Marlo thought as her ears buzzed with

her own pulse. *I got Zane into this. I'll fall down with him, our guts splattered all over the ice, but I can't let go.*

Then—just as Marlo was about to pass out from the throb of blood filling her head—Fibble convulsed, its weird wooden beams trembling, buckling, and then contracting. The frozen Falla Sea whizzed toward Marlo's head, faster and faster, as the support beams of Pinocchio wood sent Fibble free-falling to the ice like a three-ring elevator with a severed cable.

21 · BAD BREAKS
AND BREAKOUTS

THE FIVE COLOSSAL Scarecrows interlaced their sturdy ebony wings in an impenetrable wall of feathers. Their gleaming black heads bobbed as they scrutinized their captives with darting, sideways glances. Annubis, his family, and Virginia Woof backed away slowly from the blocked passage, trapped inside the Kennels.

Cerberus lunged at Lucky, who—though bristling with fury—was too weakened to rip into the three-headed hound with all the ferretish ferocity he would have liked. He managed a wet hiss, like a punctured bicycle tire filled with anger, as Cerberus stepped back through the prickling, energetic portal. One of his heads licked its chops, another snarled, and the other sniffed the air with ravenous abandon, as if the Furafter were an "all-you-can-smell" buffet.

Annubis took a whiff of the pet-pourri of scents: the stench of the Kennels, like a sharp and acidic slap, and the intoxicating aroma of the Really Big Farm, a sweet mixture of hay, alfalfa, and pine. Underneath it all the pervasive reek of crow droppings, a thick pungent paste that coated the inside of the courtyard, fortifying it like cement. Cerberus growled at Kebauet, angered by her unique blend of human and canine odors. The pointy-eared girl wrapped her arms tight around her father's leg.

"If you so much as bare your nasty teeth at my daughter," Annubis snarled, "I'll roll up the biggest newspaper I can find and smack you so hard that you'll win an Oscar for playing dead! Do you hear me, you loathsome cur?!"

Annubis could see, through the convex blur of the portal, two monstrous Scarecrows in the courtyard flapping, strutting, and pecking at the other dogs, herding them into the center of the courtyard.

"Is there another way out?" Annubis asked Virginia Woof.

The white-and-tan terrier tapped out her reply.

"Not that I know."

Cats spilled into the courtyard outside, brushing themselves against the fence, laying claim to it in their casual, dismissive feline way. The two Scarecrows perched atop the parapets anxiously paced sideways, back and forth, as they eyed the herd of cats with unease.

"Let's see if there's a back door," Annubis said as he put his arms around his shaken family. "Maybe we can find Mr. Noah and put a stop to this."

The dogs turned and trotted through the labyrinth of whimpering crates. Claws scratching concrete and tongues lolling out of mouths, the four canines scurried along the winding path, its bleak scenery of rusted, reeking cages never seeming to change, only recycle.

The dogs rounded a bend at the center of the maze, arriving at a clearing. They skidded to a stop with horror.

Three hulking, monstrous demons trudged about a spacious vat. Each of the heavily muscled creatures was nearly eight feet tall. But the most disturbing aspect of these dark red beasts was that they were headless, and sported gaping holes in their chests. They turned— swiftly, considering their bulk—and regarded the intruding dogs without need of eyes.

Tied up with twine alongside the wooden vat was an old man with a pillowy white beard, wearing sandals and a light brown robe. A look of fierce determination crinkled his otherwise kindly face.

Virginia Woof yapped and leapt in the air. Annubis gave the gagged and bound man a sniff.

Ancient . . . redolent of the sea and every flavor of beast . . .

"Noah?" Annubis muttered. "*The* Noah?"

The old man struggled futilely against his bonds.

Behind the vat Annubis noted another old man, un-tethered, dressed flamboyantly in a white ascot, navy blue cloak, and dazzling chunky pewter necklace. He stood before a shimmering, blobbish hologram that he delicately sculpted with two laser pens. The man turned and arched his bushy eyebrows at Annubis, assessing him with his gleaming eyes.

"Vell, vhat have we here?" the man asked as the demons swarmed around the dogs. The man set his laser pens down on a small table by the levitating hologram. "Vhy, are you a . . . half-man, half-dog?"

"I'm technically half jackal," Annubis replied.

The man's pupils dilated until his eyes were black with dark, self-consumed merriment.

"So prayers can be answered, even down here," he laughed in his halting yet refined accent. "Jes, you'll do nicely. And, eef at first I don't succeed—"

His beady, glittering eyes settled on Anput and Ke-bauet.

"—I can jest try and try again!"

Zane and Marlo screamed, yet the gush of wind stop-pered up their gaping mouths. Dr. Brinkley inched to-ward the rim and peered downward.

"It's working!" he gasped, amazed. "You were right, Mr. Fauster! The truth is bringing Fibble down!"

Vice Principal Barnum staggered into the quaking Big Top.

"What in blazes is going on?!" he roared, his flaming pants leaving a sooty contrail of smoke in his wake.

Dr. Brinkley hurriedly reached for the canister of liedocane tucked into his satchel.

"Time to put on the brakes," he said as he tossed the canister to the ice below, now only twenty feet away. "The sudden influx of highly concentrated lies should stop the wood from contracting."

The demon guards ran past the Gates of Fibble in fear as the can of liedocane exploded, spraying its distorting rainbow fog in all directions. The support beams screamed as the collapsing Pinocchio wood froze.

"Let go of me, Milton!" Zane yelled as the ice rushed to meet his head. Marlo, her brother's hands cramping, couldn't help but comply. Zane fell onto the ice, landing on his shoulder and rolling out of the target zone through the abandoned gates.

"No!" screamed Marlo as the mass media circus screeched to a halt just two feet from the ice floor.

"I'm fine," Zane called out. "The demon guards . . . not so much."

"Run!" quacked Dr. Brinkley as he jumped through the hole, lugging the remaining truth bombs.

"Run?" Marlo replied as she hopped onto the ice. "There isn't enough room."

"*Then crawl!* Here, take one of the bombs in case we're separated!"

Marlo grabbed the truth bomb, tucked it beneath her arm, and crawled on her knees toward Zane, sandwiched between Fibble and the Falla Sea.

Dr. Brinkley saw to his right, twenty yards beyond the rim of Fibble, eight hooves tromping nervously in place.

"Shuck and Jive!" he clucked with excitement as he wriggled toward his Night Mares.

Marlo's knees and palms burned with scrapes yet at the same time were frozen numb by the cold. She grunted yard by yard alongside Zane and Dr. Brinkley. Every labored breath felt like she was inhaling crushed ice. Above her head was the foundation of Fibble, a lattice of wooden joists and brass plumbing.

As Marlo wiggled onward, her body—*Milton's* body—was freaking out. She could feel his chest tighten, his throat constrict, and his whole body break into a sweat.

Vice Principal Barnum vaulted down upon the ice and crouched low. Marlo could hear Barnum's sizzling pants hiss and crackle beneath Fibble as if through an echo chamber.

"Tom Thumb! Louie! Kung Pao!" he bellowed. "Get your small, freakish selves here this instant and capture the runaways! Annette! Have the teachers contain the other students! Scampi! Man the Humbugger and be the biggest, baddest clown you can!"

Marlo heard a clatter of tiny feet. And those tiny feet were getting closer, unencumbered by the need to crawl, crouch, and/or wriggle.

Pushing herself harder than she ever had before, Marlo reached the edge of Fibble's foundation, just behind Zane. The skittish black Night Mares stomped and snorted, backing away in fear. Marlo straightened her aching back, then helped Dr. Brinkley to his feet. A mixture of stale smoke and salty brine filled her nostrils. Still panting, Marlo stooped down and saw a scowling midget smoking a cigar charge toward her, with four scurrying shrimp demons—tiny horns piercing their filthy rainbow wigs—at his itty-bitty heels.

Marlo cradled her truth bomb in her hand.

"Don't come any closer or I'll blow you up!" she yelled.

Tom Thumb and the shrimp demons skidded to a stop. The midget squinted and considered Marlo with his dark, jaded eyes. He took his cigar out of his mouth.

"You're bluffing," the little man replied with a cruel, underworld-weary chuckle.

"Oh yeah?" Marlo retorted, realizing instantly that this was not one of her better retorts. "What makes you think so?"

Tom Thumb laughed as he let his cigar fall on the ground.

"Because you're blushing," he said as he stomped his cigar out with his pint-sized foot.

Marlo felt her burning cheeks.

Darn Milton's goody-good body, she cursed to herself as she twisted the truth bomb's handle and hurled it underneath Fibble. The bomb clattered and rolled to the midget's feet. The shrimp demons soiled each other with fear in anticipation of an explosion that, with each passing second, seemed increasingly unlikely.

"Run!" Dr. Brinkley yelled as he speed-waddled toward his carriage.

An idea popped into Marlo's head. She leaned beneath Fibble and screamed at the top of her brother's burning lungs.

"I am lying!"

The Pinocchio-wood support beams trembled, and after several confused seconds, Fibble itself rose and fell in fierce, unpredictable spasms as the wood reacted to either the truth that was therefore a lie, or a lie that was therefore the truth.

The shrimps screamed like a pot of boiled lobsters and ran back toward the target beneath the Big Top.

Marlo and Zane trotted carefully across the slippery ice as Fibble bounced up and down—never quite fully rising, never quite completely falling—behind them. As they neared the carriage, a large shadow engulfed them, spreading out like an oil spill. Marlo looked up at the sky and immediately wished she hadn't.

Looming above, composed of glittering, electrically charged tufts of smoke, was the massive, sneering clown head.

The Night Mares whinnied with terror, their eyes bulging out of their sockets, and bolted for the horizon.

"Shuck! Jive!" yelled Dr. Brinkley as he watched his carriage disappear across the Falla Sea. A roar filled the air, so deep that it rattled every bone in Marlo's borrowed body.

"You will never leave!" the jumbo-sized clown face boomed. The head pressed close over them until it became the sky. The glittering smoke buzzed like a swarm of bees dipped in melted mirror. The sickly sweet smell of it prickled Marlo's nose. With each breath, the gargantuan, malevolent clown head became more real.

"It's . . . not . . . real," Marlo said to herself, curling her fists as panic squeezed her in its cold, sickening grip.

"It's the liedocane," Dr. Brinkley cautioned. "Pure, high-grade stuff . . . so strong that, in the end, it won't matter if it's real or not. It will be *to you*. We have to get out of here."

"But how?" Marlo asked as she scanned the bleak, frozen horizon.

The clown head laughed and swooped down upon them. Its wind knocked Marlo over and sent the doctor quacking, end-over-end. Marlo's arms were bleeding from the millions of mirror shards that cut like tiny, shining razors. Zane noticed the broken support beam a dozen yards away.

"I've got an idea," he said as he dashed toward the quivering timber. He scanned the ground and found a sharp chip of cleaved ice. Zane lifted the heavy chunk and—raising it above a section of wood—began hacking away. The Pinocchio plank screamed with each blow. Zane soon had cut the forty feet or so of wood into six pieces of equal length.

Marlo walked over to Zane, scooping up Dr. Brinkley's abandoned satchel and slinging it over her shoulder. She stared at the trembling planks.

"So . . . you're taking out your frustration on defenseless Pinocchio wood?" she asked as the leering clown head chuckled wickedly from above. Zane carved notches into the faintly whimpering planks.

"I'm makin' us a way out of this bloomin' freak show," he said, his intense gaze fixed on the wood. Finished, he set his ice chisel down. Taking two severed beams, Zane positioned them like crutches on either side of himself, then—balancing them perfectly— shimmied his way to the freshly cleaved notches toward the top.

"Britain has the best food in the world," Zane said firmly to the wood. His makeshift stilts grew to nearly three times their original size. Marlo clapped her hands and laughed.

"Brilliant!" she exclaimed.

She grabbed a pair of stilts and climbed—shakily—up to the foot notches.

"School counselors truly love their jobs," Marlo whispered to the wood. Each stilt instantly grew twenty feet tall. She wobbled alongside Zane and turned, jabbing the ground step by step until she faced the doctor.

"Quick, Dr. Brinkley!" she shouted as the clown head darkened, collecting itself like a storm cloud ready to spew lightning and vengeance. Zane and Marlo staggered away from Fibble as Dr. Brinkley grabbed two stilts and fluttered to the foot wedges.

"An apple a day keeps the doctor—" Dr. Brinkley muttered just as the clown head pounced upon him, drawing in a deep slurping hurricane of a breath.

"Dr. Brinkley!" Marlo screamed as the doctor was sucked toward the clown's swirling, cavernous mouth. "It's not real! It's just one of Barnum's tricks!"

The colossal clown's face contorted into a nightmare of a smile, its eyes a familiar dull black.

Like a shrimp's, Marlo thought. *Like Scampi's . . .*

The sucking vacuum stung Marlo's eyes as it whipped past her. To her nose, the air smelled of lightning, black pepper, and Lucky Charms.

The Humbugger amplifies and lies, so a little clown shrimp would seem huge and scary.

Marlo leaned forward to keep from falling into the slurping, chuckling wind.

"We've got to scarper, Milton!" Zane yelled. He wobbled forward, unsure at first, but with each step gained speed and confidence.

Marlo tottered and swayed until she achieved a steady clip. She glanced behind her as the clown head consumed the screaming duck doctor. Dr. Brinkley swirled inside the tornado of smoke and mirrors until he was nothing but a white, squawking blur.

Terrified, Marlo sped across the tundra in great strides. She took one last peek over her shoulder.

The clown head roared and reared, yet the sparkling smoke grew so thin that you could see the bobbing circus tents of Fibble right through it. Marlo noticed a bright, white beam of light streaming from the tip of Fibble's R & D tent, leading back to the twinkling haze of the clown-shaped vapor like an umbilical cord of pure energy. "Milton," Zane called out, huffing, sweat streaming down his face. "Where to?"

Marlo swept the horizon with her eyes. Grim sheets of vertical fog hung down from the sky, like rippling gray curtains separating miles of nothing from miles of nothing.

"I have no i—" Marlo said before stopping herself. She reached for the Smell-O-Vision goggles tucked into her hair pajama bottoms, carefully steadying herself as she teetered twenty feet above the ground. Marlo clipped the spring-hinged temples over her ears and flicked the switch on the goggles' nose bridge. She scoured the horizon through the electric Smell-O-Vision glasses and laughed.

"Scratch that," Marlo said with a smirk. "I know *exactly* where to go!"

The stocky, marbled-meat demon cinched Annubis's paws tight behind his back with twine. Another guarded Anput, Kebauet, and Virginia Woof while the last of the monstrous creatures hovered about dumbly, which made sense considering it didn't have a head. All three demons sported sturdy tree-trunk legs, sledgehammer arms, and a sort of all-beef-doughnut torso with a gaping hole where their hearts should have been.

Annubis was shoved toward the vat. Nine hemlock steps led to its rim. The vat's surface swirled with whorls of sparks, like eddies of fireflies caught forever in a draft.

"What is this about?!" Annubis barked to the dapper, demented man in the ascot.

"Jest a leedle flea dip," the man replied as he fiddled with his shimmering holographic model. "In zhe Nullification Tub."

Annubis peered across the vat at Noah, who was gagged, red in the face, and struggling against the bonds tied around his wrists and ankles.

"But . . . why? *Who are you?*"

The man tilted the brim of his black felt fedora to shield his eyes from the harsh fluorescent lights above.

He moved a sparkling, holographic clot in the air with the tip of his laser pen.

"Zhey say that art imitates life," he replied as he fixed the glistening clot of light at the center of his levitating, three-dimensional blob. "Me, zhough—Elmyr de Hory—have spent my life *imitating art,* committing forgeries so perfect that zhey are indistinguishable from original. Some of my forgeries sell *as much* as original, jess because zhey are mine! That is because I don't just match an artist's work stroke-for-the-stroke. I infuse each piece with *soul,* the spirit that guides zhe brush. . . ."

That's it, Annubis thought as he examined the twin holographic blobs that looked like a floating figure eight made of blown glass, rainbow sprinkles, and splotches of molasses. *A model of the human soul!*

"So who better than to forge the very essence of art—the human soul?" Mr. de Hory continued, confirming the dog god's suspicions.

Resting his chin on his delicate hand, Mr. de Hory judged his creation.

"But I am victim of my materials," he sighed. "To counterfeit the billions of fakes I agreed to make, I must use melted-down souls of animals—dogs, mostly—as my canvas."

"Agreed to make?" Annubis interrupted as he shook off the beefy purplish hands of the headless/heartless demon. "For whom?"

Mr. de Hory's thin lips creased into a cryptic smile.

"A patron of the arts," he replied with a shrug. "I know not who . . . I *care* not who!"

Virginia Woof—pinned between a demon's legs—managed to type out a comment on her Speak & Spell.

"Why dog?" the mechanized voice, muffled by the demon's massive calves, inquired.

Mr. de Hory clapped his hands with delight.

"Zhat is it, exactly! Dogs are so similar to zhe humans . . . so adaptable—"

A Siamese cat, a mangy black-and-tan spotted Manx, and a patchwork calico slunk around the corner, followed by dozens of other cats twitching their tails.

"No, offense, felines. You and zhe three-headed one have helped me immensely."

Cerberus trotted around the corner and hiked his leg in the air, relieving himself from his post to relieve himself on a post. The cats circled and pranced around Cerberus in a sickening display of flattery.

"But zhey—even dogs—lack zhe complexities and contrasts I need to make a convincing forgery. I need something . . . in-the-between. A missing soul link that will connect my human reproduction with zhe coarser canine materials available. I need to cast something that is both animal *and* human."

Mr. de Hory lowered his thick, black-rimmed glasses.

"Vhat I need, actually, is *you,* Mr. Jackal. Or the females."

"You wouldn't dare—" Annubis growled.

The foppish con artist waved the demon holding Annubis forward.

"The great artist is zhe who turns pain to advantage, lets suffering deepen his understanding, and grows through zhe pain."

The headless/heartless demon shoved Annubis up the steps of the Nullification Tub.

"But I am artist that makes living through zhe work of others," Mr. de Hory said, loosening his white silk ascot. "So you vill do my suffering *for* me."

22 · TOGETHER FUREVER

RIVERS OF SCENT flowed past Marlo and Zane as they strode across the Broken Promised Land atop lofty stilts of lie-lengthened Pinocchio wood. Marlo squinted through her Smell-O-Vision goggles, her eyes trained on the deep-brown/gray coil of odor she had been tracking since Fibble. Other tufts of scents—burbling blues and scattered scarlets—drifted sporadically in the dull, oatmeal-colored sky. Only the dense, brown-gray tangle of smell, though, had been a constant fixture, bunching up and thickening with each mile. At the lower left-hand corner of the goggles' lens was a tiny digital meter—a flat red arch marking "Mineral," "Vegetable," "Animal"—with the needle trained firmly on "Animal."

"Still on track," Marlo called out to Zane behind her. She could, only now, detect the faint musk herself as it tickled the back of her nose.

Marlo's legs and arms ached. With the stilts, they had probably covered five miles by now . . . or ten. Marlo had no idea, really. It wasn't like there were signs reading "15 Miles to the Furafter" staked into the ground at regular intervals. If there were, they would probably be in kilometers just to confuse Marlo. But Zane—being English and *awesome*—could probably help with that.

"Here comes another one," Marlo called out to Zane as they walked through a massive wall of swirling fog. Passing through these electrified barriers—this latest one made three, total—felt like when you lie back on the wicked cold porcelain of your bathtub after just getting in—that dull, horrible shock. It was like that, only all over, a strange, blurry chill.

This new realm wasn't much different from the last one . . . or the one before that. It seemed, to Marlo, that these in-between places, these expansive pockets of nothing, were afterlife afterthoughts. Dreary supernatural subdivisions, where even color seemed like a costly "extra" that the developers weren't going to just throw in for free.

"Can you still see the stench?" Zane asked. Marlo slipped back on her Smell-O-Vision goggles. The dense, knotted rope of pet musk snaked beside them—creepy how it was right there but she couldn't see it without the goggles—and led to a sheet of fog to their left.

"We must be close," Marlo said, willing her aching limbs to push faster, as both she and Zane slammed into the last churning fog wall.

⋆　⋆　⋆

The Badillac lurched. The passengers fell in a heap onto the floor.

"What now?!" Inga shrieked at the chauffeur.

Milton noted that, through the floor of the limo, the road sounded different. Not the steady thrum of asphalt but the crinkle of . . . *paper*.

"We're here-ish," the driver replied.

Milton climbed up off the floor and stared out at the horizon whizzing past: a flat, unbroken plain laid with acres of old yellow newspaper. A tall wood tower to the right of the Badillac shone bright with floodlights.

"*Stay!*" a mechanized voice ordered as the limo raced past.

In the distance, Milton could see a large cage of some kind. An imposing structure with big feathery gargoyles perched atop its nine walls. At least they *looked* like gargoyles, Milton thought, just as something tall and skinny skittered across the plain in the corner of his eye.

The chauffeur demon slammed on the brakes. Wood clattered across the hood of the limo. Milton could see, through the rear window, two figures fall to the ground: two boys in hairy pajamas. In fact, one of them looked really familiar.

The Badillac zigzagged across the newspaper valley before plowing into the side of the metal fortress. A broken chorus of caws thundered from above. A half-dozen

Err bags rapidly inflated in the back of the Badillac and pitched the passengers out of the car, into the arms of whatever harm awaited them.

Milton was propelled through the rear window. He bounced out onto the trunk that—as his sister's body dented the metal—popped open, breaking his fall while nearly breaking his neck. He stumbled off the Badillac and broke a heel.

"Marlo!" a boy yelled at Milton from beyond the wreckage. "It's me!"

The boy, English by the sound of it, ran at Milton, clad in coarse brown hair pajamas. Van Glorious rose from the shredded newspaper ground, mourning his expensive broken shades for a split second before tossing them aside and bounding to intercept the boy.

"You stay away from us, you little creep!" Van bellowed. "We're just like real people, with real lives. Not animals in a zoo—"

He grabbed Zane's arm, just as Zane was about to embrace Milton.

"Marlo!" he panted. "I can't believe it's you! Hey . . . let go, you—!"

Van belted Zane across the chin, knocking him to the ground.

"What did you do *that* for?" Milton asked.

Van shrugged.

"I just assumed he was the paparazzi," he explained, rubbing his fist.

"You leave her alone, you great plonkin' pillock!" Zane yelled as he leapt to his feet.

"Not the face! Not the face!" Van yelped as the two exchanged blows.

Milton leaned back against the wrecked limo. *Just when I thought things couldn't get any weirder,* he thought, *I have two guys fighting over me.*

"Milton?" a voice called out. *Milton's* voice. It sounded higher and shakier than he expected, like when he'd hear his voice on a recording. To the side of the wreck, by the fortress cage, stood . . . *himself.*

"Marlo!" Milton called back as he hobbled toward his sister. It was like rushing into a mirror.

The Fausters hugged each other, tight, as if hoping to merge into one fearless, invincible force. Tears streamed down their faces.

"I missed you," Marlo said, choking back her sobs. "I missed me, too."

She pushed Milton back, peered over his shoulder, and smiled her trademark crooked smile, a broken pink crayon even on Milton's face.

"Is Zane fighting with that dead action hero guy over . . . *me?*" she asked coyly.

Milton shrugged.

"I guess . . . Van Glorious, the dead actor, is a few shows shy of a full lineup . . . a franchise that's spawned too many spin-offs, if you know what I mean."

"I don't," Marlo replied as she tucked blue hair behind Milton's ear.

"Sorry, industry jargon," Milton apologized.

He swatted his sister's preening hands away.

"We don't have time for this," Milton said as he scrutinized the fortress behind his sister.

"Right," Marlo said as she tore her eyes from Zane, now propped up against the damaged limousine, panting alongside Van Glorious. "Time to put our freaky Fauster powers into action." She looked over her shoulder at the fortress.

"Are those . . . *crows*?" she gasped as her bulging eyes, having traveled up the bars, settled on the massive feathered guardians perched on the parapet.

The quiet of Stay! was broken by the sounds of vehicles in the distance. Tires sliced and skidded across brittle newspaper. Suddenly, the klieg lights atop the guard tower exploded with their harsh accusing glare.

"*Stay!*" the recorded voice commanded. Two vans raced closer. One of the vans, a chugging Volkswagen bus covered in nappy pink faux fur, had THE REPEAT FURRARI stenciled sloppily on its side and was playing Beethoven's "Für Elise" through a rooftop speaker. The other van, sleek and modern, sporting a satellite dish, had THE URN SHORT ATTENTION NEWS VAN detailed on its side. The vans squealed to a stop.

Marlo squinted through the bars—she just couldn't

get the hang of not having 20/20 vision—as the URN news crew set up their lights and cameras at the far wall of the fortress. Meanwhile, a half-dozen protesters spilled out of the fuzzy pink REPEAT van.

"Maybe all of this commotion can help us out," Milton said as he kicked off his painful, irritating pumps. "Provide a distraction, while we find Lucky . . ."

Marlo chuckled.

"Odds are that he's asleep," she said. "Probably having this great dream about *being* asleep while *we* have to deal with this nightmare."

Lucky reared back and hissed, arched with unfocused rage at all the awful creatures closing in around him.

Snarling, Annubis broke free of his muscular demon-captor's grasp. The other two headless demons, sensing the dog god despite their being deaf and blind, lunged at him. Annubis bit hard into the hefty arm of the nearest demon, though the creature seemed unfazed as its skin was as unyielding as a fresh rawhide chew.

"Grab him!" Mr. de Hory yelled as hissing cats pounced upon the dog god. Annubis kicked away a spitting calico. It leapt at Mr. de Hory's face, biting his mouth.

"*Mwrghleorff!*" he yelled as he tried to bat the cat away from his face.

"Cat got your tongue?" Annubis roared as he shoved the demon up the hemlock steps.

The headless/heartless demon staggered back into the vat and fell through the billowing film of sparks. The flickering layer flared angrily as the demon passed through, though the creature never emerged on the other side. It disappeared. *Vaporized.* The only remnant an oily white residue dripping down the insides of the vat, a phosphorescent grease that smelled of methane and old Certs, covered with lint, dredged from the bottom of some old lady's handbag.

"*Nulled,*" Annubis panted as he gaped into the vat. "It's true. Returned to nothing."

He looked back over his shoulder as a headless/heartless demon seized Anput and Kebauet.

"What happened, Paw-paw?" Kebauet yapped.

"There is life and there is death," Annubis sighed, his head hung low as the second remaining headless/heartless demon lumbered up the steps of the vat. "But there is also something else. And that something is . . . *absolutely nothing.*"

Lucky—coiled protectively around Kebauet's ankles—stood suddenly erect, panting, gorging on a familiar scent wafting into the Kennels, undetectable to the rest but, to Lucky, the most wonderful scent in the world. The ferret bobbed and weaved but Cerberus matched and bested his every move.

"I won't be scared, Paw-paw, you'll see," Kebauet said, more in hopes of convincing herself than her father. "Will it hurt?"

Mr. de Hory wiped his scratched, cat-spit-soaked face with a starched handkerchief.

"It vill feel like nothing," the man interjected. "Like sleeping wizzout dreaming . . . wizzout ever waking. But if your father vould jest be a good doggie . . ."

Lucky's pink eyes rolled to the back of his head. He fell to the ground at Annubis's feet. Cerberus sniffed at the seemingly unconscious ferret with all three snouts. The hound of Heck moved in closer.

Lucky lunged at Cerberus, savaging his middle face, then sprang across the floor of the Kennels, his tiny nails scrabbling across the concrete. Simultaneously whimpering with pain and yowling with rage, the dog bounded after Lucky and out of the Kennels.

Marlo watched the media event she had hatched play out through the fortress bars. She clutched her arms together and trembled. She had been so concerned with meeting Milton in the Furafter that she had no idea what to do next.

"*There's something going on,*" she murmured. "Not only here, but . . . *everywhere.* Vice Principal Barnum, Nostradamus—who knows who else—"

Lucky shot out of the Kennels, sniffed the air, and

dove into the freshly dug hole inside the courtyard. The Scarecrows cawed from the parapets, unsettled by the cameras and lights below, and shifted in their roosts.

"Something big is about to happen on the Surface," Milton said. "We'll figure it all out once we get Lucky and find Annubis so he can switch us back."

Lucky emerged from the other end of the hole, hopped up on a stack of old *GYP* newspapers, and caught the scent of his owner.

"Lucky!" Milton cried out as his ferret scrambled toward him. Lucky skidded to a stop, sniffing both Milton and Marlo. Though confused by their muddled scents, Lucky finally settled on Milton, currently inhabiting his sister's body.

"You escaped!" Milton said as he stooped down to scoop up his pet. Lucky fought the urge to hop into his master's arms, and—with a full-body twitch—doubled back and headed for the tunnel.

"Where are you going?" Milton shouted as he ran after Lucky, with Marlo close behind. "Where's Annubis? Wait!"

Milton and Marlo stepped into the mouth of the tunnel after Lucky.

"Marlo?!" Zane called through cupped hands. "Where are you scarpering off to?"

Marlo turned and gave Zane her widest, brightest smile . . . only, as she was her grubby runt-of-a-brother, her attempt to dazzle merely puzzled.

"I—" Marlo attempted before Milton jabbed her with his elbow.

"We'll be right back," Milton explained. "We're just scouting locations."

Van Glorious, rubbing his black eye, gave Marlo a thumbs-up.

"That's my girl!" he called out to Milton as he yanked his sister into the hole. On their hands and knees, Milton and Marlo crawled through the tunnel after Lucky. Marlo chuckled.

"That's my girl?" she mocked.

"Shut up," Milton replied, sweating in the cramped space that felt as if it were strangling his entire body. "I'm sure we have . . . all *sorts* of dirt on one another. We can come clean once . . . we find out what . . . Lucky is freaking out . . . about."

Lucky shot out of the tunnel and back through the portal leading to the Kennels. Milton and Marlo pushed themselves up out of the hole and into the fortress courtyard, as pressed-sawdust earth spilled back into the tunnel.

Cerberus came running out of the Kennels just as Lucky whizzed past him. Not a creature built for sudden changes in movement, the three-headed lapdog skidded and rolled on the crow-dropping-encrusted floor as each head gave its hapless body conflicting orders.

"Cerberus?" Milton murmured with alarm as he

scanned the inner courtyard for Lucky. "Here? I hope that doesn't mean—"

"There's Lucky!" Marlo yelled, spotting the wispy ferret back in the Kennels rushing down an aisle bisecting a massive pile of crates. "He went through that weird round doorway. C'mon!"

Cerberus righted himself and—his six eyes fixing upon the Fausters—galloped toward them.

Filled with disgust at seeing the horrible, three-headed lapdog that had terrorized her back in Limbo, Marlo sprinted toward Cerberus and punted him full-force into the spherical portal leading to the Really Big Farm.

"Touchdown!" Marlo shrieked as she turned to join her brother rushing toward the Kennels.

"I think you mean a goal," Milton said as he dove into the portal, his skin prickling with electricity, rushing to keep up with Lucky several yards ahead of them.

"This place is *awful.*" Marlo grimaced as she entered the wretched warehouse of imprisoned pets. "The noise . . . *the smell.*"

She pulled the collar of her hair pajama top over her face as she ran alongside her brother, their bare feet slapping against the concrete floor, racing after Lucky toward the back of the Kennels.

They cleared a winding wall of crate towers and skidded to a halt. A group of assorted creatures surrounded a large tub nestled in a clearing of crates. Ushered up the steps by a gruesome, headless meat-doughnut demon was—

"Annubis!" Milton yelled.

The dog god snapped his head back as a headless/heartless demon shoved him to the rim of the vat.

"Milton! Marlo!" he bayed. "Do something!"

Marlo, never one for thinking a plan through mentally before enacting it physically, instinctively plunged her hand into her satchel, removing the last of the truth bombs. She brought it back over her shoulder.

"What *is* that?!" Milton shouted.

"It's a bomb," she said as she pitched it over her head toward the vat.

"A bomb?!" Milton repeated with disbelief.

"Yeah," Marlo replied as she hit the floor. "No lie."

23 · THAT'S THE WAY
THE KOOKS CRUMBLE

THE THREE BLOND boys walked down Avenue 51 in downtown Topeka, Kansas. The tallest, wearing a *Teenage Jesus* T-shirt, turned back to his friends.

"Just be cool, like TJ, got it?" he said, whispering, as Topeka—which means "a good place to dig potatoes" in the languages of the Kansa and the Ioway peoples—slowly yawned and stretched in the early morning air. "I know it seems wrong, but it's one of those wrongs that's right, okay?"

The two shorter boys—one wearing a *Keepin' It Christian* T-shirt, the other a *There's a Methodist to My Madness* tee—nodded, their curly hair flopping into their eyes.

"Okay," the tall boy said as he popped a Final Judgmint in his mouth, wincing as his tongue crackled briefly with electric yet undeniably minty pain. "Here they are."

Plastered across the plywood wall of a boarded-up lot were dozens of posters touting the season finale of *Allah in the Family*. The tall boy handed his friends some black T.H.E.E.N.D.-branded Sharpies.

"Like the ads on T.H.E.E.N.D. say," he explained as he uncapped his pen, "if we want our favorite shows back next season, then they have to win the ratings war, all right? And the website gave us all those great ideas how to make that happen, even if it comes to defacing public property, which is totally against the law. But we have to obey a higher power: *television*. So let's be quick."

The boys nodded and proceeded to scrawl the word "sucks" to the posters.

"This one's out of ink," one of the boys muttered as someone behind him offered a red T.H.E.E.N.D. Sharpie. "Wow, cool. Red. Where'd you get this . . . ?"

The boys turned to find three dark-skinned boys—wearing *Allah in the Family, Wholly Shiite,* and *Malibu Mosque* T-shirts—standing behind them, glaring, biting into freshly unwrapped Doomsdanishes. The leader, a boy with black close-cropped hair and big ears, pointed over his shoulder, across the street, with his thumb.

On the other side of the avenue, against a boarded-up Liquid Paper Depot store, were dozens of *Teenage Jesus* posters, with the word "sucks" scrawled upon each one in red.

"*Why, you . . . !*" the tall blond boy said as he set himself upon the leader of the rival gang. A little boy with a shaved head walked past in his *Peek-a-Buddha* T-shirt.

"Hey, guys," the boy said with a peaceful smile. "Free yourself from this cycle of conditioned existence and suffering . . . *oww!*"

The boys dragged the peace-loving passerby into their brawl. As the seven boys exchanged blows, Lester Lobe—owner of the area's only metaphysical museum, the Paranor Mall—shuffled out onto the sidewalk to put out his extraterrestrial-shaped sandwich board.

"Hey, *not cool!*" the wild-eyed man yelled, straightening his red fez.

The kids stopped brawling and stared at the crazy old man in the pink-and-green camouflage Bermuda shorts and combat boots.

"I ain't no friend of 'the man,' but I'll yell 'sooie' and bring the pigs out here so fast, your heads'll spin around like in *The Exorcist!*"

The boys had no idea what the man was shrieking about, but rightly assumed that his rant had something to do with calling the police. They scattered.

Lester shook his head and muttered.

"Man, I'm on edge," he said as he drained his second cup of chewing tobacco juice, espresso, and blue-green VitaMold powder. "It's those KOOK tenants of mine. I feel like a stranger in my own strange land."

He pushed open the door—his entrance announced

by the five tones from *Close Encounters of the Third Kind*—and stepped into his crowded, cockeyed cathedral of curiosities.

The Paranor Mall was an 800-square-foot collection of supernatural-themed ephemera, including a big rhinestone-encrusted Psychomanthium, otherwise known as the Elvis Abduction Chamber.

But, due to the recession—which had been murder on the fringe phenomena industry—Lester had been forced to sublet half of his museum to the KOOKs, otherwise known as the Knights of the Omniversalist Order Kinship, to make ends meet.

As a condition of their lease agreement, Lester had made the KOOKs part of his Krazy Kultz exhibit just so that the Paranor Mall wouldn't lose its "flow." Puzzlingly, the new exhibit was drawing better crowds than all of his other displays combined.

I suppose it makes some *sense,* Lester thought as he flipped the sign in the window from CLOSED MIND to OPEN MIND, *with all the wackiness, paranoia, and tension in the world lately—especially with all of those weird new TV shows—people are confused, seeking answers in unlikely places. . . .*

Lester Lobe shivered as twelve-year-old Damian Ruffino emerged from his tent. He was a living exhibit, the preadolescent "prophet" of the KOOKs' religion, their bratty "Bridge to the Other Side."

The big-boned bruiser stretched, farted, then spat out a moist clump of sunflower seed husks, tinted in a rainbow of artificial colors due to a mouthful of Gummi Worms.

That boy puts the "mess" in "messiah," Lester thought with disgust.

"Aren't you going to clean that up?" Lester said as he glared at the shells scattered about the floor.

"My followers love doing that stuff for me," he replied groggily. "Makes them feel useful. And who am I to take that away from them? Oh wait—I'm their salvation, their almighty Bridge to the Omniverse. I'm also the kid who keeps your lights on, so even if you don't believe in me, you surely believe in my money, don't you, old man?"

Lester clenched his fists and gritted his yellow, nicotine-stained teeth.

"Didn't your parents ever teach you any manners, you little creep?" Lester seethed, his morning mellow irreparably harshed.

Damian ran a hand through his dark, curly hair and yawned.

"Why should kids respect old people just because they're *old*?" he replied. "They've only had more time to screw things up. Like my parents. Ever since I came back from the dead, they just don't get me. Not like they ever did, but—man, after that cheapo funeral they threw me—it was obvious. Nothing like being dead to see what people *really* think about you. So me and today's kids are just taking *what* we can *while* we can. . . ."

Lester shook his head as he dusted the twinkling papier-mâché flying saucer suspended from the museum's rafters.

"Milton wasn't like that," he murmured sadly. "Like *you*."

Damian chuckled as he slipped on his sour, crunchy sweat socks.

"Good ol' Milquetoast," he muttered as he searched for his Doc Martens. "First I send him to Heck, then he escapes and sends *me* there, then he goes back down while the KOOKs drag me up. He and I just can't seem to hook up . . . but we will. Oh, boy, *will we ever*."

Damian gave his laces an angry tug, snapping them. Lester stifled a laugh.

"I'll be out of your hair soon . . . what's left of it," the boy seethed as he leveled his dark gaze at Lester Lobe, his eyes compressing into sinister slits, as if he were trying to crush Lester with his eyelids. "And you'll *all* wish you had treated me better. You'll see. . . ."

The five tones from the *Close Encounters of the Third Kind* theme chimed as two of Damian's fellow KOOKs stepped into the Paranor Mall.

The Guiding Knight threw off his gold Members Only jacket, revealing his blue ceremonial robe. The middle-aged man's face was so angular that it could have been used for a geometry test. Next to him was Necia Alvarado, a twitchy, ratlike girl with eyes as dark and fathomless as an abandoned well. They both set down canvas bags marked VitaMold.

"Where's the rest of my flock?" Damian said, glaring at the Guiding Knight.

The thin, vaguely wizardish man (perhaps it was the robe) stiffened with irritation.

"Most of your flock have *jobs*: that's when you agree to perform a certain task in exchange for pay," the Guiding Knight replied, his tone like an overly starched shirt. "And, on top of that, you have us all selling this VitaMold stuff."

"It's not *selling*," Damian corrected. "It's providing marketing opportunities. At least that's what my lawyer says, Algernon Cole—"

"Lawyer!" laughed Lester as he combed out Bigfoot's back. *"Right, and I voted for Nixon. . . ."*

"Just tell my flock to show up when it's *convenient* for them to worship me as their Bridge," Damian continued. *"He who will cross over to prepare for their imminent arrival in the Next Life, and hasten the Last Days, which serve as our new beginning."*

The Guiding Knight set his bag down.

"Speaking of 'hastening,'" the man said as he unfolded a card table and set out a stack of *Get KOOKy: Why It's AWESOME to Be in a Death Cult!* pamphlets, "your flock is getting restless."

"Yeah, yeah," Damian said as he strung a black tie around his neck. "You just tell my flock that I've been really busy on their behalf. Sure, we have had some setbacks, like getting kicked out of Mazel Top-to-Bottom after Milquetoast's dumb ferret Lucky got killed—"

Necia's eyes grew wet. She wiped her nose with her bony, clawlike hand.

"He wasn't dumb, O Bridge," Necia said as she unbuckled her black wool coat. "Lucky was sweet. Just vicious and unpredictable."

"Well, it was the excuse Grizzly Mall needed to kick us out," Damian continued. "But look: we're actually part of a museum now. In downtown Topeka, not that yahooville Generica! And Algernon Cole is working hard on settling my multiple suits against Generica General Hospital and the Barry M. Deepe Funeral Parlor. In the meantime, he helped me to invest our membership dues into something *big*—now we're the regional distributor for VitaMold fungus-based nutriticeutical drinks!"

"Have you actually *tasted* this stuff?" The Guiding Knight grimaced as he kicked his VitaMold bag in the corner, where it joined three dozen other bags. "It's like licking an old basement."

Lester Lobe shrugged as he drained his cup.

"I actually like it," he said as he blew the tassel of his fez out of his eyes. "It's got an . . . earthy taste."

"See?" Damian shot back. "Freaky old hippies like it! And no, I haven't tasted it, but that doesn't matter. Vita-

Mold is a conversation starter, a way to get suckers interested in the cult."

The Guiding Knight tugged on his droopy blue silk hat while Lester clipped pictures from a stack of tabloid magazines and glued them to the side of the Psychomanthium.

"Maybe, but—" the Guiding Knight interjected.

"*But nothing,*" Damian interrupted. "I've also got that book idea brewing. And once that's finished, it'll not only make us some money, it'll be the first wave of propaganda for the cult. Better than those lame pamphlets."

"Have you even *read* a book?" the Guiding Knight replied.

Damian scratched at a tiny white feather growing out of his chin.

"It's like VitaMold," he replied. "I don't have to taste it to sell it. Sure, I haven't had a lot of luck writing the book myself. That's why I found a ghostwriter."

"Oooh, spooky!" Necia replied as she helped Lester snip pictures from magazines.

"No," Damian said, pressing his thumbs into his temples, "a writer to write the book for me: Dale E. Basye. The guy that writes those dumb Fartisimo Family books."

"My mom won't let me read those," Necia said as she cut out a picture of a bat-boy flying over the Great Pyramid. "She says that their . . . *gas* . . . is a metaphor for demonic possession."

"The point is that I'm doing a lot while all you folks do is sit around and complain," Damian continued. "Now I need some time to myself. *Business* . . ."

Damian pulled out a Ouija board, a pad of paper, and a pen from his tent. Sitting cross-legged on the ground, Damian set the heart-shaped planchette on the board, touched it delicately, and closed his eyes. The wooden heart quivered momentarily, then slowly slid to the letter *Y,* then *O,* then *U* . . .

Damian opened one of his eyes and reached for his pen and paper with his other hand. He strung the letters together on the pad.

Y-O-U-R P-A-R-T-Y I-S C-U-R-R-E-N-T-L-Y U-N-A-V-A-I-L-A-B-L-E. P-L-E-A-S-E T-R-Y Y-O-U-R C-A-L-L A-G-A-I-N. . . .

Damian sighed. This was the third time he had received the exact same message when trying to contact Satan in the not-so-great beyond. He flipped back through the pad of paper.

T-O-T-A-L R-E-W-R-I-T-E—August 18
A-R-E Y-O-U S-E-R-I-O-U-S?—August 30
G-E-T A G-H-O-S-T-W-R-I-T-E-R—September 16
N-O, N-O-T A R-E-A-L G-H-O-S-T—September 17
A R-E-A-L W-R-I-T-E-R. G-E-T O-N-E N-O-W O-R N-O
D-E-A-L—September 19

Damian shoved aside the Ouija board and paper.

Forsaken by Satan, he thought as he threw himself back on a white beanbag chair. *Well, I've got it all covered. He'll be so proud of me. Can the devil be proud? Pride's a sin, so yeah. Then he'll give me everything I want: absolute, corruptive power over all. Send more souls his way by lying to kids, telling them how fun and awesome the afterlife is. And then let me rule over them. The only thing Satan doesn't see coming is that I'll train these stupid kids to be my personal army, and when we turn eighteen, the devil is due for a big, bad surprise. . . .*

The Guiding Knight glowered at Damian, who was slouched back on his white beanbag chair spitting sunflower seed husks onto the floor like some lazy, freakishly large chicken with a raging superiority complex. *A chicken,* the Guiding Knight mused as he recalled, with regret, the moment he and his fellow KOOKs had brought Damian back from the dead using the sacrificial energies of twenty-seven Rhode Island Reds. Damian seemed, himself, a big chicken in the "letting a religious cult take your life so that you may prepare the everlasting everyplace beyond for its 14,217 believers across the Northern Hemisphere" department. Worse than that, the boy's attitude was having a devastating effect on cult morale, especially among the elder members.

The Guiding Knight sighed and picked at the nachos stain on his midnight-blue robe.

If the Bridge of the Knights of the Omniversalist Order Kinship, subordinate chapter of the lower Midwest sect, won't play nice by letting me slit his obnoxious throat up on the altar so that he may cross to the other side and we can get this whole death cult thing moving along, the Guiding Knight mused, *then he leaves me no choice but to give him a firm shove through death's door. . . .*

24 · THE CATASTROPHE'S
MEOW

"WHAT WAS THAT?" Barbra Seville asked her crew as she peered into the fortress courtyard. Her cameraman, a paunchy fellow with a receding gray hairline, shrugged his shoulders.

"Sounded like some kind of explosion," he said with a hand-rolled cigarette balanced between his lips.

Five REPEAT protesters jogged to the fence—their ANIMAL RIGHTS/PEOPLE WRONGS, CRUEL AIN'T COOL, and NEVER FUR-GET! signs resting on their shoulders.

"An atomic flea bomb?" the group's dowdy leader, Brigid Brophy, speculated.

Another protester—a freckle-faced woman with pigtails and overalls—frowned.

"I don't, you know, think so," she murmured as she

eyed the energetic portal to the Kennels. "There'd be, like, tiny portobello-sized mushroom clouds."

Barbra beckoned her crew toward the fence, crooking her finger.

"This is Barbra Seville with URN News—no snooze, just news—reporting to you *live* from the Furafter," she said, holding her microphone urgently as she wedged herself into the line of protesters. "I am at the epicenter of a raging volcano of controversy, a pro-pets protest that is testing the patience of authorities here, if the sound of explosions can be believed. The only question is how this band of animal-loving—"

Barbra examined the five drab, visually unthreatening women and crinkled her brow.

"—*Amazons* will retaliate. . . ."

Annubis stirred to consciousness. He rolled on his side to see his family, motionless beside him.

"Are you all right?!" he yelped as he clutched Kebauet's emaciated arm.

His wife and daughter nodded groggily. Annubis sighed with relief as he eased himself upright.

Crates lay strewn about the Kennels, coated with a clinging, silvery vapor that drifted across the concrete floor, then climbed up the crates on hazy, glittering tendrils.

Virginia Woof lay on her back at the base of the Nullification Tub. She sneezed herself awake and rolled over, having played dead a little too convincingly for her liking. The Speak & Spell strapped to her side was crushed and useless.

Annubis sniffed the air. The fog tickled his nose and smelled faintly of menthol. He could detect the acrid stench of animal fear wafting from the crates, but not the dark, uncomplicated musk of the headless/heartless demons. Annubis peered into the vat. Beneath the flitting eddy of sparks was a dull film of translucent sludge.

The demons must have tumbled in, Annubis thought, *and were energetically undone. Their soul residue is so weak . . . barely there at all.*

Milton and Marlo lay on the concrete floor under a small pile of fallen crates. Lucky rippled forward like a Slinky sheathed in a fuzzy white sock. He licked Milton's face. Milton opened his eyes, reaching out of habit for the glasses he no longer needed, seeing the world through his sister's sharp, kleptomaniac's eyes.

"We're . . . ?" he mumbled before sitting up with a start. *"The bomb!"*

Marlo stirred sluggishly awake.

"The bomb?" she mumbled. "No one says that anymore. . . ."

She bolted up.

"The truth bomb!"

Annubis strode toward the Fausters and knelt down before them.

"You saved us . . . me and my family," the noble dog god relayed as he placed his paws on the Fausters' shoulders. "For that I am eternally grateful. And, as I am a several-thousand-year-old demigod, the phrase 'eternally grateful' really means something. . . ."

Milton wrapped his arms around Annubis and hugged him tight. Annubis felt solid. *Real.* And—as Milton wasn't exactly himself, awash in a raging river of lies—holding on to the dog god felt like clutching a life preserver. Reassuring and hopeful. Annubis patted Milton's head.

"Ah, Milton . . . that's right," he said with his curled dog smile. "I almost forgot I had switched your souls."

He turned to address Marlo.

"Tell me about the device you used to thwart our nullification," Annubis said. "It had a peculiar explosive power, seeming to vanquish only those in need of vanquishing."

"Nullification?" Milton asked. "You mean, that vat would have neutralized you?"

"Yes," Annubis replied somberly, looking back at his family. "But about this bomb—"

"*Truth* bomb," Marlo replied as she rubbed an aching lump on her forehead. "I got it from a doctor back in Fibble. A big duck. He made it using liquid truth and little white lice, that—when smooshed together—make a big explosion."

Annubis rubbed his bristly chin in contemplation.

"A volatile blend of fact and fission," he said with a nod. "Lobbed in the nick of time, too."

Someone moaned from behind the vat. Virginia Woof bounded toward the slow, pained groan. After several seconds of delighted yaps, an old man rose to his sandaled feet.

"Mr. Noah," Annubis muttered as he stood tall, straightening his tunic and smoothing down his ruffled fur.

Milton and Marlo helped each other to their feet and stared, slack-jawed, at the ancient man with the flowing white beard and robe as he scritched the terrier in his arms.

"Mr. Noah . . . as in *the* Noah?" Milton asked as he tucked his sister's unruly blue hair behind his ears.

"A robe, huh?" Marlo replied with a smirk. "I guess I always expected him to be wearing *floods* . . . get it? You know, cropped pants that aren't quite capris? Because of the ark and—"

Milton nudged Marlo hard in the side.

"Show some respect," he whispered as the Fausters followed Annubis to the Nullification Tub. "Especially since he'll think you're *me*."

Annibus extended his paw-hand to Noah, who—after setting Virginia Woof gently down to the ground—shook the dog god's hand warmly, his restraints hanging, shredded, from his wrists.

"Mr. Noah," Annubis said with reverence. "My name is Annubis. Can you tell me what happened here?"

Noah scratched the thick hair coursing out of the rag cinched around his head. Milton had never seen a face with so many lines carved upon it before. It looked like a street map of New York etched on skin. The ancient man smiled a toothless grin at Milton.

"Never seen a nine-hundred-fifty-year-old man before, little girl?" Noah laughed.

He cleared his ancient throat, unearthing a ball of phlegm so old that it may have been of archaeological import.

"I had noticed that some creatures—dogs, mostly—had begun to disappear from the Really Big Farm. And the Scarecrows had been acting . . . odd. Listless and distracted . . . I thought they had, perhaps, gone raven mad!"

Noah looked at Milton's, Marlo's, and Annubis's faces for signs of mirth, yet there was none to be found.

"So I investigated the Kennels—a place I abhor and would eliminate if I could convince the Powers That Be Evil otherwise," he continued. "I only use it when trying to rehabilitate difficult animals before releasing them into the Really Big Farm. And that's exactly what I was doing when I discovered, back here, this dreadful vat, those hulking, horrible titans, and the man with the shiny necklace. The necklace that controls the Scarecrows."

"What man?" Milton asked.

Noah pointed to a fallen row of crates to the side of the Nullification Tub.

"*That* man."

A smooth white hand, one that had never performed a moment of honest work in its life, twitched beneath two crates: one holding a sandy-colored dingo, and the other a feral Chartreux. Annubis walked over to the mound of crates and pushed them aside with his foot, freeing the man beneath.

"Mr. de Hory!" Milton exclaimed as he saw the man's dapper, disdainful face. Annubis snatched the dazzling pewter necklace and turned to Milton.

"You know this man?" the dog god asked as Mr. de Hory came to, the man's dark eyes fixing upon the faltering holographic soul model projecting weakly just beyond him. The fuzzy, multicolored light sculpture winked on and off in the air by a large wooden crate marked DO NOT OPEN: EVER.

Milton shrugged as he watched the man creep forward, painfully, on his hands and knees.

"Sort of . . . I saw him on TV."

A group of black cats slowly oozed around the bend, followed by Napoleon Bone-apart. The blithe Italian greyhound nudged his See 'n Say.

"The cat says . . . *meow!*"

Milton and Marlo stared at one another. Marlo reached to pinch Milton, hard, on the side of the arm.

"Oww!" he yelped. "Why did you do that?"

Marlo shrugged.

"I wanted to see if I was dreaming . . . this is all too weird."

Milton watched as the mist wafted up the steep wall of crates.

"This place is beyond awful," he murmured. "Just leaving all these pets here, forgotten, seems like the worst kind of abuse. And what are they being punished for, anyhow? Because they weren't as domesticated as their owners expected? Like that's *their* fault?"

Lucky coiled up Milton's leg and shot into his arms. Milton stroked his ferret as, eyes wet, he gazed upon the countless, caged animals.

"We've got to do something," he continued.

Annubis shook his head sadly while the cats skulked closer, slinking from shadow to shadow.

"There just isn't enough time in eternity to open all of these cages ourselves—"

The spirals of luminous silver mist whirled about the crate doors like tiny hurricanes. Suddenly, with an explosive clatter, the doors of *every* crate sprang open.

Most of the animals vaulted instinctually out of their cages, while the smarter ones carefully climbed down to the floor. Many, however, had been caged for so long that they had forgotten what freedom even looked like.

The black cats hissed, arching their backs so that they

were spiky black croquet hoops of aggravation. Milton and Marlo stepped back from the crate walls as furry creatures spilled forth like a mewling, yapping waterfall.

"But—" Milton said before his sister interjected.

"The truth," Marlo offered in a spooky hush as animals wriggled past her ankles, *"shall set you free."*

Annubis's cryptic dog smile vanished as he saw the wooden sides of the huge crate marked DO NOT OPEN: EVER collapse. Inside was a rectangular green igloo adorned with yellow quartz cat's-eye gems and etchings of ancient, pampered felines wrapped in gauze tunics cleaning themselves.

Noah shuddered.

"Pandora's Cat Box," the old, old man gasped.

"Pandora's Cat Box?" Annubis repeated. "But that's only a myth."

"Apparently not," Noah replied. "This place has often served as a dumping ground for unwanted artifacts too terrible even for museums. But I never thought that it would house this . . . this *vessel* containing all of the plagues, pestilence, burdensome worry, and unrest that cats have never known. Locked away in an era when felines were revered as gods incarnate . . . what lies within is potentially cataclysmic."

Filled with curiosity—despite its potentially deadly effect on cats—Chairman Meow, Frankenpuss, and a dozen other felines padded cautiously to the crate. Milton eyed the box with unease.

"Where did it come from?" Milton asked, now knee-deep in squirming, thrashing animals.

"Egypt, by way of Katmandu," Annubis replied. "It is said that the ancient Egyptian cat gods partook in the burdens of the world, then, um, *passed* them into this cat box so that their feline progeny would be free of all worry, woe, and the onus of obligation."

Marlo scratched at her brother's forearms, which were ready to hatch a litter of cat-allergy-induced hives.

"Are we safe?" she asked, her gaze glued to the centuries-old box packed tight with despair and disease.

"Yes," Noah said tentatively as more cats circled the box, their vague interest blossoming into obsession. "As long as what is within—"

Frankenpuss stuck his blocky, calico head into the box. Chairman Meow, Hannibal Lickter, and thirteen other cats soon followed suit. Clawed Yereyesout gave the box a few dainty sniffs, rubbing his side against it indifferently, before—suddenly—he and the other cats bolted inside.

"—*stays* within," Noah added miserably. "If only I had a spray bottle. *That* would dampen their enthusiasm."

The sound of furious scratching echoed from the box. Out darted the cats, their ears pinned back to their head, frisky in that "I just did something terrible in there like you wouldn't believe and it's your problem now" cat way.

"Bad kitties!" Annubis yelled. "Pandora's Cat Box is not for . . . *that!*"

The box trembled, its eerie green glow throbbing and pulsing, ever quicker. The last of the cats emerged, pupils dilated, tails twitching.

Some of the freed pets in the higher crates took brash leaps downward. They struck the sea of animals below with squeals of pain.

"This is getting out of control," Annubis said as a surge of animals nearly swept his daughter away.

"Paw-paw!" she yelped as Annubis grabbed hold of her arm. The scrabbling swells of pets grew higher, to the dog god's thighs.

Pandora's Cat Box quaked, hissing like a neglected teakettle.

Noah stood atop a mound of vacated crates.

"Two at a time! Two at a time!" he shrieked through cupped hands above the din.

Milton struggled to stay on his feet as cats, dogs, rabbits, guinea pigs, and assorted other animals clawed their way past his hips.

"That will take too long," he muttered against the tumult of yelps and growls. "I think it's going to be every pet for itself."

Milton saw Mr. de Hory struggle to his feet and teeter toward his shimmering soul simulation.

"Mr. de Hory!" Milton called out. "We've got to get out of here!"

The man cinched his white scarf tight around his neck, then picked up his laser pens with unruffled determination.

"Theez place is mine . . . *adverse possession*," the faux artist proclaimed. "Squatter's rights, I believe you say. Eet is perfect studio in which to create perfect forgery."

Mr. de Hory peered through his cracked eyeglasses and set to work amidst the riot of fur and fear.

"Art eez long and life eez short and I vill only leave when I have made my ultimate artistic statement!"

Suddenly, Pandora's Cat Box—a brimming heap of utter nastiness—erupted in a green, fiery ball of burning cat litter, smoldering feces, and swirling, noxious vapor.

"And his 'ultimate artistic statement' will be 'Oh the excruciating pain!'" Annubis said, gripping Mr. de Hory's crow-controlling necklace in one paw-hand and grabbing Milton by the other. "We can't help it if that fraud is willing to die—*again*—for his sick, shady art. We must go . . . *now*!"

"*It's Van Glorious!*" one of the REPEAT protesters squealed, dropping her sign so that she could better pat her burning cheeks in star-worship. Van—his smile beaming like an artificial sun—stepped before the camera and pried the microphone from a stunned Barbra Seville.

"Thank you, Barbra," Van said smoothly, like hot buttered rum poured over a silk tie. "I love what you do . . ."

He turned to the protesters, pressed his hands together, and bowed before them with overtheatrical reverence.

". . . and I love what *you* do," he continued. "It's . . . *important*. Making sure that even the dead animals no one cares about anymore get their fair shake."

Barbra tilted her microphone, now in the possession of Van, to her mouth.

"So Mr. Glorious—"

"*Please,*" Van replied as if mortally wounded, which he knew a thing or two about. "It's *Van*. That Mr. Glorious stuff is for my lawyers."

Barbra giggled, despite herself, before regaining her journalistic composure.

"Okay then . . . *Van,*" she continued. "So you've always been an animal rights supporter?"

He nodded emphatically.

"Yep. Even as a kid we only ate meat from animals that died of old age, or who formally agreed—with an attorney present—to be our dinner."

"But—?"

"Oh yeah, we ate it all—snout to tail—out of respect, you know? Nowadays I'm all about the tofu: Tofutti, Tofurky . . . I even do kung-tofu in my next action flick . . . I'm messing with you. But look, get a shot of my shoes . . . they're made out of one hundred percent fruit leather. . . ."

A mixed herd of cats, dogs, and assorted mammals shot out of the Kennels. The startled Scarecrows flapped their enormous wings and cawed.

Brigid dropped her sign and shrieked, pointing to the courtyard.

"The animals!!" she shouted in near breathless joy. "They've been *freed*! We did it!"

Ambulating Abyssinians, bolting bunnies, careening corgis, and dashing dachshunds streamed out of the crackling electric portal. They flowed into the courtyard, most choosing—after a few quick sniffs—to race toward the Really Big Farm. At the heels of the stampede came Milton, Marlo, Noah, Annubis, and the dog god's family, followed by a blast of vile, wicked wind. Putrid, angry lumps of molten disease poured out of the ravaged shell of Pandora's Cat Box and into the courtyard, like a team of genies gone bad, flying out of a lamp that was rubbed the wrong way.

"Boys, we're packing up," Barbra Seville told her crew as she gazed at the flaming, snot-green energy spewing from the Kennels. "The secret to becoming a successful newscaster is to never, ever *become* the news."

The news crew collected their gear, dashed toward their van, and drove away as a blast of foul wind ripped the REPEAT signs from the astonished protesters' hands.

The Badillac's chauffeur demon stepped out of his vehicle to gape at the noxious gale.

"I'm not insured for this!" the creature grumbled as he ran to the back of the limo and tossed out the video equipment. Scooting back behind the steering wheel, the chauffeur demon punched the gas, swerved the limo in a squealing 180-degree turn, and sped away from the Furafter as fast as his multipoint injection V9 engine would take him.

Van and Inga chased after him.

"But what about *us*?" they yelled in a cloud of up-turned dust, just as the cat poop *really* hit the fan.

25 · THE STY OF THE STORM

"QUICK!" NOAH YELLED to the Scarecrows as biting gales of hurricane-force woe assailed the frightened, freshly freed pets in the fortress courtyard. "Herd them all to the Really Big Farm! Saint Francis—the patron saint of animals—will receive them."

Milton's eyes stung with ammonia as he tried to make sense of his chaotic surroundings. His face and arms itched and burned as the hot, creepy-moist wind chafed against them. He looked up at the Scarecrows on the parapets, clutching the bars tight with their talons, their faces impossible to read.

"Why don't they *do* something?" Milton shouted as the wind gained ferocity, filling his mouth with a blast of putrid fish-diaper smell. "Aren't they . . . supposed to . . . protect this place?" he added between dry heaves.

Noah kneaded his gnarled white beard as he stared up at the normally stalwart stewards of the Furafter.

"Yes, that is their calling. But they have been dazed and confused."

Noah's eyes rested on the glittering bauble in Annubis's paw-hand.

"The necklace. Perhaps I can regain their control."

Annubis tossed the shiny, mesmerizing necklace to Noah, just as a burning hunk of black goo shot out of the Kennels, heading straight for the old man's head.

"Watch out!" Marlo bellowed. "Flaming turd at nine o'clock!"

Noah ducked in a swift, surprisingly athletic dip while, simultaneously, snatching the necklace as it raced past, buoyed by a blast of shrieking, sickening wind.

Milton, Marlo, and Annubis stared with dumbfounded awe.

"I work out," Noah said casually as he approached the fence.

"Scarecrows of the Furafter!" he bellowed, his robes fluttering in the storm, as he swung the necklace in tight arcs over his head. The Scarecrows gazed down at the whirling necklace that threw back light in such a beguiling, irresistible way. "Listen to me! Form a wall protecting the Really Big Farm and flap for all you're worth!"

The Scarecrows rustled on the parapet, anxious, fluffing and unfluffing their gleaming black feathers until, as one, they took to the air in an explosion of great flapping wings.

Meanwhile, corrosive bile gusted out of the Kennels, stripping the REPEAT Furrari of its pink fur.

Milton gripped the iron bars of the nine-foot-tall fortress walls and shouted over the howling wind.

"Van! Inga! Um . . ."

He turned to Marlo.

"What's your boyfriend's name?"

Marlo slugged Milton in the arm, in the same spot she slugged him earlier: her patented sadistic sister technique.

"Zane is *not* my boyfriend!" she replied before leaning close to Milton.

"Do you think he likes me?"

Milton rolled his eyes and called out through his cupped hands.

"*Zane!* And you protesters . . . get in here! There's a hole by that stack of newspapers over there, where the Badillac was. And Van . . . grab the video camera! *Hurry!*"

The people outside the fortress knelt down, running toward the tunnel entrance as sheets of glowing snot-green rain pelted their backs.

Milton gaped at the bilge surging out of the Kennels. Swirls of radioactive cat litter and clumps of flaming excrement vomited out of the portal, with no sign of abating.

Annubis watched the people outside the fence climb into the tunnel as the storm whipped into a nasty, squalid squall.

A burst of humid wind heaved the fallen REPEAT van across the peeling newspaper ground. Its metal hull screamed as it was picked apart and dragged by the gust. It finally came to rest on top of the tunnel entrance.

"I guess its a one-way tunnel now," Milton muttered. The bars of the fortress wobbled and whistled as Van, Inga, and Zane emerged from the tunnel. Annubis trotted over to meet them.

"Follow me . . . now!" he ordered.

The Scarecrows swirled above in the treacherous air, pecking angrily at the smoldering hunks of debris that left trails of oily smoke crisscrossing the sky. They alit in the courtyard outside the portal leading to the Really Big Farm.

Noah gave Mr. de Hory's crow-controlling necklace a twirl.

"Flap!" he roared at the top of his antediluvian lungs.

Wings extended magnificently from tip to tip, the Scarecrows dug their talons deep into the ground and flapped. The rhythm was slow and labored at first, then gained in tempo, with each synchronized beating of wings becoming more fluid and confident.

The fluttering wall of wings bent the foul, stinging gusts back, squealing, like invisible steel bars at the hands of a circus strongman. Gradually, the wind was diverted away from the Really Big Farm back to the abandoned Kennels, where the toxic gale threw crates about in a blustery tantrum.

Milton pressed his hand against his sister's back.

"We should go," he said as they ducked down and ran for the Really Big Farm.

A spectacular imitation sun streamed down like sweet melted butter. The rich, prickly scent of grass, the dry honey of hay, and the thick sugar tar of pine overwhelmed Milton's nose, while the sunlight and cool gentle breeze caressed his skin.

Somehow, as he gazed across the ridiculously colorful terrain—the fiercely green trees and grass, the uncompromising blue of the sky—Milton couldn't help but feel like this beautiful place didn't want him here. It was subtle, but Milton felt—quite correctly—that the Really Big Farm wasn't calibrated to contain humans, so everything, while picturesque and pure, seemed a little *off*.

Lucky wriggled out of his arms and bounded across the soft green knoll. The only human Milton could see, besides himself and his sister, was a gaunt man in a thick brown robe, whistling sweetly as he tossed seed to the birds that flocked about his sandaled feet.

Milton joined Marlo beside one of many towering dogwoods. The trunk of the tree, like every tree Milton had encountered so far in the Really Big Farm, was well marked—"signed" by centuries of happy perished pups and hounds. Each tree was a living yearbook, auto-graphed with dog pee.

Milton settled by a cluster of flowering catnip plants. He and his sister locked eyes, before blurting out at once:

"They're planning the end of the world!"

Milton tucked his sister's stubborn blue hair behind his ear. "You go first," he said, seeing that his sister was about to go first.

Marlo closed her eyes and drew in a deep breath.

"Okay," she began. "First, Fibble's vice principal, P. T. Barnum—get this, the guy has flaming pants and electric hair."

"What?"

"Let me finish," Marlo continued. "So Fibble is this crazy advertising agency, and he—Barnum—uses the kids as his focus group, which is dumb since all the students are compulsive liars. So he unveiled all of these creepy products, like Doomsdanish, Apocalypstick, and Final Judgmints—"

"I've heard of those—"

"Shush. And these freaky-deeky products are some-how connected to the end of the world. Armageddon. I even heard him talking to Nordstromdumbus—"

"Nostradamus?"

"That's what I said," Marlo continued, breathlessly caught up in her story. "So they were talking about a way to shoot realistic illusions up to the Surface, using a ma-chine called a Humbugger. It runs on something called liedocaine so that people are fooled into thinking the illusions are real. And then there's the Truthador . . . don't interrupt—"

"I wasn't!" Milton replied.

"You just did," Marlo said, rocking back and forth with nervous energy that had nowhere to go but her mouth. "So the Truthador is this guy that was on this pirate radio station that kept blasting through the PA speakers. His songs were kind of like those songs Dad would listen to—"

"In his den when he was feeling depressed?"

"Yeah, only the Truthador's songs don't actually *cause* depression. His lyrics are some kind of code, about a salesman selling humanity out to aliens, fooling us into moving to a drab, awful new home—"

"*The Man Who Soldeth the World,*" Milton muttered, his blood turning to ice water despite sitting in a beam of simulated sunlight.

"And how we don't need a feather to take us where the crow flies—I don't really get that one," Marlo continued beneath the canopy of dark pink blooms, "and that we shouldn't follow cheaters, honesty's our leader—"

Milton reached into his shabby canvas tote and pulled out a stack of T.H.E.E.N.D. scripts.

"Satan has this new TV network beaming up to the Surface," he explained as he handed them to Marlo. "It's called T.H.E.E.N.D.: the Televised Hereafter Evangelistic Entertainment Network Division. All of the shows pander to a specific religion—"

"Like that show *Eighth Heaven Is Enough?*"

"*Worse,*" Milton replied while Marlo shivered. "But all the shows air at the same time and are, somehow, impervious to DVR. So it's started this religious ratings war. Everything is all tense up on the Surface. And all the shows are heading for these brutal, dismal finales—"

Marlo leafed through the scripts.

"Ugh," she said. "I may be Goth, but this stuff is even too dark and depressing for *me.* How did you get these?"

"I worked for Satan as a production assistant for the network, though I never met him, and had to deal with actors like Van Glorious, hang out on the sets . . ."

Marlo glared hard at her brother.

"So *that's* where I would have ended up if you hadn't made Annubis switch our souls?" she said. "Instead I was in some cheapo-circus wearing hair pajamas infested with little white lice?!"

"Um, well . . . it seemed like a good idea at the time," Milton replied as a stray crow feather wafted by. Marlo snickered.

"Madame Pompadour had me pretty messed up," she reflected. "I probably would have made things even *worse.*"

"And there was this surreal reality show but with cool special effects about some unseen man or creature who was going to clean off the Earth so he could sell it,"

Milton continued, spooked. "It sounds just like what your Truthador was talking about: someone's end game being the *End Times*."

"But why go through all this trouble?" Marlo asked. "I mean, destroying the world is one thing, but running a TV network—dealing with writers, actors, producers, directors, and sponsors—I mean, what a pain! Surely there are easier ways to wipe us out. . . ."

Milton shrugged as Lucky ran back across the grass and leapt into his arms.

"Maybe Satan is working with this guy—or actually *is* the Man Who Soldeth the World," Milton speculated. "Making it seem like humanity is wiping itself out all on its own, not like the Apocalypse is being . . . I don't know, *orchestrated*. Maybe he'd get in trouble with the Galactic Order Department."

Marlo flipped the pages of the scripts on her lap, stopping suddenly. Her eyes—even though they were *his*, Milton thought—burned with a fervor that was thoroughly *Marlo*.

"What if we rewrote these scripts so that they all had happy, non-end-of-the-world-for-no-good-reason endings?" she said with a mischievous grin.

"I tried that," Milton replied, shaking his head. "Only Satan can edit the scripts, and he apparently uses blood and a crow's quill and has really unusual handwriting—"

Marlo rolled her eyes.

"That's what they *want* you to think," she said as she

examined the grass around her. "It's like security cameras in department stores. Most of the time they aren't even hooked up. They just want you to *think* that they are. So we just need the edits to look as close as—"

Marlo found a long crow feather rolling in the breeze.

"—possible."

She snatched it up, then found a sharp rock wedged in the reddish dirt.

"Put your thinking cap on, bro," Marlo said with a smirk, " 'Cuz we're going to rewrite some *serious* wrongs."

Marlo dug the jagged stone into her palm. Milton winced with sympathetic pain, perhaps because the palm that was now currently gushing blood was *his*. She took the crow's feather with her other hand, dipped the tip in blood, and laid the first script across her lap.

"Okay," she said matter-of-factly, as if she wrote with her own blood every day, "let's hurry before I pass out. *Allah in the Family* . . ."

She scanned the last few pages.

"Hmm . . . the father is trying to get his family out of the house before his judgmental Uncle Mahdi comes at the appointed hour because he's afraid they'll embarrass him—especially his modern daughter—and spoil his chances of inheriting the family estate in the country. But the father *doesn't* and they all get in a big fight and, while all the relatives are screaming at each other, the whole house is accidentally torched by a prayer candle and . . . ugh. *De*pressing!"

"Wait, I know," Milton interjected. "How about the daughter brings home a Christian boy, and at first the father is really mad, but then they all get to talking and realize they have a lot more in common than they thought? Then Uncle Mahdi drops by and is furious but no one cares. The father doesn't inherit the country estate, but the family is cool with that because they're so happy in their old home."

Marlo scribbled over the last pages with the quill.

"Corny, but satisfying," she said as she dashed out Milton's edits. Marlo threw the script off to the side and picked up the next.

"*Queen of the Shebrews,*" she mumbled as she tapped the tip of the quill on her tongue. "Hmm . . . New Jersey superheroine Bat Mitzvah freaks out when a band of thieves called The New Order move into Newark and cut off the power for a week until their demands are met: that Bat Mitzvah has her credit cards taken away and is driven out of town forever. . . ."

Marlo stared off across a rolling hill, where a pack of dogs with toys strapped to their sides were chasing squirrels up a tree.

"First, *no* girl should have her credit cards taken away," Marlo said while dipping her quill in fresh blood. "That's just cruel."

Milton paced in front of the tree.

"*I know,*" he said, holding his finger up in the air. "Bat Mitzvah joins forces with her archenemy, the Jersey Jokester, united now that they both face a greater threat. Then they'll take back Newark, and the Jersey Jokester will reveal that she's Bat Mitzvah's long-lost sister, Kabbalah, who fell off a horse during an equestrian event at boarding school and lost her memory. Then they hug and go shopping."

"Brilliant!" Marlo replied as she scribbled away, getting paler with every sentence. She picked up another script.

"*What's Mayan Is Yours,*" she said, a little dizzy. "An ancient Mayan family living in Central America freak out because the calendar on their refrigerator runs out of months . . . that's dumb."

Marlo made a few quick edits to the script.

"There, they find a big box full of cool *new* calendars and the whole town celebrates by inventing astronomy. Okay, next . . ."

She picks up another script.

"*Peek-a-Buddha* . . . Buddha and his parents, Sidd and Hartha, are on a road trip to visit this cool amusement park near Vanna—must be some city—but the Wheels of Life on their Karmann Ghia blow out."

"Simple!" Milton exclaimed, padding across the grass in his stockinged feet. "They find four spare Wheels of Life in the trunk, go to the amusement park, but it turns out to be overly materialistic so they drive around and around, aimless and happy, taking in the beautiful countryside!"

Marlo's eyes fluttered, a loopy grin smeared across her face.

"Boom!" she laughed as she made her brother's edits and grabbed another script.

"Marlo?" Milton asked as she squeezed more blood from her hand.

"What, me . . . I mean, bro?" she replied, her face deadly pale.

"I think maybe you should stop," he said, kneeling down beside her with concern.

"But there are a few more—"

"I think maybe the well has run dry, plasmaticly speaking."

Marlo nodded groggily.

"Maybe you're right," she said before swiftly jabbing the point of her quill in her brother's thigh.

"*Oww!!*" he squealed, clutching his leg. "Why did you—?"

Marlo worked the feather into Milton's wound a bit before removing it and opening the last few scripts.

"Just needed to draw some more inspiration. C'mon, let's finish these, Bleedy McInkwell . . . we're on a drop-deadline."

★   ★   ★

The Fausters, pale and drained, hobbled together back into the fortress courtyard as the Scarecrows beat back the toxic wind.

Saint Francis stood beside the portal leading back to the Really Big Farm. The gentle friar gaped at the gruesome wake of Pandora's Cat Box, smeared across the Furafter.

"It's like something out of Revelation," he said in a near whisper.

Milton cocked one of his sister's not-plucked-for-a-month-or-so eyebrows.

The Man Who Soldeth the World . . . he had "Revelation 12:7" written on a doily, Milton thought. "Excuse me, sir, but what's Revelation?" he asked.

Saint Francis pulled his brown hood over his sharp, angular head and eyed the horizon with quiet apprehension.

"The last book of the New Testament. The last breath of humanity as flesh and blood *humans.* The divine undoing of creation."

"Cheery," Marlo said, still a bit loopy from blood loss. "All the cool stuff I miss by sleeping in on Sundays."

"What does the '12:7' mean?" Milton pressed.

"Chapter 12, verse 7," Saint Francis clarified. *"And there was war in heaven. Michael and his angels fought against the dragon, and the dragon and his angels fought back."*

Milton shuddered. Had he and Marlo stumbled into

the middle of some kind of "heavenly" war—either real or staged—with mankind as the likely casualty? He didn't have time to grapple with the enormity of it. The only thing Milton *did* have now was a plan . . . and that would have to do.

"Well . . . thanks," Milton said abruptly as he dashed over to Noah, who stood before the Scarecrows like a synchronized-flapping coach.

"I, h-hello, Mr. Noah," Milton stammered as Marlo staggered to his side. "Um, thanks for saving us all from the flood. . . ."

Marlo snickered.

"Thanks for saving us all from the flood," she whispered back at Milton, twisting his words into a taunt.

Milton punched his sister in the arm.

"You'll be sorry," she grumbled as she rubbed her shoulder. "You bruise easy."

"I'm Milton Fauster, a friend of Annubis. And it's really important that I get this stack of scripts back to Hellywood, Infernia, to a Mr. Orson Welles. The fate of the Surface may hang in the balance."

"Milton?" Noah answered, his confusion somehow squeezing another wrinkle in the incredibly wrinkled man's face. "That's a boy's name. At least it was . . . well, back in Bible times. . . ."

"It's a long story," Milton replied as he self-consciously picked at the holes in his tights. "Could one of your crows deliver these now?"

Noah scanned the sky. Swirls of thick, soupy gas uncoiled from the smoldering Kennels, reaching out as if to strangle any sign of good.

"Well—believe it or not—it looks like the worst of the storm has passed . . . and if *anyone* should be able to gauge the relative threat of a meteorological event, it's me," he replied before giving a quick nod. "Okay."

"Awesome!" Milton replied as he quickly wrote a note, pricking his throbbing thigh one last time with the crow's quill.

Mr. Welles—

Here are my final edits for the finales. It is imperative that these be staged exactly as written and—to save money, time, and to give the shows an urgency and excitement—performed live. You know: "evil" backwards.

—Satan

Milton secured the note to the stack of scripts with a rubber band, dropped the pile in his canvas tote, and handed it to Noah.

"Thank you!" Milton said with a wave as he turned to Marlo.

"Wait, you forgot one," Marlo said, pointing to the script tucked beneath Milton's arm. He gave Marlo a conspiratorial grin.

"*This* one we're going to do ourselves," he replied mysteriously.

Milton gazed at the destruction outside in the Furafter. Black rain poured down in dire, dismal sheets. Bitter wind howled and screamed. It looked like the end of the world, which—to Milton—was *perfect*.

26 · A LiE FOR A LiE

THE SKY CRACKLED and seethed, like a roaring fire fed with kerosene. Greasy, black-brown globs of fiery yuck hailed down, hitting the ground with corrosive splats that set the newspaper floor aflame. Milton panned across the Furafter with the video camera before rushing back into the Really Big Farm to get a close-up of his star.

> Teenage Jesus bolted awake from beneath a tree, his honey blond hair damp with perspiration.
>
> "Auntie Christ!" he yelped. "I had this terrible dream! You and me were fighting . . . like, *really* fighting. Not our usual arguments, but a knock-down, drag-out battle to the end. But we were more than just us. We were *everybody.* And everybody, suddenly, died. For no reason . . . none whatsoever."

Auntie Christ shook her head as she sat beside him beneath the tree, knitting.

"It's probably a warning," Auntie Christ scolded with pursed lips as she purled. "A peek at what's to come now that you've stirred everything up with your crazy ideas."

Teenage Jesus stretched and took in the sunlit beauty of the unspoiled countryside around him.

"No, it was just a dream," he said as he turned to his aunt, his blue eyes blazing. "And it doesn't have to be anything more than that. We live in this gorgeous place. All of us, together. Why does it have to end?"

Auntie Christ snickered, as if her nephew had said something incredibly foolish. "Everything ends," she replied. "Everything has a beginning, a middle, and an end. That's just how things are."

Teenage Jesus paced in front of the tree.

"*Fairy tales* have beginnings, middles, and ends," he explained as his sandals flopped against the brilliant green grass. "And, for some reason, we started to think that our lives have to be stories, racing to some prewritten conclusion. But life is *more* than that. It's *billions* of different stories, writing themselves as they go along, every moment a new sentence, a new celebration of us being alive."

He knelt down before his frowning aunt and grabbed her swollen hands.

"Your story is different than mine, mine is different than yours," he explained. "And that's more than okay—

it's *perfect*. Our lives are too big and sloppy to be squished between the covers of one book."

Teenage Jesus untangled his fingers from those of his aunt.

"We have the freedom to decide our fates," he said as he got up from his knees. "And why would we decide to destroy ourselves and this amazing place so full of joy and possibility? Maybe some people are just scared— they can't handle the responsibility. They'd rather have their story written for them; then they could just flip to the back of the book to read the ending, which is cheating and ruins everything. They want to ruin *your* story with *their* fear . . . and don't let anyone sell you fear. Hope and wonder are a much better investment."

Teenage Jesus looked up at the sun through the trees. The radiant beams cast through the colorful leaves made his face look like a church's stained-glass window.

"It's time we all stopped taking everything so flippin' seriously, excuse my Aramaic," he said with a faraway grin. "If you're holding something as precious as life, you don't squeeze too tight. Speaking of squeezing . . ."

Grinning mischievously, Teenage Jesus beckoned his plump aunt over.

"I feel a hug coming on!"

Auntie Christ shook her head, smiling so that her plump cheeks dimpled, as she embraced her nephew.

"You're crazy," she clucked as Teenage Jesus lifted her off the ground.

"It must run in the family," he grunted under the strain of his ample aunt's bulk. Teenage Jesus looked over her shoulder straight into the camera and added with a wink: "And aren't we all just one big crazy family?"

The two continued to cling to one another for a few moments.

"Cut!" Milton yelled as he turned off the video camera perched on his shoulder.

"That was beautiful," Saint Francis sniffed from a nearby tree as he walked over to Van, handing the sweaty actor a shroud.

Van wiped his face as he set Inga down with a grunt.

"Wow . . . live TV . . . beamed out to the whole world," he said as he handed Saint Francis back his scrap of sheet. "What a rush!"

Saint Francis stared in awe at the shroud that had Van's pancake face makeup smeared inside.

"Wait, you're not really . . . *Him*?" the kindly deacon asked, looking up at Van with his soulful eyes.

Van chuckled as he sat beneath a tree and stroked a chocolate Labrador retriever.

"Nah . . . I'm not a messiah," he replied. "I just play one on TV."

Milton set the heavy video camera down on the vibrant green grass.

"I just hope this does the trick," Milton mumbled to his sister.

"It *has* to," she replied, scratching underneath her hair pajama top. "But now we have some unfinished business back in Fibble. Barnum's machine . . . he can still beam up horrible things to make people think the world is ending, even if we sent this message that it *shouldn't*. People on their own are dumb enough. Put them together and they can do some seriously stupid things. Remember the state fair Mom made us go to when we first moved to Kansas?"

Milton shuddered.

"Yeah," he replied spookily. "That stampede on the All Manner of Things Deep-fried and Placed on a Stick pavilion. I can still hear the screams. . . ."

"So we should hurry," Marlo interjected, "but maybe Annubis can do his ol' switcheroo thing on us before we am-scray."

Milton beamed from ear-to-ear.

"Awesome!" he exclaimed. "Getting back in my own body will be like coming home after a long trip. Cozy and familiar, even if it isn't the greatest house ever."

"What are you guys on about?" Zane asked, suddenly appearing behind the Fausters. Marlo instantly went red.

"We—um—have a secret twin language," Marlo lied. "See, I—I mean Marlo—was born first, then I—Milton—due to complications, didn't pop out for another fifteen months. But we still have this creepy connection. . . ."

"Excuse us," Milton said as he dragged his sister to the garden shed Annubis had set up for his family. *"Why* do you have to go out of your way to make up this stuff?" he whispered as they crossed the deep green-blue grass. "Isn't it a pain to keep track of all your lies?"

Marlo shrugged as they stepped up to the charming, moss-green cottage.

"It keeps me sharp," she replied as Milton knocked on the door. "It's like Exaggercise."

Annubis poked his head out the door.

"Hello," he whispered. "My family is resting . . . perhaps for the first time in months. It's hard to sleep when you fear you may never wake."

"I'm sorry to interrupt," Milton said, giving a quick look over his shoulder. "But we were wondering if you could . . . *switch us back*. Before we go back to Fibble."

Annubis nodded.

"Of course," he replied as he emerged from the cottage, closing the door softly behind him. "It's unnerving, at first, but fascinating to see you both forced to work with each other *as* each other."

"Well, it's getting *way* old," Marlo said as Annubis led her and Milton to a secluded, nearby dogwood.

The dog god motioned for the Fausters to sit. He knelt before them, rubbing his paws together in a quick, circular motion until his paws smelled like popcorn.

"Lay down all thought and surrender to the void," Annubis coached as he set one warm paw on Milton's chest and the other at the base of his neck.

Harsh, explosive caws shattered the placid calm of the Really Big Farm.

Milton whipped his head to face the portal to the courtyard.

"Something's going on outside!" he exclaimed.

"Duh . . . *a Catbox–ageddon* . . ."

"No, something new. C'mon!"

Milton and Marlo raced out to the courtyard.

The cawing was deafening. Beyond the veil of sooty wind and puke-green drizzle, Milton could see a stage-coach on the horizon led by a team of Night Mares. A demon driver cracked his licorice whip over the horses' snarling heads, but his team was so spooked by the output of Pandora's Cat Box, they could barely trot. A sizzling fireball whizzed over the vehicle, illuminating, briefly, a passenger within: the ghastly, unmistakable silhouette of Principal Bubb.

"It's Bubb!" Marlo gasped. "We've got to get out of here *now* or it's curtains for the Surface!"

Milton wracked his mind for a way out. The tunnel in the courtyard was blocked off by the overturned RE-PEAT Furrari, and there wasn't time to dig a new one. Marlo squinted through the dismal murk outside of the fortress, searching for her Pinocchio-wood stilts.

"I should have taken the stilts with me," she muttered.

"Stilts?" Milton asked.

"Yes," Zane interjected, as he walked up beside Marlo holding four small pieces of wood in his hands. "*Stilts.*"

Marlo laughed and moved to hug Zane, but—after catching sight of Milton staring back at her with her own eyes—Marlo was too weirded out to carry out her squeeze play.

"So those little things are stilts?" Milton asked suspiciously.

Zane nodded, his deep brown eyes twinkling.

"I'll show you how to use them," he said, inching closer to Marlo. "Because I'm going with you . . . I know the layout of Fibble even better than your brilliant brother."

Milton sighed.

"Okay, whatever. You and Mar . . . you and *Milton* can use those weird things to get there since I don't have a clue. Now *I've* got to find a way to Fibble."

"Hey, doll face!" Van shouted with a grin as he sandal-flopped across the courtyard to Milton. "What a scene, huh? Live TV, running around, sticking up for causes," he added, motioning to the REPEAT protesters behind him, who were helping the sick and wounded pets from the Kennels.

"Yeah, it's a real blockbuster in the making," Milton said as his sister's blue hair whipped about in the wind, "but I've got to get out of here. Something is going on in

Fibble . . . it's part of this whole T.H.E.E.N.D. thing, a plot to clean the Surface of humanity."

Van grabbed Milton by the arm. His eyes blazed crazy blue, like a swimming pool full of Ty-D-Bol at a mental asylum.

"I'm coming with you," he said. "I'm like an actor-slash-activist now. It's what Teenage Jesus would do. I *get* it now. And besides, if my show has caused any trouble up on the Surface, then *I'm* the only one who can fix it."

Milton sighed. Van's logic, like his complexion, was flawless.

"*Fine,*" Milton said as he stared into the blur of energy leading back to the Really Big Farm, hoping that a new avenue of escape would somehow pop into his head. Through the portal he could make out Cerberus—easy to identify, what with his three heads—nuzzling a curly-haired dog with a dense black-and-white mottled coat. For a moment, it looked as if they were one long dog. Then—as the waves of portal energy cleared—Milton saw, to his intense disgust, that Cerberus's three snouts were firmly implanted beneath the other dog's three wagging tails. A tall, slender blur walked urgently through the portal.

"Annubis!" Milton called to the dog god as he crossed into the fortress courtyard. "Principal Bubb is here! And we could really use your help in Fibble, but I'm not sure how you would get—"

Milton saw Cerberus frolicking with his tri-haunched girlfriend back in the Really Big Farm behind Annubis's shoulder. The two cavorted happily, rolling across piles of fresh dung.

"Maybe we could hold Cerberus hostage!" Milton exclaimed. "Perhaps Bubb would back down!"

Annubis shook his jackal's head soberly.

"It would never work," he replied. "She'd only double-cross us . . . perhaps triple-cross us, with Cerberus involved. Besides, I know exactly how we can use Cerberus to our advantage."

"How?" Milton asked.

"We leave him in the Really Big Farm."

Milton's jaw fell open.

"Why would you reward that horrible, three-headed beast an eternity in pet paradise?!"

Annubis smiled as he cradled, in his paw-hand, the latest copy of *GYP.*

"Justice will be served, I assure you," he said. "But you and your party must go . . . Fibble is at least thirteen miles away, as the crow flies."

Marlo and Zane were suddenly—inexplicably to Milton—teetering atop their now-towering stilts at Milton's side. He squinted his eyes in the foul wind, watching the stagecoach, helplessly, as it slowly approached the fortress.

"As the crow flies," Milton muttered. He turned to watch Noah flapping his arms in front of the eight re-

maining Scarecrows. "I think I know how we can get out of here, Van. But be prepared to fly coach."

Annubis watched the stagecoach swerve back and forth in the flaming poop storm, diverted from the Kennels by the Scarecrows and focused out beyond the gates.

"I will be joining you soon," he replied mysteriously. "But you and your friends must leave. *Now.* Or all will be lost."

Milton nodded as Lucky bounded toward him.

"Lucky," Milton said, kneeling down, as he gazed into his ferret's crazed pink eyes, "you don't have to come with me. You can stay here in the Really Big Farm. I'd . . . understand."

Lucky spun around in a circle and sniffed the air. After a moment's hesitation, he leapt into Milton's arms. "Thanks for the vote of confidence, Lucky," Milton said, beaming, as he gently placed his pet at the bottom of his tote bag. "I need all the luck I can get. Let's go!"

27 · FOLLOW THE MiSLEADERS

THE COLOSSAL SCARECROW clutched Milton's shoulders tight with its talons as it glided across the bleak mosaic of dried hexagonal plates below. The pain was incredible, though it helped to take Milton's mind off the fact that a giant crow was clutching his shoulders, whisking him high across some grim no-man's-land toward certain doom.

The Scarecrow fluffed its gleaming black crest and swooped down to join the Scarecrow pinching its talons into Van. Just below were Marlo and Zane, sweeping the edge of the Broken Promised Land atop their elongated Pinocchio-wood stilts.

They were now safely beyond the ammonia-soaked apocalypse unleashed from Pandora's Cat Box, though it seemed to have died down to a mere dense, eye-stinging mist with the occasional chance of flaming turd-fall. The toxic output of feline-spurned ills, toil, and sickness had provided excellent coverage for which to escape the Furafter undetected. Milton, however, was conflicted: he was both relieved and thrilled to be fleeing the Furafter, yet had no clear idea how to deal with what awaited in Fibble . . . whatever that was. If only he and Marlo had some support—beyond a dead British boy with an incomprehensible crush on his sister (whose weird body was unfortunately the current resting place of Milton's eternal soul) and a has-been actor with a sense of self so inflated that it could lead the Macy's Thanksgiving Day Parade.

Just then, Milton noticed below him a bank of three gray machines, like drab metal refrigerators. Surrounding them were dozens of castaway bottles, like the kind that the PODs, the Phantoms of Dispossessed, used to collect—

"Liquid silver!" Milton yelped, the wind nearly stuffing the words back into his mouth. "Those are the deposit stations the PODs used to trade that weird glittering fluid they collected for supplies."

Milton grasped the Scarecrow's ankles.

"Down, please," he asked the sturdy bird as it ceased flapping its majestic wings and drifted down toward Marlo.

"I swallowed a necklace before we switched!" Milton yelled to his sister. "Did it . . . come out?"

She looked up at her brother.

"Yeah," Marlo replied as sweat trickled down her brow. "I barfed it up in the Fibble boys' room."

"Do you still have it?"

"Yeah . . . why?"

"I'm requesting backup. You know: calling in the cavalry," Milton replied. "A bunch of friendly phantoms said to call if I ever need any help. I just hope they come in the nick of time, like on TV. . . ."

"Here comes . . . another fog wall," Marlo said while maintaining her steady stride. "I think it's . . . the last."

Milton, Marlo, Van, and Zane pierced the billowing barrier of electrified vapor. The cold, tingling fog wiped Milton's mind clean. However, after he passed through the wall, his jumbled thoughts and feelings quickly returned. It was like his brain was a rebooted computer.

At the edge of a valley of fractured salt plates was Fibble, bordering the rim of the frozen Falla Sea.

"There it is!" Zane called out, though with his British accent, it sounded more like *"theri tizz."*

The three tents of Fibble jostled about like demonically possessed Hippity Hops.

"Why is it bouncing up and down like that?" Milton yelled.

"It's . . . because the wood that supports it . . . is made of Pinocchio people . . . ," she panted with exhaustion. "Man . . . *I* get to go by . . . crow . . . next time."

Marlo leaned close to her stilts and whispered.

"I wish I were still alive," she murmured sadly as her stilts instantly collapsed into two pieces of wood roughly the size of school rulers.

The Scarecrows dropped Milton and Van from a few yards above ground before soaring back into the sky. After a quick circle of Fibble, the majestic monster birds flapped back toward the Furafter with nary a caw for goodbye.

Milton and Van landed hard on their knees, rolling to a stop, as Zane tumbled from his pair of rapidly contracting stilts. Milton rose and tugged down his irritating creeping-terror-of-a-dress, joining Marlo and Zane at Fibble's perimeter. Wind gushed in a steady rhythm, squished out from between the ground and the platform supporting the tents.

Zane studied the festively striped tents of Fibble as they tossed and joggled.

"It's as bonkers as when we left," Zane explained. "Fibble rises about fifteen meters, then comes whooshing down, stopping about thirty centimeters from the ground, and then flies back up."

"Caught between a lie that's a truth, and a truth that's a lie," Marlo muttered.

A plume of silvery smoke drifted out from the Big Top's tip, snaking up into the sky and birthing a confusion of glittering tendrils.

"What's that?" Milton asked as the smoke clotted and

coiled high above his head, gradually blocking the light as it thickened.

Marlo gulped.

"You're not scared of clowns, are you?" she said as she wrapped her brother's gangly arms around her.

The sparkling cloud spread out across the sky and darkened, slowly coagulating into a massive head leering out at the horizon. It turned an angry shade of red and sprouted a pair of horns.

"That's like no clown I've ever seen," Milton murmured. "It looks more like . . . Satan. *Almost*. But not quite. The horns are shorter, his complexion is lighter . . ."

"You're right," Marlo whispered. "And you know how much I hate saying that. But it was totally a clown before."

The demonic head roared up at the sky, exposing a pair of lightning-white fangs. Its eyes belched fire.

"Let's get out of here!" Van yelped as he turned to make a run across the frozen Falla Sea. Marlo grabbed him by his talon-soar shoulder.

"*We're right underneath it*. If we run away, it'll see us. The best thing for us to do is to break into Fibble as planned. C'mon."

They crouched as they jogged to the perimeter of Fibble.

"Follow me, mates," Zane said as he fell to his hands and knees and crawled swiftly ahead past a squealing contracting/expanding Pinocchio post. "We'll want to get just under the Big Top."

Milton hunkered to the frosty, murky ground. It was hard not to flinch all over when Fibble zoomed down, only to stop inches above their backs.

"You're sure this place isn't going to squash us?" he asked as he crept behind Zane.

"Not to worry, luv," he replied, looking back with a sly wink. "I've got you covered."

I'm not sure which is worse, Milton thought as he scrabbled along in the icy muck, *being crushed by Fibble or crushed on by Marlo's boyfriend.* Several yards to his right, Milton noticed a glinting cylinder.

"It's one of those . . . bombs," Milton panted to Marlo. "Like you used . . . in the Kennels."

Marlo crawled over to the truth bomb, snatched it up, and put it into her satchel.

"Could come in . . . handy," she replied. "Nothing like a little truth . . . to clear a room. Like . . . a fart. Kinda feels good to let one out. But then . . . everything stinks and no one likes you anymore."

They crawled through the freezing mud on their hands and knees, past the fractured gates of Fibble—its broken, rainbow-hued neon lights sputtering like sick electric snakes—and beneath the torn paper center-ring of Fibble's Big Top.

Milton stared at the underside of Fibble, its lattice of wood and brass bobbing up and down at him like a yo-yo.

"How do we get up there?" Van asked, his vestments

covered in muck. "One second it's there, then it's not . . . like my agent up on the Surface."

"We just time it, sync up to the rhythm," Milton replied as the flapping paper entrance to the Big Top brushed his head, "then jump inside."

Milton rose, tightly reining in his instincts that told him to lie flat.

Maybe I'm not as scared because I'm Marlo, he thought as the top of his head popped into the hole on the Big Top floor—springing inside like a jack-in-the-box—before Fibble shot back up into the sky. Milton crouched down, his legs coiling like springs.

"One-two-three . . . one-two—"

He leapt inside the Big Top, as hard and as far as he could.

"Three!" he yelled as he rolled onto the sawdust floor of the darkened, empty tent.

Soon after, Van, Zane, and Marlo were lying beside Milton on the orange sawdust floor, panting, the latest attractions of Barnum's Three-Ring Media Circus.

They emerged into a darkened hallway in Fibble's second tent, leading to the classrooms. The projectors that normally cast the drab walls with flickering opulence were dark.

"It's so quiet," Milton said as he snuck down the jerking hall behind his sister.

"They must have all the blokes confined to their bunks," Zane speculated. "Because of what we did to this mental place."

"Where are we going?" Milton asked.

"To this secret room, behind Nostradamus's classroom," she replied. "Maybe we can eavesdrop on Barnum and learn where his Humbugger machine—"

A tall, robed figure burst into the hall from, seemingly, nowhere. The hem of its immaculate white cloak dusted the floor.

The Man Who Soldeth the World! Milton screamed inside his head as he, Marlo, Van, and Zane clung to the wall and held their collective breath, willing themselves invisible. Sizzling just behind the mysterious figure was—what *had* to be, Milton thought as he gaped at the man's slacks of flame—Vice Principal Barnum. They both disappeared into a classroom.

Marlo felt along the wall until she came to a large, barely noticeable beige rectangle. Voices—tense and testy—spilled out of the classroom several yards away. Marlo turned back to the boys and held her finger to her lips.

"This way," Marlo whispered as she pressed her palm to the door and slipped inside. Zane, Van, and Milton followed, with Milton closing the secret door behind him. They clustered behind the large, chalkboard-sized two-way mirror looking into Mr. Nostradamus's classroom.

On the other side of the mirror were Vice Principal Barnum, Nostradamus, and the Man Who Soldeth the

World: a basketball player–sized creature with broad, quivering shoulders, completely concealed by a luminous white silk robe and cloak.

"It's . . . *him. I just know it!*" Milton exclaimed.

"Who?" Van whispered.

"The guy from the TV show we watched in the limo," Milton replied. "He's *real.*"

Van shrugged and sat back in the cheap plastic chair.

"As real as any actor can be, that is."

Milton couldn't believe his sister's eyes.

"So I trust trying out the Humbugger yourself soothed your ruffled feathers," P. T. Barnum proclaimed as he paced across the room in his sizzling slacks.

"*Feathers?*" the man replied abruptly in a voice as booming and smooth as an explosion in a velvet museum.

"It's just an expression," Barnum replied tartly. "The point is—as you just experienced yourself—the machine to beam your doom-laden visions straight to the Surface is still online. Those schematics you provided were nothing short of groundbreaking technology—"

"It was a Promethean task . . . *literally,* as Prometheus designed the machine himself," the man replied laconically, crossing his legs as he sat on the edge of Nostradamus's desk. "Now that my plans have changed, the Humbugger is more important than ever. . . ."

"Changed?"

"The unscripted finale of *Teenage Jesus*—the highest-rated TV show *evereth*—has dampened the apocalyptic fervor I was toiling to achieve—"

Van was just about to whoop with delight until Milton silenced him with a hard punch in the arm.

"—so I am forced to evicteth the squatters on the Surface by *force* . . . employing our Humbugger machine to terrify them into a stampede toward the interdimensional openings I've created. *Putting the fear of God into the monkey people.* 'Tis a crude maneuver, but it appeareth to be the only option left available. . . ."

"Of course," Barnum interrupted. "Then we should really—"

"The plan was as neareth perfection as I," the man continued as he stared off into space, his face obscured by the shadow of his white hood. "Which is why I captured every moment of it. So that—when it was far, far too late—the Powers That Be would see how *easily* they were duped. And that a certain all-seeing/all-knowing being never even saw it coming and knew not what hit Him. . . ."

The man's gaze rested on the clock on the wall, reading a quarter to eleven. " 'Tis almost *the eleventh hour.* The Big Guy Upstairs was once the one who could bring about the end of days. Now man can do it himself. Everything has changed. I was intended to be their champion, their majestic defender. But now humanity isn't *worth* defending . . . so I must fulfill the divine Revelation myself."

Revelation? Milton thought in the darkness of the secret room.

Nostradamus stared, mute, into his crystal ball paperweight as if it contained fate itself, coiled tightly, waiting to spring out and bite—which is exactly what it did. He shoved himself away from his desk, his filmy eyes bulging with fear.

"In five minutes, Fibble will be destroyed!" Nostradamus yelped.

The man glared at Vice Principal Barnum.

"What is this fortune-telling flake on-eth about?" he asked, recrossing his legs beneath his robe so that his lap looked like an angry ocean of milk.

"Though Mr. Nostradamus's prognosticative powers are a little worse for the wear," Barnum replied, "he *can* see five minutes into the future."

The man glared at the trembling pseudo-seer.

"Explain thusly to me what you meaneth by 'in five minutes Fibble will be destroyed.' "

Nostradamus smoothed his pointy gray beard with his long, arthritic fingers.

"Four minutes and fifty seconds," he corrected. "Up in the Boiler Room, above the secret Focus Group viewing chamber, where the Humbugger is . . ."

Milton looked above him. On the ceiling was a round hatch; behind him, a beige ladder hidden against the beige wall.

"Up there!" he whispered to the others.

". . . four youths will undo this place," Nostradamus continued. "Turning lie to *truth*."

Marlo gaped at her brother.

"Us? But we wouldn't even know where to go if Nostradamus hadn't told us—"

Milton shrugged, beaming.

"Don't argue with fate," he replied as he clambered swiftly up the ladder.

In the classroom, Vice Principal Barnum's pants blazed with purpose.

"Mr. Nostradamus," he croaked. "Evacuate the teachers—"

"And children?" the wizened teacher interjected.

"Fine, them too," Vice Principal Barnum replied crossly.

The man abruptly rose to his feet and strode in elegant sweeps for the door.

"If your crystal-gazing crank is correct," he replied, "then this whole area will soon be buzzing with Galactic Order Department representatives like bureaucratic flies on procedural excrement. Which means that I'll leaveeth you, Mr. Barnum, to handle this mess. For if you *don't,* and my plan doesn't go down as planned, then *you'll* be going down. To h-e-double-hockey-sticks, where the really, *really* bad folks go. I haveth connections . . . an old coworker, you could say. Do I maketh myself clear?"

The vice principal swallowed, though he needed to

tug at his lapel to accommodate the downward passage of the lump in his throat.

"Yes, sir," Vice Principal Barnum replied unsteadily. "I'm like an abacus: you can count on me."

Milton pushed open the hatch and scaled another ladder, ultimately leading to a second hatch. He twisted the handle and climbed onto the wooden floor of Fibble's Boiler Room.

The round, cramped room was crowded with brass tubes and metal tanks that hissed with steam. The tubes coiled up the walls in a spiral, ending at the tip of the pointed roof. Across from Milton, on the other side of the room, hung what looked like a periscope, only instead of the conventional viewing goggles was a dangling mask. Marlo crawled into the loud, sweltering room beside Milton.

In front of the periscope mask was a tall, steel-backed high chair. The chair swiveled around with a startled squeak. Scampi the shrimp demon, his face smeared in clown makeup, gaped in shock at the intruders with his trembling, distended eyes.

"Is that a . . . *shrimp*?" Van asked as he crept into the room.

Marlo nodded.

"Yeah, but he's fairly harmless," she replied. "He's just a prawn in Barnum's game."

Zane pointed to the mask, smeared with whiteface and lipstick.

"The great, nasty demon clown that ate up Dr. Brinkley!" he exclaimed. "That's how they do it . . . *it's just a mask!*"

"Yes!" Marlo cried. "Barnum has Scampi—the shrimp demon—stick his face in that Humbugger machine and, somehow, it becomes this gargantuan, freaky, scare-the-soiled-pants-off-you clown head! It's the big, exaggerated *opposite* of whoever sticks their face in it, which is why he needed a tiny, totally unscary shrimp!"

"But that thing we saw outside wasn't a clown, it was like . . . *Satan.* Or a demon of some kind."

"Do you think the man in the robe is Satan?"

"I don't know," Milton replied. "But whoever's plan it *is*, we've got to stop it. And fast."

Milton noticed a number of masks, disguises, and toys littering the console beneath the periscope: a collection of beards, four horsemen figurines on rainbow-maned ponies, an angel mask . . .

"*This is how he's going to do it,*" Milton exclaimed. "He's going to stage the Apocalypse right here, and scare everyone through those interdimensional portals the man was talking about!"

Scampi edged his feelers subtly, so as to not attract attention, toward a large red button labeled PANIC. Zane bolted up and spun Scampi's chair around, fast enough to fling him to the floor. Zane picked up the wriggling demon by the ruffle of his polka-dotted clown blouse. He held him over the open portal on the floor.

"Down the hatch," Zane said with a smirk as he dropped Scampi into the chute.

Marlo kicked close the hatch. "Let's destroy this Humbugger thingie before Barnum gets a chance to use it," she said.

Marlo ran to the console and tried pulling out one of the pipes.

"Wait!" Milton called out. "Don't destroy it!"

"But why?" Marlo asked. "Nostradamus even *said* we would."

Milton shoved Van toward the dangling mask.

"Teenage Jesus was able to help calm things down up on the Surface," Milton explained. "So maybe he can use this thing to keep people from passing through the inter-dimensional portals to that lame planet across the galaxy."

Van chewed his full, bee-stung lip.

"B-but I don't have a script," the young, usually over-confident actor stammered.

Milton put his arm around Van's shoulder.

"Think of it as . . . improv," Milton said. "Besides, you're the star of the biggest TV show in history. Your fans just want a little *more*."

"Right, of course," Van replied as he flung back his lustrous blond mane and positioned the trillion-volt periscope to his head.

Milton examined the console. The Humbugger had

been set to "Exaggerated Negative." Milton flipped the switch to "Exaggerated Positive."

The metal tanks vibrated, the pipes screamed, and puffs of smoke and ground mirror seeped from the seals connecting the ducts and tubes. Heat radiated from the strained plumbing and cisterns.

"People of Earth," Van said. "This is . . . Teenage Jesus. I . . . I just wanted to say that you should just . . . *chillax*. You know, and enjoy the world my dad made for you all . . ."

Marlo cocked her eyebrow and looked dubiously over at Milton.

"This guy has the biggest audience ever and all he can say to them is to *chillax*?"

Milton shrugged.

"Judge not lest ye be judged," he replied as Van grabbed a long black beard.

"Hey, everybody," Van continued, "here's my good friend Mohammed."

He slipped on the beard, hooking the wires behind his ears.

"Thank you, Teenage Jesus," Van said in a passable Middle Eastern accent.

Fists pounded against the floor hatch.

"I just wanted to say that, regardless of your beliefs," Van continued, "this wonderful place we've inherited is like a . . . *business*. And we're all shareholders. So as long as we all exchange love, respect, and goodwill with one another, we'll always show a profit. And if there's one thing Teenage Jesus and I know about, it's *prophets.*"

The hatch nudged open. Barnum wedged his froggy face into the Boiler Room.

"Stop trying to stop this right now!" he shouted as Zane rushed across the room. "I'll cut you brats in for a percentage if you just let—"

Zane leapt onto the hatch as Barnum and his demon guards tried to get inside.

"Thank you, bro," Van said as Teenage Jesus, trading his black beard for a white one. "Whoa, we've got a real special guest for you now, it's . . . um . . . it's . . . G.O.D. . . . you know: Good Ol' Dad!"

Demonic fingers wormed into the Boiler Room through the hatch. Marlo stomped on them as best she could, but she realized that she needed a more long-term solution. She reached into her satchel and pulled out the last truth bomb. Milton looked at his sister gravely.

"Doesn't that thing have to explode on impact?" he asked. "Which means we'd all go too if we threw it in this small room?"

Marlo pinched her brother's cheek, *her* cheek, while smiling a lunatic grin.

"I got it all worked out, my gullible apprentice," she said, her pure Marlo-ness radiating from beneath Milton's face.

"I'm doomed," Milton mumbled under his breath as the demon guards wedged the hatch open.

Van laughed like a creaky old Jewish Santa Claus.

"But seriously," he boomed in a deep, craggy voice, "it's much easier for all of us who art in Heaven if you good people arrive just one at a time, *not all at once.* It helps with processing and assures that you have the smoothest, most pleasant hereafter experience possible. Look, we know you have a lot of afterlife options, so thank you for choosing Heaven as your everlasting eternal reward. When kingdom comes, come here . . . but not just yet. Enjoy the nice planet we worked so hard making for you all. . . ."

Marlo yanked Van out of Scampi's chair.

"And *cut!*" she shouted as she set the truth bomb in the chair. She grabbed the mask from Van's face and pulled it down to the bomb, hooking it through one of the mask's eyeholes. Marlo then took her two stubby Pinocchio-wood stilts and wedged them on either side of the truth bomb, cinched between the sides of the chair. The demon guards burst into the Boiler Room, sending Zane and Milton tumbling to the floor.

"Grab them before they destroy us all!" Vice Principal Barnum roared as he poked his head through the hatch. Marlo held her hands above her head.

"You guys got us, fair and square," she said as she walked over to one of the burly chameleon demon guards. Marlo whispered out of the side of her mouth to Zane and Milton.

"Trust me," she said, "just make sure I'm the last one out of here."

Milton's eyes widened.

"You aren't going to . . . to," he stammered, "*blow yourself up,* are you?"

Marlo gave a sly smirk that clashed with the trace of trepidation in her eyes.

"Stop worrying," she whispered. "You'll give me wrinkles."

The demon guards led Zane, Milton, and Van down through the hatch. Vice Principal Barnum gave the Boiler Room a cursory glance, not seeing the truth bomb hidden behind the high-back chair.

"Well, I guess Mr. Nostradamus was wrong," the smug, stout man said as he lowered himself, with difficulty, back through the hatch. "Fibble is safe and sound, and once I get these brats out of here, I can finish some unfinished business."

The last demon guard led Marlo down into the shaft, its crazy lizard eyes twitching in every direction. Just before it closed the hatch, Marlo popped her head back into the Boiler Room.

"Adults have all the answers!" she screamed at the top of Milton's lungs. The Pinocchio wood yelped and sprang into the sides of the pipe bomb, sending shards of truth shooting in every direction, until everything went silver.

28 · THE PLOT SiCKENS

THE BUFFALO BILL International Airport just outside of Generica, Kansas, was teeming with laughing, happy people hugging one another tightly. This in itself wasn't *that* out of the ordinary, as airports are often full of cheerful people who have finally gotten their insufferable visiting relatives onto a plane.

But here in the terminal today—Dale E. Basye thought—it was somehow different. Perfect strangers openly embraced and traded smiles as if they were suddenly the best of buds, their friendships as bright, clean, and full of promise as a new car. These people, of every imaginable race and creed, crowded together in airport restaurants such as Tom O'Foolery's Dublin Pub 'n' Sub Shoppe and Little Hofbrau on the Prairie as the credits to various T.H.E.E.N.D. shows scrolled across banks of television screens. People were toasting each other, singing ponderous songs with too many verses, and generally carrying on like a mass karaoke version of "We Are the World."

Dale E. Basye shrugged and went to retrieve his luggage. A Barbie-esque FAUX news anchor appeared on one of the omnipresent televisions throughout the airport.

"Reports of . . . *giant talking heads*"—the woman smirked, shaking her head without upsetting her lacquered blond helmet of hair—"continue to stream in from all over the world. While it's unclear if these sightings are the result of bizarre weather conditions, mass delusion, divine intervention, or an elaborate publicity stunt perpetrated as part of T.H.E.E.N.D.'s final broadcasts, one thing is certain: people all over the world seem to be drawn a little bit . . . *closer.* Next up . . . *The Oh Really? Factor . . .*"

Dale stared, fixated, at the luggage chute where suitcases of all sizes squeezed through like poop from the business end of a Clydesdale. While the rumpled, middle-aged man waited for his tiki-themed tote to rotate languorously within reach, two sandy-haired boys with beady blue eyes—twins, by the looks of it—appeared at Dale's side.

"Hey, mister," the boy on the left uttered around the wad of neon purple gum in his mouth. "Are you that Fartisimo Family guy?"

Dale E. Basye smirked. He always seemed to get spotted by fans when he wore his "Author of the Fartisimo Family Series" T-shirt.

"Why, yes, I am," he replied.

"Can we be in your next book?" the boy on the right asked with a mischievous grin.

Dale could never understand why people asked to be in his books. His books were about an awful family plagued with chronic intestinal gas. Besides, awkwardly wedging fans into a book is about as vain as inserting yourself into your own story.

"Well, I—" Dale replied.

"Here's our audition," the boys laughed as they farted loudly in unison. Then, like bank robbers fleeing the scene of a crime, they ran away.

Dale E. Basye waved clean the air around him as he reached for his pocket notebook, adding Gassy twins masquerading as fans to his list of fears.

The Guiding Knight hoisted up the hem of his midnight-blue robe and crept into the Psychomanthium: the large rhinestone-and-tabloid-photo-festooned box formerly known as the Elvis Abduction Chamber. The cadaverous, sharp-featured man was suddenly split into six by the half-dozen mirrored walls in the spacious converted photo booth. He held a mason jar brimming with multicolored jellyfish beans: an almost-instantly recalled Japanese candy responsible for a host of fatalities and profoundly crippling allergic reactions.

"*Thank you, eBay,*" he muttered as he set the jar down between two Elvis beanbag chairs, one showing the King at the height of his career, the other, at his widest. The Guiding Knight's attempts at hurrying Damian, his cult's Bridge, from this world to the next had been less than successful. He had first tried a toaster, baited with Damian's beloved millet-seed bread, submerged in a shallow pool of water, but all that had resulted in was wet toast. Next was a Slip 'N Slide set outside of the bathroom while Damian took his weekly shower. Unfortunately, Damian had developed a phobia about getting his feet wet, so he showered with his boots on. It was supremely frustrating, the Guiding Knight thought as he turned to leave. Somehow that cruel, arrogant, unrepentantly horrid lump of a boy was always one step ahead—

"What are you doing?" Damian demanded with an accusatory cluck as he opened the chamber door. "I have a meeting here in five . . . and *not* with you."

The Guiding Knight nearly crossed over to the Other Side himself with shock.

"I was just . . . fluffing your beanbag chairs," the hollow-cheeked man replied, noting a small, downy feather sprouting from Damian's chin. "You know, *feathering your nest.*"

Damian yanked a cord dangling inside the booth, filling it with red light. He examined the interior of the Psychomanthium suspiciously.

"Okay, well, you can fly away now," he replied, scowling. "There are some tourists out there, loitering between Krazy Kults and Mrs. Bigfoot. Go try to convert them into KOOKs . . . or at least unload some VitaMold."

The Guiding Knight nodded.

"As you wish, my," the gangly man replied before adding sarcastic air quotes, "'Bridge.'"

The Guiding Knight swished away in his flowing robe. Damian made a horrible face—even more horrible than his own—behind the man's back.

Nearby, Lester Lobe was busy dusting a heap of pseudoscience artifacts.

"Hey," Damian said to the twitchy curator, "can you put on that cool old rock station, the one that plays those heavy hippie tunes?"

Les tipped his fez to one side and gave his gray, scraggly head a scratch.

"You like the classics?" he asked suspiciously.

Damian nodded, trying to widen the cruel, inscrutable slits he used for eyes into something approaching sincerity.

"Yeah," he replied, forcing a smile. "I think that stuff is . . . *groovy.*"

Les grinned a mouthful of dark brown, nicotine-stained teeth.

"Sure thing, kid," he said. "I'll uncork some right-eous tunes, pronto!"

Les trotted over to his camouflage-painted boom box and cranked the volume. Droning guitars oozed out of the speakers like musical mud. Clumsy, thumping drums and shrieking vocals, like someone strangling a screech owl, followed.

Damian plugged his ears and waited for his lawyer, Algernon Cole, to show up. Damian *hated* the awful music but—somehow—it seemed to unlock the powers of the Psychomanthium, granting him the ability to connect with the underworld. And since Satan refused to pick up his Ouija board, Damian was going to up the ante, whatever it took—short of a face-to-face visit, Damian wasn't ready for that just yet—to get the devil on the horn and renegotiate his book contract.

"Hello, hello." Algernon Cole, a spry man wearing khaki shorts, white socks, Birkenstocks, and a pink dress shirt, walked into the Paranor Mall. "Sorry if I'm a bit tardy. My No Fuelin' hybrid is in the shop so I had to take the bus. But you know what they say: better *litigate* than never!"

Lester Lobe hopped off a stepladder, having replaced the black light over the UFOria! exhibit so that it continued to exude its otherworldly glow.

"Hey, legal seagull—"

"You mean *eagle*," Algernon replied haughtily.

"Do you know how I'd go about getting a restraining order against someone who keeps making *unannounced* visits?" Les added, folding his arms together and leaning against a large, heavily muscled "Abdominal Snowman" mannequin in gym shorts.

"Well," Algernon Cole went on, "first you would file a formal complaint with your local county court . . . hey, wait a second . . ."

Damian grabbed his lawyer's arm and led him to the Psychomanthium.

"As fun as it is to watch two old farts get snippy with each other, I asked you over here for a reason," Damian said gruffly as classic rock filled the museum.

"Say one, say two, I can't get enough of you!"

"Yes, I know," Algernon replied, "to renegotiate your book contract with that eccentric publisher of yours, Louie Cipher . . . *oww,* you're hurting me."

Damian released his exceptionally powerful grip on his lawyer's bony arm.

"Sorry," Damian offered as they reached the mysterious chamber. "I'm just a little on edge. Luci, um, *Louie,* can be a little . . . *intense.*"

"Say three, say four, one look and I'm done for!"

Damian turned the chamber's brass knob, stomped into the Psychomanthium, and plopped down in the Fat Elvis beanbag chair.

Algernon, still seething from his encounter with Les Lobe, clasped his hands together and stood unsteadily on one foot like a wobbly crane in an attempt to center himself.

"That irritating hippie crackpot," he muttered. "You know, you and your KOOKs could take this whole place away from him. Squatter's rights, or adverse possession as we say in the law biz. There's some mnemonic device, a handy acronym to remember the components of an adverse possession action, but it escapes me at the moment. . . ."

Damian yawned and rubbed the dark circles under his eyes with a grubby fist. Algernon broke his pose and examined Damian over his tortoiseshell designer glasses.

"Hey, you don't look so good," he commented. "Here, try a swig of this." Algernon held out a plastic bottle emblazoned with the fuzzy green VitaMold logo. "It'll kill whatever ails you, and *then* some."

"Say five, say six, you're the grooviest of chicks!"

Damian grimaced.

"No thanks," he said as he scooped up some sunflower seeds from the plastic bag in his pocket. "I'm good."

"*Hardly,*" Algernon muttered underneath his breath as he settled back on his Skinny Elvis beanbag. "So, how do you turn this thing on?" the barely certified lawyer said, gesturing to the six mirrored walls surrounding them.

"Say seven, say eight, you are my far-out soul mate!"

Damian pulled out a crumpled piece of paper from his jeans.

"Last time you mentioned Milton saying something about," Damian scrutinized the paper in his hands, *"guardians of the spirit realm hearing his cry, and summoning those spirits from the other side . . ."*

The heavy rock song exploded with a percussive avalanche of drums, a tuneless blizzard of distorted guitar, and a high-pressure front of blustering, blistering vocals.

"Say nine, SAY TEN . . ."

The music rattled the chamber. The six mirrors surrounding Damian and Algernon ruffled, like reflective fur being rubbed the wrong way. An icy wind blasted through the Psychomanthium.

". . . you've gone and blown my mind again!"

Algernon's eyes widened as his reflection was pulled apart, as if by invisible wolves. Damian smiled with wicked satisfaction as the frigid wind sculpted his greasy hair into a crown of shiny spikes. A flat, nasal voice leaked, eerily, into the chamber through the mirrors surrounding them.

"Your call is being forwarded."

Damian's reflection melted into a warped, pulsating blob. The blurry, restless shape calmed into a dull lump while the rock music outside the Psychomanthium downgraded from "Deafening" to only "Terribly Loud."

"I've run out of fingers and my heart's run amuck,
My love for you lingers, and I just gotta say . . ."

"Yuck!" Algernon Cole exclaimed as Bea "Elsa" Bubb's image was brought into tight, unforgiving focus in the mirrors. "It's that . . . *woman*," he continued, stretching the barely descriptive word in hopes that it would cover the beastly image before him.

Principal Bubb's putrid yellow goat eyes bore twin holes through the mirror.

"Mr. Ruffino?" she rasped. "What are you doing in the shiny windows and gleaming door handles of my stagecoach?!"

Damian scowled.

"I was trying to contact . . . ," he replied, giving the shaken Algernon a sideways glance, *"Louie Cipher . . .* you know. *The Big Guy Downstairs."*

Principal Bubb expelled a frustrated sigh.

"You and half the underworld," she said.

Damian grumbled as he flipped through the pages of his manuscript, *Heck: Where the Bad Kids Go,* on his lap.

"I need to renegotiate my deal with . . . *him,*" he spat. "This book thing is going to be *big*! And I need an advance to match . . . like, right now!"

Principal Bubb laughed uproariously.

"Renegotiate a contract?!" she repeated. "With the creature who *invented* contracts? You can't be serious. . . ."

"Of course I'm serious!" Damian roared. "I even have my lawyer here with me. . . ."

Algernon rubbed the lenses of his glasses with his sleeve, hoping that the six ghastly images of Principal Bubb surrounding him were just a smudge to be wiped away. Trembling, he set his glasses back on his nose and gaped, slack-jawed, at the mirrors.

"Is that . . . *a dog in a tunic?*" he muttered weakly.

To Principal Bubb's side on the sealskin seat sat Annubis.

Damian scooched his overstuffed beanbag closer to one of the mirrored walls.

"*Hey,*" he murmured. "That's the dog that took out my soul and weighed it, back in Limbo."

Annubis's dark lip curled up against his fang.

"The darkest soul I've ever seen for someone so young," the dog god recalled with disgust.

"I'm just a prodigy, I guess," Damian replied. "Like Mozart, only meaner and without all the fruity music stuff."

"Look, I don't have time for this," Principal Bubb hissed impatiently as she shrugged out of her pony-leather shrug. "Annubis here is leading me to some old *friends* of ours, who are apparently up to no good, as usual. They are one heck of a problem—"

"A *HECKUVA* problem!" Algernon interjected. "The elements of adverse possession: Hostile, Exclusive, Continuous, Known, Uninterrupted, Visible, and Actual! HECKUVA! I just remembered. . . ."

Damian glared at his lawyer with his fathomless black slits.

Algernon hopped up from his beanbag chair.

"See, the *H* stands for 'hostile,' as in trespassing. The *E* is for 'exclusive': holding the property to the exclusion of the true owner. The *C* is for holding the property 'continuously,' the *K* is for 'knowledge,' as in the legal owner knowing that the squatter wants to take over the property, and the *U* is for—"

"*You've* got to be kidding me!" Principal Bubb gasped, rolling her eyes like a pair of loaded dice.

"It actually stands for 'uninterrupted'—"

The music outside the Psychomanthium suddenly stopped.

"I can't *stand* this song," Lester Lobe muttered. "Just because it's old doesn't make it classic."

The six mirrors shimmered and rippled, with the dark swirling blobs therein returning to the shocked, clammy faces of Damian and Algernon.

"That could have gone better," Algernon murmured with a nervous smile of artificially whitened teeth.

The freaked-out lawyer took a swig from his Vita-Mold bottle.

"These people you work for at Brimstone Publishing," Algernon continued shakily, "they're . . . *unnerving*. Really committed to their image, though."

Damian emptied the bag of sunflower seeds into his mouth.

"Yeah, but cheap as used, imitation dirt," he said. Suddenly, he grabbed his throat.

"I'm . . . ch-ch-ch," he said as he slowly turned purple.

Algernon handed Damian his bottle.

"Here!" he shouted. "Take a drink!"

Damian nodded and tilted the VitaMold back into his throat until dark green ooze spilled out of the corners of his mouth. Damian gasped as he struggled for breath.

"I think that did it," he managed before his face went from purple to a sickly green. His cheeks puffed out as he shot to his feet, running out of the Psychomanthium, blowing chunks all the way.

Algernon Cole sat back into his beanbag chair and settled himself with his kundalini breathing exercises.

"Never a dull moment here," he said between deep, goggled breaths. "And to think, some people practice law in a stuffy old office building."

He sighed wistfully.

"I've *got* to get a stuffy old office someday," Algernon murmured, his eyes settling on the jar of jellyfish beans. "But until then, I'll take my perks where I find them."

He scooped up a handful of the deceptively merry, multicolored treats and plopped them into his mouth. Almost immediately, Algernon's face was covered with patches of angry red hives. His lips swelled around his lolling, swollen tongue, and he clutched his throat just before his air passage closed.

"I . . . *object*," he whispered before falling dead on the Psychomanthium floor.

"This is address you gave, I assure," the cab driver said as he pulled up beside the ambulance and police cruiser parked outside the Paranor Mall. "I'm not pulling legs."

Dale E. Basye took in the scene dubiously.

"Fine," he replied tentatively. "Just in case, could you wait here for a bit?"

"Stay here, I will," the cab driver replied as he turned on the radio, filling the taxi with relentlessly buoyant Indian pop music.

Dale tread cautiously across the sidewalk and into the Paranor Mall. He was immediately paralyzed by the commotion surrounding him, his feet stuck to the floor as if it were covered with wall-to-wall flypaper. Paramedics hovered over a burly boy puking his guts out into a bucket. A body covered in a sheet was wheeled out into the waiting ambulance. A frantic ex-hippie was waving his arms as he was questioned by police. A tall, gaunt man in a blue floor-length robe, his arms cinched behind him with handcuffs, was led away by two police officers. Several other creepy people in robes fidgeted in a corner behind a desk stacked with religious pamphlets and nutritional supplements. And all of this craziness was happening within the craziest place Dale had ever seen, like a lunatic asylum lavishly decorated with space aliens, UFOs, and painted in every shade of weirdness imaginable.

Dale's heart palpitated. His chest tightened. The Paranor Mall began to slowly spin around as if it were an elaborate carnival ride.

He reached for his notebook, hoping that jotting each of the irrational fears currently being hurled his way would stem his budding panic attack. His hand shook. The notebook dropped to the floor.

As he bent to pick it up, he saw a manuscript splayed out beside it.

Heck: Where the Bad Kids Go.

Without thinking, the middle-aged man grabbed the manuscript and fled the Paranor Mall, telling himself—between gritted teeth—that good authors borrow, great authors steal, and desperate authors take whatever they can get their hands on.

29 · ASUNDER THE BiG TOP

MILTON, MARLO, ZANE, and Van slid down the metal ladder as Fibble collapsed around them. They whizzed past the stunned lizard guards that were stuck fast to the walls of the constricting tube leading back to the secret Focus Group room, their protruding eyes scanning, desperately, for some way out. The foursome were soon sprinting out into the hall, the walls bowed and bent as their Pinocchio-wood frames violently shrank.

Vice Principal Barnum was nowhere to be seen, though Marlo noticed a faint, dissipating plume of smoke snaking down the hall.

"What's happening?" Milton asked as he ran alongside his sister to the Big Top.

"The truth bomb," she replied, panting. "It blew up . . . amplified by the Humbugger machine. I thought it would wash out Barnum's lies . . . so they wouldn't make it to the Surface."

Marlo gaped at the incredible shrinking circus toppling down around her.

"But the Humbugger must've also been keeping Fibble together," she continued as they sped around the corner to the Big Top, "feeding the weird wood with fibs . . . so it stayed big. And once the truth got into the ducts—*boom*. It was like Fibble was a gigantic silk camisole . . . that someone washed in hot water."

"What?"

"Girl stuff . . . anyway, unless we make it out the main ring in time, we're going to get squashed along with everything else!"

They skidded across the orange sawdust of the Big Top. Through the tattered paper bull's-eye they could see the frozen Falla Sea—inches below, then lurching hundreds of feet away.

Milton held his hand out to his sister.

"One," he chanted as Marlo grasped his hand, then held out her other hand to Zane.

"Two," Van joined in as he held his hand out to Milton who, reluctantly, took it.

"*Three!*" they shouted as they sprang through the ring.

They fell to the silver ice on all fours. Fibble zoomed back up, though—Milton noticed as he crouched and crawled, scraping his sister's knees raw—only a dozen feet or so this time.

The truth is winning out, Milton thought as Fibble returned, threatening to crush him and his partners-in-undoing-crime. Inches above his head, the lattice of tormented, living wood and brass pipes that made up Fibble's foundation quivered and strained as it compressed dangerously tight. Milton noticed the anguished whorls in the grain of the wood, like screaming faces frozen and trapped inside.

The sound of footfalls spilled out across the ice behind Milton, Marlo, Van, and Zane. Six lizard demons slithered swiftly toward them. They led a huddled mass of freshly evacuated students and faculty close through Fibble's battered rainbow gate.

"Those children!" Nostradamus shouted. "They are responsible for this! Guards, seize them!"

Milton emerged from beneath Fibble's quaking foundation and sprinted across the Falla Sea. Beneath his feet he noticed waves of liquid silver lapping up beneath the ice floor, pools of swirling, gleaming, agitated "truth" cracking the shifty surface.

"*The ice,*" Milton panted as the others scrabbled to their feet. "It's cracking!"

A demon lizard guard, its skin mimicking the grimy frost beneath it, sprung at Marlo and seized her ankle with its tongue.

"Help!! This leapin' lizard's got me t-tongue-tied!" she yelled.

Zane stomped the long, sticky tongue and pulled Marlo away. As the guard and the rest of its squad rose to their feet, a great geyser of liquid truth shot up out of the thawing Falla Sea. The demon lizards were tossed about like toys—hundreds of feet into the air—by the foaming blast.

The teachers and students clambered out from beneath Fibble's shrinking foundation as screams of creaking wood split the frigid air. Drenched by fountains of silver truth, the tents of Fibble crumpled, sagged, then fell in on themselves in a heap of gnarled, striped canvas.

"Look!" Zane yelled, pointing to a tubby man with blazing pants walking across a cable suspended between two straining tent posts above the mound of buckled tents. "It's Vice Principal Barnum!"

The chunky charlatan wobbled across the tightrope, followed by his shrimp demons Scampi, Louie, Kung Pao, and Annette. "When the world has got hold of a lie," he shouted against the roar of gushing liquid, "it's astonishing how hard it is to kill it!"

The stout man edged himself across the wire toward a pole that, Milton could see, had several rockets strapped around it and a snub-nosed capsule on top.

"An escape pod!" Milton exclaimed.

A cloud of black, buzzing energy swooped overhead,

rushing at P. T. Barnum. The vice principal ducked as the angry cloud attacked, but Scampi, Louie, and Kung Pao weren't so lucky. They were swept off the tightrope and tumbled down into the crumpled wad of tents below. A fresh geyser of truth stabbed the shriveling foundation of Fibble. The silver gush smashed apart the lattice of wood and piping, sending broken planks and twisted tubes flying into the air.

"What's that mean black cloud all about?" Milton asked Marlo as Vice Principal Barnum frantically waved away the darting globs of energy.

"Must be his lies," Marlo replied with a shrug. "And it looks like they're coming back to bite him on the butt."

Another surge of seething lies dove down to attack the vice principal. He staggered yet retained his balance upon the swaying suspension wire, though the vengeful cloud claimed the last shrimp demon, leaving Vice Principal Barnum crossing a tightrope without Annette.

"More persons are humbugged by believing in nothing than by believing in too much!" he shouted as two more geysers burst through the ice, splintering Fibble's rapidly shrinking foundation, now about the size of a large raft. A swarm of dark, stinging lies consumed Barnum, knocking him off the wire.

"And there's a sucker born every minute!" he bellowed as he plummeted down into the shredded wreckage of Fibble just as it was consumed by liquid silver and dragged down into the Falla Sea.

"And a sucker is *unborn* every minute too," Marlo mumbled to herself.

The Falla Sea's icy surface was savaged by gushing liquid truth, cleaved into floes, then consumed by gleaming swells of silver. The neon gates of Fibble fizzled out as truth devoured lie. A thick vapor spilled forth from the silvery froth and formed a shiny canopy overhead.

Sandwiched between the gleaming ice and glittering cloud cover, Marlo felt as if she were pressed in between two gargantuan mirrors, reflecting themselves into infinity.

Milton, meanwhile, as the small ocean calmed itself smooth, examined it for any sign of the Man Who Soldeth the World. The frosty rim, the last remnant of the frozen Falla Sea, melted away. Milton stepped back from the quickly dissolving shoreline to the dried mud of the Broken Promised Land.

Just then, a familiar squeal and clatter broke the profound silence. Milton turned and saw, over a ridge of cracked mud plates behind him, a rolling fleet of shopping carts, pushed by a motley chorus line of haggard phantoms: the Phantoms of the Dispossessed.

"The PODs!" Milton shouted with joy as he ran toward their lanky, dark-haired leader, Jack Kerouac. The wild-eyed phantom cocked his eyebrow at the girl with the blue hair racing toward him.

"Jack!" Milton cried as he embraced the baffled Beat poet.

"Um, have we, like, met before, pigeon?" Jack asked.

"Oh, right . . . my body," Milton replied. "It's me, Milton. I'm my sister now. See, we had our souls switched in h-e-double-hockey-sticks . . . it's complicated."

Milton noticed a blind phantom with wild white hair and a Viking robe that flapped in the wind like the flag of a land long erased by time.

"Moondog!" Milton cried out as he embraced the haunted old man. "Surely you have to know it's me!"

Moondog smiled as he took in Milton with the eerie sixth sense of a career medicine man.

"Yep . . . it's our little unborn," Moondog replied. "But don't call me Shirley."

The phantoms pushed their shopping carts toward the cascading fountains of gleaming truth.

"So you got the note I left?" Milton asked.

Jack smiled a boyish grin.

"Looks like we crashed this crazy clambake a little late," he said. "But, yeah, Popsicle, we lamped on your note—the pendant you borrowed grabbed Divining Rod's divining rod and took us straight to it. Then, like in your note, we took liquid silver and put some in every deposit station we found," Jack explained. "Like, gallons and gallons of it."

Moondog drew in a deep breath and grinned, basking in the refreshing spray of honesty.

"I always had a strange feeling about the liquid silver, that it was, somehow, pure truth: that rarest of substances down here," he said in a craggy wheeze as the wind parted his beard.

"Truth is the unshakable shake, the unquakable quake that topples all of man's lies built atop it," Jack added with a lopsided smirk. "We must've overloaded the plumbing—which, like, led straight to Fibble, by the looks of it. Makes sense: if you're going to make lies, you gotta know what the truth is. But this place couldn't handle the truth, not when it came, like, *flooding,* pure and strong. . . ."

Milton and the PODs reflected upon the mirrored horizon, until the sound of wheels slicing through dry mud snagged their ears. Through a fog wall, a thousand yards away, Principal Bubb's black stagecoach came whizzing toward them. A lump of cold lead formed in Milton's belly.

"It's Principal Bubb," he murmured dismally.

Jack squinted at the luxurious, horse-drawn SUV.

"Yeah, the *death* of the party, from what I've, like, heard."

Moondog tilted his head toward the glimmering cloud cover above. "And she's not alone," he said as he eyed the clouds with sightless eyes.

Through the silver mantle overhead descended a luminous milk-white chariot with great, flapping wings on either side.

"A Plymouth Valiant!" Jack exclaimed, slapping his thigh. "Wow, that is one sweet ride!"

The sculpted car with its dual headlights and grinning chrome grill settled to the ground just beyond the PODs' line of shopping carts. The door swung open and, sliding out from the chariot's white simulated-leather interior, emerged a seasoned gentleman in a white silk suit, with majestic white wings folded behind him.

The angel stared at the space formerly occupied by Fibble. He cocked his dark, bushy eyebrow and scratched beneath the gold halo hovering just above his head.

"Ah, yes," he said to himself in an upper-class English accent. "Truth is the ultimate mirror. When it meets itself, it makes infinity."

Principal Bubb's stagecoach pulled up alongside the winged Plymouth Valiant as Marlo, Zane, and Van joined the scene. The angel elegantly glided to the stagecoach in an eerie way that seemed familiar to Milton, just as Principal Bubb kicked open the doors with her gleaming hooves.

Her rancid, custard-colored eyes settled, simmering, on the Fausters.

"Principal Bubb," the distinguished angel said cordially, offering his hand. "Always a pleasure."

The principal tore her gaze away from the children, painfully, like ripping off a scab.

"We've met?" she asked as she lowered her bulk from the stagecoach to the dried mud ground.

"Yes, briefly," the angel explained. "A corporate off-site years ago. The name is Gabriel. Archangel and representative of the Galactic Order Department."

Principal Bubb nodded as her demon guards—snarling, bat-faced creatures with cobra-like hoods flared out on the sides of their necks—piled out of the stage-coach behind her.

"Now I remember," she said with vague recollection. "Sorry, but with the wings, I can scarcely tell you heavenly creatures apart."

Gabriel maintained a smile despite the slur.

"Of course," he said, unruffled. "Well, I am here to declare Fibble—a circle of Heck under your purview, I may add—a disaster area—"

"It's these Fauster children!" Principal Bubb hissed. "I know that they are at the heart of—"

"Please, let me continue," Gabriel said, interrupting Principal Bubb's interruption. "With the truth flooding this den of lies, Fibble is so irreparably permeated with pure, high-grade honesty that the Galactic Order Department is forced to proclaim this realm an official annex of Heaven."

Principal Bubb's jaw dropped open, revealing her yellow-brown Stonehenge of gnarled teeth.

"Heaven?!" she croaked. "My circle of Heck zoned as Heaven?!"

She grabbed Marlo, thinking her Milton, roughly by the shoulders.

"So help me, I will throw the full weight of my

abused authority upon you . . . both of you!" she screamed.

"Please, Principal Bubb," Gabriel urged, "this is most unseemly."

"I will have you tried, do you hear me?!" she continued, her face as red as a mandrill's bottom. "*Tried as adults!* Then I'll send you both packing to h-e-double-hockey-sticks!"

Gabriel pulled Principal Bubb off Marlo.

"You will do *no* such thing," the smooth, cultured angel commanded. "We will have no vigilante injustice here. All I'm interested in is the *truth.*"

Milton stepped forward.

"Mr. Gabriel," Milton said. "I can explain."

Principal Bubb scowled.

"*Wonderful,*" she fumed, "another dramatic work of fiction from one Marlo Fauster. . . ."

"Shhh!" Gabriel scolded. "Please, young lady, continue."

Milton quickly exchanged glances with Marlo, who was smirking at her brother for being addressed as "young lady."

"It began when I was working with Mr. Welles on T.H.E.E.N.D.," Milton summarized swiftly. "*The Televised Hereafter Evangelistic Entertainment Network Division.* I started to realize that all the shows seemed to have these apocalyptic finales."

Gabriel snapped his fingers.

"*That's* where I recognize you from," the angel said, pointing to Van. "Teenage Jesus! I have to say, your portrayal is positively riveting!"

"Thank you, sir," Van said with an uncharacteristic trace of embarrassment.

"Anyway, young lady," Gabriel said, "I am aware of the unrest and fervor those shows have stoked upon the Surface."

"So I figured that Satan was up to something awful—"

"That's only his *job*," Principal Bubb mumbled under her sour breath.

"—but then I began to suspect the Man Who Soldeth the World, this mysterious creature who had a weird show that no one watched. He was right here in Fibble, but he must have gotten away—"

"*Convenient,*" Principal Bubb interjected.

"He was working with Vice Principal Barnum, apparently, trying to bring about the end of the world."

"The end of the world?" Gabriel gasped. "Do I look like a cherub? I wasn't reborn yesterday. . . ."

Marlo stepped up.

"No, it's true . . . I had been hearing all of these crazy songs in Fibble through the PA," Marlo blurted breathlessly. "These songs about the Apocalypse and how Satan or someone was plotting to trick mankind into thinking it was the end of the world and then shuttling everybody off to another planet—"

"Songs?" Gabriel said with a look of divine bafflement across his face. *"By who?"*

"Some guy named the Truthador," Marlo explained.

Just then, through the north fog wall in the distance, sped a pirate sloop on mag wheels, masts furled tight and a satellite dish lashed to the bow. Painted on the side of its varnished wood hull in red letters were the words: THE TRUTH OR BUST!

The sloop rolled to a stop in front of Gabriel's chariot. A rope ladder was cast out to the cracked mud ground by unseen hands. Then suddenly, popping out of the forehatch, was a slim, dark-haired angel with bright gray-green eyes and an electric harp slung across his chest.

"Sariel?" Gabriel said, thunderstruck—an unusual reaction for him, as angels tend to spend the majority of their time *above* cloud cover.

Sariel, aka the Truthador, leapt off the sloop and onto the cracked mud plates of the Broken Promised Land. He swung his harp onto his back, stretched his wings, and popped his chewing gum.

Gabriel stepped up to the four-wheeled pirate ship.

"I thought you were . . . *up there?"* the distinguished archangel said, pointing to the sky.

Sariel gazed past Gabriel at the splendid, silver showers of truth springing forth like hope eternal.

"Heavah cool," he replied, with a pop of gum for punctuation. "Like Vegas, only more real . . . anyway, *nice to see you too,* Gabe. So, like, right after our last quarterly meeting of archangels—remember, when you and Uriel ducked out early?"

Gabriel gave a quick, nervous nod.

"Yes . . . go on . . . ," he replied evasively.

"So Michael called an emergency meeting, saying that Satan was up to no good . . . or down to *yes bad* . . . something like that. And that it was time for *drastic measures,* which meant working on an undercover assignment so secret we couldn't even discuss it with the Big Guy Upstairs. . . ."

"Or me, apparently," Gabriel interjected testily.

"Yeah, Michael said that you and Uriel were too close to *Him,* and it would compromise the operation."

"But keeping something like this from the Big Guy Upstairs is, to put it lightly, *really bad*—"

"That's what Michael said . . . but he also said it was for the greater good. . . ."

Michael, Milton thought. *There's that name again. The angel from Revelation.*

"*Michael said, Michael said,*" Gabriel replied with a nettled shiver of his wings. "Did *you* and the other archangels have anything to say about all of this?!"

Sariel uncapped a water bottle tucked into a holster on his side.

"Well," he said hesitantly, pausing to take a swig of water, "you know how righteously persistent Michael can be."

Gabriel smoothed back a wayward tuft of silver hair.

"Yes, indeed I do . . . but what else would we expect from someone whose name, in Hebrew, means 'who is like God'? So near-perfect in his near-perfection."

Near-perfection. The phrase clung to Milton's mind like Velcro as the crowd of bedraggled, displaced teachers and students converged around him.

"So the other archangels and I were sent to the far corners of creation to keep our heavenly peepers open for . . . *something,*" Sariel continued. "We just weren't sure *what.* And, as I wandered the dreary Wastelands, I, like, realized I totally couldn't contact anyone on my halo," he added, pointing to the dim bronze ring atop his head. "Luckily that's when I hooked up with *me mates.* . . ."

Two pirates poked their scarred, matted heads out from the sloop hatch to listen.

"The broadcasting buccaneers of ARGH—Ahoy Rogues, Guerillas, and Hearties!—radio," Sariel explained with a grin. "They'd been picking up all sorts of odd transmissions on freaky transdimensional frequencies about some shady surreal estate deal. After sifting through the intel, all grubby fingers pointed to some powerful creature, most likely Satan, selling out the human race. But, disconnected from my heavenly counterparts, and bound by the ANGEL Act—"

"Angelic Nonintervention with the Galaxy's Evolving Lifeforms," Gabriel interjected.

"I thought, while I can't just blunder into this with shaky accusations, I *could* subtly influence things—let the corruption take its course while cryptically commenting on it through song—hoping that someone embedded in the underworld would take action and expose this plot. And, since I was in the area, I thought I'd aim my whole Truthador shtick at Heck. In particular . . ."

Sariel leveled his blue-green gaze at Marlo.

"Milton Fauster."

"Me?" Milton chirped, before remembering whose body he was currently in. "I mean . . . my geeky brother?"

Gabriel swallowed nervously as his deep brown eyes quickly darted to Marlo—now Milton.

"What do you know of Milton Fauster and why he's here?!" the refined angel exclaimed, unsettled.

Sariel shrugged.

"Chill, Gaby baby. Simply that he's different. Not defined by the label of who he *supposedly* is. Not like the other kids down here. Plus, after what he did in Limbo, I thought maybe he'd be smart enough to figure out what was going on—"

Milton and Marlo clutched onto each other through a shared, sideways glance.

"—and do something about it from the inside," Sariel continued. "And apparently I was right. Though—wow—I never thought the kid would hook up with the Phantoms of the Dispossessed and wash away the wickedness with truth, or join forces with his sis. I thought she was too far gone down the River Styx, according to my intel."

Marlo smiled sadly.

"Me too," she said softly.

Gabriel rubbed his chin in contemplation.

"This is all very interesting, Sariel," the archangel said, "but what I'm concerned about is this surreal estate deal: selling the Earth to . . . *aliens?*"

"Yeah," the young—scarcely older than twenty-one millennia—angel replied. "Even though it seems like the Fauster kids helped to prevent a phony Armageddon up on the Surface, we still might have shiploads of ETs coming, expecting to move in. And they won't be too happy with all the humans squatting in their new home—"

"Squatters," Milton muttered. "Squatter's rights . . . *adverse possession.*"

Gabriel absentmindedly polished the triangular G.O.D. badge pinned to his lapel.

"What was that, young lady?" the archangel inquired.

"Something I keep hearing about . . . squatter's rights and adverse possession . . ."

Gabriel rubbed his temples, keeping his heavenly headache at bay.

"I'm afraid I have no clue what you're on about—"

"It's a HECKUVA problem," Principal Bubb interjected, unthinkingly thinking aloud.

"It certainly *is*, Principal Bubb," Gabriel replied with irritation. "Now if you don't mind, we need to figure out a way to solve this mess—"

"No, HECKUVA," she clarified. "The elements of adverse possession: Hostile, Exclusive, Continuous, Known, Uninterrupted, Visible, and Actual. "See, the *H* stands for 'hostile,' as in trespassing. The *E* is for—"

"Excellent!" Gabriel exclaimed. "I see what you're getting at—"

"It actually stands for 'Exclusive,' " the Principal of Darkness muttered.

"You're saying that a squatter—or the human race, in this case—can acquire title by remaining on the property," Gabriel said. "*The Earth*. Which is exactly what they've done for more than twenty centuries, making the planet legally *theirs*!"

Gabriel patted Bea "Elsa" Bubb on the small hump on her back, before abruptly removing his hand with thinly veiled disgust.

"I must go to the Surface, immediately, and broker a meeting with these aliens when they land!" the archangel pronounced as he discreetly wiped his hand off on his luminous white suit. "I never thought, Principal Bubb, that the key to thwarting an evil plot would be found in your despicable claws. No offense."

"None taken," the principal replied, baffled at the sudden rush of events.

"And, considering that Satan is obviously behind this,

there might be an . . . opportunity for you," Gabriel said as he hopped onto the hood of his Plymouth Valiant.

"People and assorted creatures!" the archangel shouted to the crowd in his lilting British accent. "A transport will be along shortly to take you somewhere fitting."

Jack wandered over to the archangel as the divine creature climbed off the hood and opened the door to his chariot.

"What about us?" the lanky leader of the PODs asked. "I mean, *neigho* pops on us being taken anywhere. We've been lampin' to find somewhere fitting on our lonesomes for, like, *ages.*"

Gabriel furrowed his immaculate brow, not understanding Jack's words but divining his meaning nonetheless.

"Your people, *the PODs,* are always searching for truth, is that right?" Gabriel posed.

Jack nodded.

"You got it, pops."

Gabriel smiled and extended his arms and wings majestically to either side.

"Then I can think of no better place for you restless phantoms to rest than . . . *right here!*" he said, his golden halo bobbing atop his impeccably trimmed, salt-and-pepper hair.

The Phantoms of the Dispossessed gazed at each other with shock and wonder.

"Solid!" Jack whooped. "This can be, like, our Margins! Where nomads and know-mads make their rightful home at the very edge of wrong, and puzzling jigsaw spirits become one glorious whole!"

Milton and Marlo went to join the throng of children and teachers milling about the edge of the immaculate sea of truth.

"Not so fast," Principal Bubb growled as she seized each Fauster by the arm. "*We've* got some unfinished business."

30 · THE MOMENT OF TRUTH

THE GROTESQUE HEADMISTRESS of Heck dragged Milton and Marlo to her waiting stagecoach.

"You did it . . . you really did it!" Milton called out to Jack through his sister's crooked grin as Principal Bubb's claws pinched into his shoulders. "You made it to the Margins!"

Jack waved. "Stay cool, Popsicle!" he shouted. "Whatever you do, don't get caught up in this scene, dig? It's just a lot of dust and drag and means nothing in the end!"

Zane bobbed up from the teeming mass of children as the teachers led them away. Marlo elbowed her brother.

"*Wave at him and smile my prettiest smile,*" she whispered.

Milton rolled his eyes, sighed, and waved at Zane,

beaming a feigned, toothy smile that—judging from Zane's dimpled return grin—was convincingly warm, at least from a distance.

Principal Bubb threw the Fausters to the ground with a ferocious disdain. "Get those terrible children into the stagecoach!" she shrieked. The bat-faced demon guards prodded Milton and Marlo inside with their pitch-sporks.

Breaking free of the other students, Colby brushed his stringy hair from his face and peered into the stage-coach.

"Wolf!" the boy cried, his trembling arm pointing.

Mr. Nixon pulled the boy back into the mob.

"*Like anyone is going to believe you,*" the ex-president said, shaking his doughy head.

Milton tumbled into the coach.

"Annubis?" he asked as he was prodded into his seat. "What are you doing here?"

Principal Bubb smiled as she, with great difficulty, hoisted her bulk into the stagecoach.

"How do you think I found my way here?" she sneered. "To the scene of your latest crime-against-all-that-is-indecent."

Milton's jaw dropped with the shock of betrayal.

"How *could* you?" he gasped.

Annubis shrugged his sleek shoulders.

"She would have found out sooner or later," he explained.

Marlo scowled at the dog god. *"Bad doggie,"* she hissed.

Annubis, despite his regal bearing as an ancient demigod, still found himself cringing slightly at this deeply cutting canine rebuke.

"Don't be too hard on him," Principal Bubb said with a sneer. "Even though he led me to you, he's still got a date with a rolled-up newspaper, for his unauthorized excursion to the Furafter."

Annubis straightened his tunic and held his long, elegant nose up high with a dignified air.

"Speaking of newspaper," he said as he pulled out the latest copy of *GYP* from underneath his belt, "I believe I have information regarding something you've lost . . ."

He held out the full-page HAVE YOU SEEN ME? ad at the back of the paper.

Principal Bubb's goat eyes widened as she looked down, lovingly, at the picture of Cerberus.

"You know where my whiddle fluffle bottom—ahem—*Cerberus* is?" she gasped.

Annubis nodded.

"I'll take you to him right now, if you like," he answered coolly.

"Yes, oh sweet candied cudgels, yes!!" Principal Bubb blurted emotionally before composing herself. "I mean, that would be satisfactory. Now tell me . . . *where is he?"*

Annubis locked eyes with the principal as he flipped the paper so that it faced her.

"First I need reassurance that if I hold up my end of the bargain"—he pointed to the last line of the ad.

Reward: Your Freedom

"That you will hold up *yours*."

Principal Bubb glared at the ad.

"B-but . . . there was a d-disclaimer . . . ," she stammered. *"Fine print."*

Marlo smiled, not only realizing what game Annubis was playing, but that he had won before even punching the Pop-o-Matic.

"There wasn't room when we placed your ad in *GYP*," Marlo explained, dripping with feigned sincerity. "There's a strict character limit, as clearly detailed in the Terms of Disservice agreement."

Principal Bubb gritted her teeth. They squeaked like a mouse caught in a trap.

Milton, grinning from ear to ear, leaned close into Annubis.

"So *this* is what you were up to all along," he whispered. "Leaving Cerberus in puppy paradise so that you could tell Bubb and get the reward. Plus, that hound from Heck is dragged away from the only true happiness he's ever known."

Annubis winked slyly.

"But wait, there's more," he whispered before turning to the fuming Principal Bubb.

"And since the Fausters aided me in locating your *whiddle fluffle bottom*—"

"*There's no way I'm releasing them!*" the principal spat. "After all, they're minors!"

"Then I want your assurance that they will be dealt with in the normally-cruel-yet-not-unusually-so way," Annubis requested firmly.

Principal Bubb coiled her thick arms together like two lovesick anacondas.

"*Fine,*" she seethed.

Principal Bubb waved her claw at her stagecoach driver before rolling up the Scarecrow poop–encrusted window.

Gabriel had mentioned an opportunity, Principal Bubb recalled as the team of snorting Night Mares pulled the stagecoach away. And, considering that Satan was—more than likely—behind the plot to sell the Earth, this meant that there would be a vacancy . . . *down under.*

A secret electric thrill surged through Principal Bubb. She had spent the bulk of her career scaling the corporate ladder of the underworld, fighting fang-and-claw for each hard-earned rung. But even in her wildest nightmares, Bea "Elsa" Bubb never thought that that ladder would lead all the way *down.*

"I have an idea how you can punish the Fausters *with-*

out punishing them," Annubis said slyly as he leaned into the principal, bursting her reverie. "It will also keep them disoriented, making it harder for them to get into mischief."

Principal Bubb's sickly yolk-colored eyes clouded with suspicion.

"I'm listening," she replied.

Annubis smiled.

"I can *switch* their souls," he said, folding his elegant arms together. "Make Milton *Marlo* and Marlo *Milton*. Think of it as an extra layer of awkwardness and confusion slathered across their already awkward and confused afterlife adolescence."

Annubis looked at the Fausters and prodded them with his gaze.

"Um . . . *oh no!*" Marlo cried out, feigning tears. "Anything but that!"

"No, how awful!" Milton blubbered, joining in. "*I can't think of anything worse than being my brother!!*"

A sneer birthed itself underneath Principal Bubb's glistening snout as the two children pretended to sob.

"Oh, stop your sniveling, you wretched—"

"An *excellent* idea," Annubis interjected. "Sending them both to Snivel. A dismal place for them to stew in their own anguish . . ."

Principal Bubb stroked her bristly chin.

"Yes," she murmured. "Snivel would definitely dampen their spirits."

She crossed her thick, stumpy legs.

"All right then: *switch their souls immediately,*" she commanded with a snap of her claws.

Annubis nodded as he drew in a deep breath.

"As you wish," he said, closing his eyes and turning toward Milton.

Annubis rubbed his paws together in quick circles as the stagecoach drove across the cracked terrain of the Broken Promised Land.

Rolling his eyes back in his head in that creepy way dogs do when they're deeply asleep, Annubis gently— with the precision of a surgeon—pressed his paws into Milton, where they disappeared as if into human Jell-O.

Milton shuddered as Annubis carefully felt inside Marlo's body for Milton's soul. He could feel his spiritual essence quiver as Annubis prodded it gently with one paw toward the other. Milton felt a wave of shock shoot throughout Marlo's body—like someone throwing a water balloon at you while you're asleep on the beach— as Annubis seized his soul and cradled it in his paws. A horrible, numbing emptiness, a metaphysical gush of Novocain, welled up inside of him. Annubis deposited Milton's soul into his cupped hands to hold while the dog god went about removing Marlo's spiritual goo.

Milton looked down at the jiggly soul in his hands with a vague, faraway interest, like something that you've been told is terribly important but just doesn't *feel* so, like making sure that the toilet seat is down. His soul had a few more black flecks in it than it had when he'd first seen his soul in Limbo, but it also contained more of those brilliant, shimmering rainbowish-white globs, as if Milton had simultaneously become more good and more bad. Not that he cared right now. He didn't really care about *anything*.

Annubis, having removed Marlo's soul, took the twitching, glittering glob from Milton's hands and gently placed it inside of Milton's *real* body.

"Oww!" Milton yelped as a medley of new aches, cuts, bruises, chafing hair-shirt rashes, and assorted wounds assailed his nervous system.

"Oww . . . flippin' *monkey flippers!*" Marlo yowled as she, too, seconds later, suffered a host of new scrapes, pains, and contusions.

Principal Bubb glanced over at the Fausters with a flash of disdain, before resuming her glassy-eyed vigil staring out the stagecoach window, deep in thought, reconciling her conflicted feelings for Satan with her unquenchable thirst for power.

Marlo examined the bottom of her sore foot.

"Would it have *killed* you to wear shoes?" she grumbled as she examined the holes in the foot of her tights.

"At times it sure felt like it," Milton whispered as he scratched a maddening itch beneath his prickling pajamas. "Those things were like portable, strap-on torture devices."

Milton stared out the stagecoach window. The

monotonous terrain of cracked brown mud flats whizzed by, broken up by the occasional swirling gray fog wall.

Milton and Marlo had gotten their bodies back, averted an ersatz Apocalypse, rescued countless pets from being "nulled" in the Kennels, brought the pernicious Three-Ring Media Circus of Fibble down to the ground, put the kibosh on a crooked intergalactic real estate deal, and even made Heaven just a little bigger.

But something felt just a little bit *off* to Milton, like when he wore socks that didn't match.

Near-perfection. Revelation. He Who Is Like God.

The last, missing freight car of Milton's confused train of thought coupled into place.

Back in Fibble, he, Marlo, Van, and Zane had been greeted by a gargantuan, Humbugger-projected image of a snarling, wrathful demon that wasn't *quite* Satan. Next, they had overheard—in Barnum's secret Focus Group room—that the Man Who Soldeth the World had been the last creature to wear the Humbugger mask. And when they had stormed the Boiler Room, atop the second tent, the machine had been set to "Exaggerated Negative," projecting the exact, magnified *opposite* of whatever wore the mask.

So that meant that the Man Who Soldeth the World—whom Milton was *convinced* was truly behind all of this—was the exact *opposite* of something *nearly* as evil as Satan, making him almost as good as God . . .

Nearly perfect. He Who Is Like God.

"*Michael,*" Milton muttered in horror. "*He's* the one who tried to sell the world!"

Principal Bubb shot Milton a darting, hateful glance.

"What are you blathering on about?" she hissed, licking the scabby patch around her mouth that she outlined with lipstick.

Milton slunk back in his seat and folded his arms. He knew, deep down, that no one would believe him about Michael. He had problems believing it himself. Why would an archangel, of all creatures, do something like that? Milton sighed.

The stagecoach passed through another electric fog wall with a whoosh and a crackle, fragmenting Milton's thoughts. Judging from the sickly green sleet that washed the congealed crow poop off the window, they were back in the Furafter to pick up Cerberus and release Annubis so that he could live happily ever after with his family.

Maybe Gabriel would believe me . . . but why was he so weird back in Fibble, snapping at Sariel about what the angel knew about me and why I was here? Perhaps Annubis . . .

Milton looked over at the dog god. He was panting faintly with excitement, his eyes and nose wet and shiny as he anticipated his future. Annubis had something true held tight in his heart that kept him going despite the deceit that raged around him. The last thing Milton wanted to do was drag the dog god into another mess, after all he and his family had been through. That left Principal Bubb. . . .

Milton glanced at the hideous, detestable demoness that glowered back at him through pus-colored eyes.

Once you live a life of lies, there's no going back, Milton thought sadly. Likewise with the truth. In that moment, Milton vowed to never lie to himself, so he could remain true to his purpose—to right the wrong that was Heck—perhaps the entire *afterlife*. And there was no use feeling sorry for himself, Milton reflected as the stagecoach slowed. There would be plenty of time for that in Snivel.

BACKWORD

There is a popular legend that has George Washington—
the first president of the United States of America—
purportedly chopping down the backyard cherry tree
as a child, unprovoked, then relaying the shameful details of his perplexing deed to his father, uttering the
immortal line: "I cannot tell a lie . . . it was I who
chopped down your cherry tree." For reasons unclear,
this parable of truth—later exposed as a lie fabricated
by a pastor—has been held up for centuries as an example of nobility. To me, it feels more like a disarming,
preemptive strike akin to "Hey, pops, I shaved the cat,
switched your shampoo with Nair, and glued my sister
to the ceiling . . . wow, it feels good to get that off my
chest! Can we all go out for ice cream now? Except my
li'l sis, of course, as she is stuck fast and squirming by
the chandelier." And how, pray tell, did young George

come to be in the possession of an ax to begin with? I blame the parents, but then again, I always do.

Just because it's the truth doesn't make it all good. ("You've got a candy corn stuck on your tooth. Oh wait: that is your tooth.") And just because it's a lie doesn't make it all bad. ("No, Mom: seriously. You still look good in jeans.")

It's a question of intent. In the hands of the cruel, the truth can be a weapon either sharp as a dagger or blunt as a hammer. Likewise, a little white lie delivered with compassion and love can make someone's day (into what, exactly, is up to that special lied-to someone).

The most important thing to keep in mind is that, while the biggest lie about lies is that some people never tell them, the truth about the truth is that we often can't handle it. Absolute truth is like absolute zero: bitter, cold, and unlikely to garner you many friends. It's like getting a shot: it hurts at first, but it's the only way to cure the creeping malady that rots you silently from within, invisibly, until it's too late.

So whether real hard to swallow or real hard to hear, the truth is, above all, real. And, when push comes to shovel or George Washington's ax, real is all we really have.

ACKNOWLEDGMENTS

I WOULD LIKE to formally acknowledge that I have not always been completely truthful in my life. There have been times when I have misrepresented myself ("my" pilfered computer science final project comes to mind . . . as does the time when I told an ex-girlfriend that I wrote Echo and the Bunnymen's "Killing Moon," completely underestimating her ability to read liner notes), and they have almost always ended badly.

I would like to acknowledge that I am confused by the fact that, despite honesty being supposedly so good, there are so many types of lies—everything from little-white to barefaced, which (one would assume) are in flagrant opposition to the fully-clothed-faced truth.

I would like to acknowledge that a little white lie isn't *always* a bad thing, in that—while honesty may be a delightful policy—without at least a few fibs, most family gatherings would probably end with police intervention.

I would like to acknowledge that, to this day, being consistently truthful is a challenge, and sometimes I fall prey to telling a lie, or—in some cases—writing a whole book of them.

I would like to acknowledge that, in closing, perhaps I missed the point of the "Acknowledgments" portion of this book.

ABOUT THE AUTHOR

DALE E. BASYE (the "E" stands for "Eeeeeeeeee") has written stories, screenplays, essays, reviews, and lies for many publications and organizations. He was—and still *is* when the price is right—an advertising copywriter, winning numerous awards for his campaigns, especially those that his clients initially feared. Dale E. Basye has also written a number of independent films, none of which you have seen. Heck, *he's* barely seen them.

Here's what Dale E. Basye has to say about his fourth book:

"The truth is like the dark. It can be really scary at first, but if you tread carefully and wave your arms in front of you, you actually come through it okay. Sure, sometimes you will stub your toe, but there's a reason people say that something 'smarts': it's a way—though a painful one—to learn and grow. Lies . . . not so much.

Lies are like a strobe light. They daze and disorient by omitting vital information but pretend not to. Heck is like that. And, no matter what anyone tells you, Heck is real. This story is real. Or as real as anything like this can be."

Dale E. Basye lives in Portland, Oregon, in a small house that exists solely in the dream of a feral cat named Molly Ringworm that Dale is understandably wary about waking.

SNiVEL

THE FIFTH CIRCLE OF HECK

AVAILABLE MAY 2012